The Sha

An award-winning and highly acclaimed writer of fantasy,
LENE KAABERBØL was born in 1960, grew up in the Danish
countryside and had her first book published at the age of 15.
Since then she has written more than 30 books for children and
young adults. Lene's huge international breakthrough came
with *The Shamer Chronicles*, which have been published in
more than 25 countries selling over a million copies worldwide.

TEEN AND YA FICTION FROM PUSHKIN PRESS

THE RED ABBEY CHRONICLES

MARESI

NAONDEL

MARESI RED MANTLE

Maria Turtschaninoff

Translated by Annie Prime

'Combines a flavour of *The Handmaid's Tale* with bursts of excitement reminiscent of Harry Potter's magic duels'

Observer

THE BEGINNING WOODS

Malcolm McNeill

'I loved every word and was envious of quite a few… A modern classic – rich, funny and terrifying'

Eoin Colfer

THE RECKLESS SERIES

1. THE PETRIFIED FLESH
2. LIVING SHADOWS
3. THE GOLDEN YARN

Cornelia Funke

'A wonderful storyteller'

Sunday Times

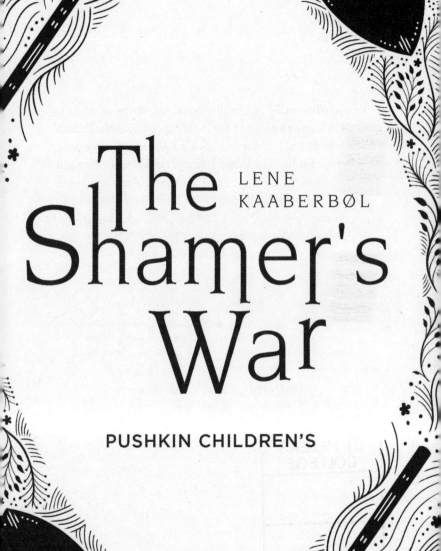

LENE
KAABERBØL

The Shamer's War

PUSHKIN CHILDREN'S

Pushkin Press
71–75 Shelton Street
London WC2H 9JQ

Original text © 2003 by Lene Kaaberbøl
English translation © 2005 by Lene Kaaberbøl

· *The Shamer's War* was first published as *Skammerkrigen*
in Copenhagen, by Forlaget Phabel in 2003

First published in English in 2005 by Hodder Children's Books

First published by Pushkin Press in 2019

1 3 5 7 9 8 6 4 2

ISBN 13: 978-1-78269-231-7

Designed and typeset by Tetragon, London
Printed and bound by CPI Group (UK) Ltd, Croydon, CRO 4YY

www.pushkinpress.com

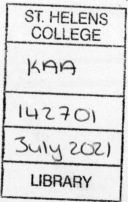

CONTENTS

My Name Is Davin

My name is Davin. My name is Davin. My name is Davin.

I kept repeating it to myself, over and over again. Trying to hold on to everything it meant: Dina's brother. Melli's brother. My mother's son, and Nico's friend. A human being. Not…

… your name is murderer…

… Not what the voices were saying. Not what they were whispering to me in the darkness when I was trying to go to sleep.

… your name is murderer… your name is coward…

I sat up in bed. My palms were sweaty and cold. I wrapped my arms around my head as though I was afraid someone would hit me, but I knew I couldn't shut out the voices. They were inside me. They had sneaked in, burrowed in, the days and nights I had been locked in the Hall of the Whisperers, surrounded by stone faces with empty eyes and yawning mouths that kept whispering and whispering, over and over, hour after hour, until one would rather die than keep on listening.

The house was dark. Darker still here in my small enclosure. I couldn't stand the darkness anymore because I kept seeing things that weren't there. Faces. Dead eyes. Dark blood seeping from a half-cut throat….

I leaped to my feet and yanked the curtain aside. Bluish slivers of moonlight came in through the cracks in the shutters, like pale knives. As soundlessly as possible I opened the door and went out. The trampled grass of the yard was damp and hoar-cold against the soles of my bare feet, but I had no time for shoes. I ran. Slowly at first, then more quickly, along the path to Maudi's farm, past the old black pear trees in her orchard, up the next hill, and on up into the naked heights that seemed so close to the sky it felt as if I could pick the stars like apples just by reaching for them. I didn't stop. I just kept running, so that my breath came in deep jerks and I could feel my heartbeat in every last inch of my body. I wasn't cold, despite my bare feet; my blood was pumping too hard, and pure sweat was running down my back and chest inside the nightshirt.

It took perhaps an hour before I had run the voices out of my head and the horror out of my body. Then I turned, trotting back to Yew Tree Cottage at a more leisurely pace. I stopped at the pump in the yard to wash the sweat from my cooling body, and to drink my fill.

The cottage door was open. In the dark doorway, Mama was waiting. She didn't say anything; just held out a glass of elderberry juice and a woolly blanket. She knew I would start shaking the moment I stopped sweating. For the briefest of moments she rested her hand against my cheek. Then she went back to the end room where she and Melli slept, still without speaking a word.

It wasn't every night I ran like this, but perhaps one out of two or three. It was the only thing that helped once the voices had hold of me. Mama woke up every time—not necessarily when I got up, but by the time I came back, she was always awake. It was as if she had some instinct telling her that one of her children was no longer in the house. I hadn't told her about the voices, but she had probably guessed that my sleeplessness had something to do with the Sagisburg and the Hall of the Whisperers. In the beginning she had asked me if there was anything wrong, but I always said no, and now she had stopped asking. She was just there, waiting, with the blanket and the sweet elderberry juice, and then the two of us went back to bed.

I lay down on the cot in my enclosure and wrapped myself in the blankets. My feet were hurting me now, but that didn't matter. In my head there was only silence, and I fell asleep almost at once.

The Flute

The flute rested in the grass next to me. I didn't dare touch it. I hardly dared to look at it, and yet… and yet it was as if I couldn't quite help myself.

My father was dead. The flute was all I had left of him.

Finally, I reached for it after all. Touched its shiny black surface. Picked it up.

There was a sound inside me that needed to get out. Wild as a bird's cry, heavy as a thundercloud. A sound I couldn't make myself. But the flute could.

The first note piped through the air and went chasing up the hillside, and it was as if everything around me fell silent, listening. I hesitated. Then I blew again, harder this time, with harsh, wild defiance.

My father was dead, and nobody cared. Most of them were probably relieved. But he was half of me. He had searched for me for twelve long years, and at last he had found me. And he might not be the greatest father in the world, and he might have given my mother good reason to be scared, and he might have done things in his life that were neither right nor nice nor fair, but he was still my father, and he had held me when I was most scared, and he had sung to me. And he was the one who had played open the gates of the Sagisburg so that Nico and Davin and the other prisoners could get out, and he was the one who had piped dreams of freedom and change into a hundred cowed and desperate children in the House of Teaching so that they found the courage to escape the Educators. So if I felt like mourning him, who had the right to stop me? If I wanted to play the flute he had given me, who could prevent me?

"Dina!"

I gave a start, and my fingers slipped in the middle of a note. *Pfffuuuiiiiihh*, it said, a thin, off-key, and startled sound.

Mama was standing behind me. Her face was hard as stone.

I didn't say anything. I just clenched my hands around the flute so tight that it whitened my knuckles.

It was Mama who finally broke the silence.

"I think you should put it away," she said.

I still didn't answer.

"It's not a toy."

"I know that!" Better than anyone. I had seen what it could do, good *and* bad. I had heard it save lives. And I had heard it take a life, too. Oh, I knew. I knew it was no toy. Better than she!

And so she finally spoke the words we both knew she had been thinking for weeks now:

"I don't want you to play that thing."

She had never mentioned it before. She had wanted me to understand on my own that it was wrong, and that it was harmful and dangerous to me. But now she had had to say the words out loud, and it felt almost like a victory to me. As if there had been some sort of contest between us, like when Davin and I used to see who could stare at the other the longest without blinking. That was before my Shamer's gift kicked in. Now no one played games like that with me.

No one played that game with my mother either. She looked at me, and her gaze was rock hard and yet sharp enough to cut right through me. Cold and hot at the same time. A gaze that made you feel about three inches tall.

I clutched the flute defiantly. It's not for you to decide, I thought, but silently.

I think she heard it all the same.

"*Do you hear?*" she said, this time in her Shamer's voice. And images came crowding into my head, sights I would rather not have seen.

Sezuan was sitting with his back against a quince tree. Shadow's head rested in his lap. But Shadow's body was limp and lifeless, without a heartbeat, without breath....

"No!" No. I didn't want to think of it. Didn't want to think of the worst thing I had ever seen my father do.

"Dina. Look at me."

It was hard to refuse. It was impossible. I looked into my mother's eyes, and the images thrust themselves into my head even though I didn't want them there.

Sezuan slowly rose. He came toward me and might have wanted to comfort me, to hold me. But I could only see his hands, his slender, beautiful flute player's hands that had just killed a living human being....

It was wrong. I didn't want it. And even though I couldn't stop the images from coming, even though I couldn't help thinking about those terrible minutes, I still knew that it wasn't right.

She wanted me to be ashamed of being Sezuan's daughter.

And I wouldn't.

It wasn't *right*.

I don't know how I did it. When my mother used her voice

and her eyes, no one got away until she was finished. And yet I was no longer standing still. I backed away from her, stumbled, righted myself. And turned to run.

"Dina!"

But I wouldn't listen. I stopped my ears with two fingers and ran, eyes half shut, so that I could barely see where I was going. I ran as hard as I could, up the hill, down the other side, across the brook.

"Dina. Dina, stop!"

I could hear Mama calling behind me. Her voice was no longer the Shamer's, just Mama's, and she sounded completely desperate. But I couldn't turn back. I kept going until I couldn't run another step.

The sky was darkening. My fingers were stiff with cold. Every single bit of me was stiff with cold. I was sitting with my back against one of the stone Giants of the Dance, looking down at our little cottage. Someone had lit the lamp, and the windows had been left unshuttered, so that the light made yellow squares in the yard. I knew this was so that I would be able to find my way home more easily. I knew Mama was down there, in the kitchen probably, and beside herself with worry. Melli would have asked for me. About a thousand times, I imagined. And Rose, and Davin... it would not be easy for her to explain.

Mama was terrified that I would turn into someone like my father. She knew I had the serpent gift—*his* gift—just as I had her Shamer's gift. But she didn't want me to become a Blackmaster.

I didn't either. But... but... I didn't know what else I could be. I didn't know what sort of a being I was: Mama's daughter, Papa's daughter, or some other thing completely.

The chill was spreading through my body. There was a sheen of hoarfrost on the grass. If I stayed here all night, there might be no need to think of Shamer's eyes or serpent gifts, or indeed a future of any kind at all. If I didn't get up soon and try to get some life back into my numbed legs… the Highland cold could kill you, I knew. Callan had said it over and over: "Find shelter. Light a fire. And if ye cannot keep warm in any other fashion, walk. Move. Sitting still can kill ye."

I could go down and sneak Silky out of the stables. Ride off. Go. Go to Loclain, perhaps, where they didn't know I had the powers of a Blackmaster. Or to the Aurelius family in Sagisloc who would surely take me in, what with being so grateful because we had brought Mira back to them. They would welcome me, I knew.

Rose. Melli. Davin. Mama.

I couldn't do it.

Slowly, I got up. My legs were so numb I had to lean against the dark dappled granite behind me. My feet were two lumps of ice. Could there be frostbite already? I began tottering around the giant stone, one hand against the rock so as not to fall. Slowly, life seeped back into my lower legs, and then my feet, though I still couldn't feel my toes.

It was a long way down the hill to Yew Tree Cottage and the windows and their warm yellow light. When I finally pushed open the door, Rose's dog, Belle, was the only one to welcome me in her usual manner, with eager little yaps and a furiously waving tail. Rose and Davin were staring at me as if they thought I might be ill. Melli had long since been put to bed. Mama sat by the fire, her back turned, saying nothing. She didn't look at me at all. And I was just as careful not to look at her.

Planning a Murder

Ziiiiing. Hwiiisssj. Hwiissj-ziing-swok.

Damn. Another hit.

The steel blade hissed through the air, in long sweeping arcs, in short brutal stabs. Whenever it found its target, there was a wet, rather disgusting sound, and in Maudi's empty sheep shed there was by now a penetrating smell of beet juice and sweat.

I was breathing in short, deep gasps now, and my side stung so hard I could barely stand upright. But I wasn't about to give in, not now. Not as long as there was even the tiniest hope left.

Hwiissj-ziing... swok.

My parry failed completely, and another beet bit the dust, in two uneven halves. I had only one left now, perched on its stick like the head of a scarecrow, defenseless except for me. Some defense I had been so far. If Nico managed to hit the last beet, I was done for, and he had won.

"Come on, Davin," he said, and yes, he was breathing hard, but not as hard as I was. I could probably run longer and faster than he could, but when it came to fencing, Nico moved more easily and spent his strength more wisely. "You can do better than that!" He egged me on with his free hand.

Easy for him to say. His dark hair was black with sweat, but there was no uncertainty in his movements. Considering that he didn't even *like* swords—

I saw the attack coming at the last moment and blocked the blow with a lightning parry.

Claaang.

I felt an involuntary smile pull at the corners of my mouth. Not this time, Nico. This time I was too quick for you!

But where—

No!

Oh *damn*. If only he'd stay in one place.

Swockkk! The last beet tumbled to the ground. And I stood there, arms shaking and sides heaving, and had to face the fact that I had lost.

Nico wasn't the sort to rub my nose in it. He merely wiped the beet juice off his blade with a rag and gave me a brief nod, like a kind of salute.

"Again?" he asked. "This time I'll defend, and you can attack."

He knew very well that I liked to attack. But my arms were hanging from my shoulders like two leaded weights and I wasn't sure I would ever be able to lift them again.

"No thank you," I said. "I think I've had enough for one day."

He nodded once more. "Tomorrow, then."

"Are you coming back in with me?"

"I think I'll just run through a couple of exercises."

"Nico, don't you think you've had enough?" He might be less reckless with his strength than I was, but I could hear his breathing even through the sound of the rain drumming against the shed's turfed roof, and glistening trails of sweat ran down his bare chest.

"Just one more time," he said, his jaw clenched. As he raised his sword, I could see his arm tremble. Yet he still began a series of lunges and parries, now with an invisible opponent instead of me.

I shook my head, but he didn't see.

"I'll get us some water," I said, pulling on my shirt.

"Nico?"

He had finally put down the sword and was standing in the doorway, gazing at the autumn rain. His shoulders slumped, and I was pretty sure his legs must be shaking. Mine certainly were.

"Yes?"

I passed him the bucket and the ladle, and he drank greedily of the cold water.

"Why… why the rush?" I had never seen anyone train as doggedly as Nico did. Day in, day out. With the sword or the knife in the mornings, with the bow in the afternoon. Sometimes he saddled his brown mare and trained mounted combat with a long wooden lance he had carved for himself, but it was clearly the knife and the sword that held his main interest.

Something moved in his eyes, something bitter and dark.

"I suppose you think we have plenty of time?" he said.

"What do you mean?"

He looked away. "Nothing."

"Nico—"

"Wasn't it your idea anyway? That we should train, I mean?"

He had a point. It had been me, a long time ago, before Valdracu, before the Educators and the Hall of the Whisperers.

"Yes, but there's no need to half kill yourself. What's your hurry?"

"Weren't you listening? That letter. Your mother read it out to us. Surely you haven't forgotten."

"The one from the Widow?"

"Yes, that." He said it in a what-else tone of voice, and it wasn't as if we had letters coming in every week, I had to admit. And of course I remembered what the letter said. Arkmeira had fallen, by treason it was said. It had been the only city in the coastlands not under Drakan's fist, and now he had Arkmeira too. But there had been resistance, and Drakan did not let resistance go unpunished. He had had every fifth man in the city executed, wrote the Widow. Not necessarily those who had resisted the most, just every fifth. *One, two, three, four, you die.* There was a sickening lurch inside me every time I thought of it, as if it was somehow worse for being so calculated.

"People die," Nico said in a strange voice I couldn't remember having heard him use before. "People die every day."

I didn't like the new voice. I didn't like the look on Nico's face—his eyes so unnaturally dark they hardly looked blue anymore, and his skin so pale under the sweat.

"And what exactly are you planning to do about it?" I asked.

"There is one obvious and sensible solution, isn't there? Logically speaking."

"Which is?"

But he was suddenly done talking.

"Forget it," he said. "Just the rain getting to me, I suppose. You can't really go out, and yet sitting indoors drives you crazy, doesn't it?"

"Nico—"

"No, forget it. I'll be along in a minute. You go on ahead."

I went. But I didn't forget. He had some plan, I thought, some plan he didn't want me to know about. But I knew Nico very well by now. You can't spend several days and nights together in the Hall of the Whisperers without learning a thing or two about each other. And when someone who hated swords suddenly began to practice fencing with such dogged persistence, it had to be because he figured he would need a weapon soon. And all that talk of an obvious solution… I suddenly halted. Killing Drakan. That was the obvious solution, simple and logical if one didn't consider the fact that Drakan was surrounded by thousands of Dragon soldiers and anyway was no slouch with a blade himself.

It would have been easy for Nico to gather a rebel army around himself. The Weapons Master and the Widow had often talked to him about it, and Master Maunus, who had once been Nico's tutor, missed no opportunity to point out to Nico that it was his duty as the rightful heir to Dunark. But Nico kept refusing. Just the other day, the day the letter came, they had had a row about it. It offended Master Maunus's sense of proprieties horribly, but Nico said only that he was no warlord, and that he had no intention of asking hundreds of people to die in his name.

I knew what he didn't want. But what was it he wanted?

I had to keep an eye on him. Because if Nico had some plan to get close to Drakan, I wasn't about to let him do it without me.

The rain had almost stopped, but my trousers were soaked to the knee from walking through the wet heather. Dina and Rose were picking juniper berries on the hillside between our cottage and Maudi's farm, and both of them had kilted up their skirts to avoid the mud. Rose had very nice legs, I noticed. A pity they were rarely on show. And then I suddenly felt embarrassed. Rose was… Rose was a sort of foster sister, wasn't she, and it wasn't right to look at your foster sister's legs in that way. Was it?

"Where have you been?" asked Dina.

"Training with Nico."

"You do that all the time now."

I was beginning to think so too, but I didn't say so.

"Dina, you sometimes talk to Nico, don't you?"

"Sometimes. So do you."

"Couldn't you keep an eye on him?"

"What do you mean?"

"Just keep an eye on what he's doing. And then tell me."

Dina gave me a look that was close to being the old Shamer's look, very straight and with the punch of a mule kick. "Spy on him, you mean?"

"Not spy, exactly. I just… if he behaves any differently from the way he usually does, I'd like to know."

"Why?"

I squirmed. I hadn't intended to say even as much as I had, but I had forgotten Dina's gift for prying the truth from people. "Only so that he doesn't do something stupid."

"Stupid? Nico is one of the most sensible people I know."

I thought of the things Nico had said about "an obvious and sensible solution." I was pretty sure that that wasn't what my sister meant by sensible.

"If you see him packing stuff. Or something," I finally said. "Tell me. Please."

Now I had her worried too, I could tell.

"Davin. Tell me what it is you think he'll do."

I didn't mean to. But I suddenly found myself telling her the whole thing, about the too-hard training, about Drakan and the sensible solution, about the plans I was almost certain Nico had. Plans for murder.

Both of them were staring at me now.

"Alone?" said Rose finally. "You think he'll go alone?"

"I'm afraid he might."

"But we won't let him!" Rose's eyes were glittering with a very familiar stubbornness, and I remembered how hard it could be to get rid of her when she had her mind set on something. It might not be such a bad idea to sic the girls on Nico. Let's see you get away from *them*, I thought with some satisfaction.

Mama called from the cottage door. Dinner was ready, and the same could certainly be said for my growling belly.

I took two of the baskets from the girls, and we walked down the hill together.

"Should we tell Mama?" asked Dina.

I shook my head. "Not yet," I said. "She has enough to worry about."

A Knife in the Dark

It wasn't long before Nico made his first move. It probably began with Katlin the Peddler's visit. She came by with her handcart, complaining to anyone who would listen that trade was bad these days, people had nothing to sell or buy. And it was certainly true that her store had shrunk to a bit of woolen yarn and some badly crafted pots. We had no need for any of that—it was no better than what we could make ourselves. But she must have had something for Nico, after all, because I saw him give her a coin before she traveled on.

"Keep an eye on him," I told Dina. "He's up to something."

And lo and behold. The very next day, Nico suddenly wanted to go on a shopping trip, or so he said. To Farness.

"Farness?" said Mama. "Why Farness?"

"It's about the only place left where you can get proper goods," said Nico. "And we're short of about a hundred things."

True. Iron nails were hard to come by now, and there seemed to be a shortage of rope as well. And the salted herring that Maudi usually bought by the barrel for winter stores had been impossible to get. Worst of all, though, was the lack of decent flour. It had been months since we had seen a proper trader's cart, and the Highlanders were beginning to realize that this was no coincidence.

"It can't go on like this," said Mama. "Drakan can't decide who is allowed to trade with us on both sides of the mountains!"

Nico grimaced. "Apparently, he has succeeded in scaring Sagisloc and Loclain into cutting off our trade."

Drakan had tightened his fist so hard that barely a jar of preserves got through, let alone a herring barrel. It hadn't been a huge problem as long as we could still get goods from Loclain, but if Nico was right, it could mean a very hungry winter in the Highlands.

It made good sense to go to Farness to get herring and nails and suchlike while it was still possible. Farness was a seaport, one of the few the Highlanders had, and some of the ships that put in there came from afar, from Belsognia or Colmonte or places even farther away. Towns that had not yet felt the pinch of Drakan's long fingers and did not know that they were supposed to be afraid of him. It made sense, yes, but I didn't think it was a coincidence that Nico was so keen to go himself.

I caught Dina's eye across the table. She nodded almost imperceptibly—she was on to Nico too.

"Maybe we should all go," she said. "We need the cart anyway, for the herring barrels and the rest, and if we brought some herbs and things to trade, it might not be so expensive."

Mama's eyes went to Dina briefly, and then to me. She had a sense that something was going on, I think, but she wasn't certain what it was. And she was being extremely careful not to look at Dina for too long, I had noticed. Something was wrong between my mother and my sister, I needed no magic to see that. And I was almost certain it had something to do with Sezuan Puff-Adder. Dina hadn't been the same since she found out about her father and what he could do.

"It would be nice to get away for a bit," I said. "Have something to do."

Mama's glance softened. She was probably thinking of all the nights I went running because I couldn't stand lying still, listening to the Whisperers.

"Go, then," she said. "I'll stay here with Melli. That's best, I think."

Melli still wasn't quite her old self after our headlong flight from Sezuan that summer. She clung to Mama more, and often seemed younger than her six years.

"But Callan will go with you!" Mama added.

I frowned. "Who would look after you, then?" I asked, because Callan Kensie had been my mother's bodyguard during all the time we had been with the Kensie clan.

"Killian or one of the others. You can choose, Davin. You can go with Callan, or you can all stay home."

I sighed, but I knew that was the end of it.

"We'll go with Callan," I said.

A cold and stubborn rain poured steadily onto our heads and was slowly but surely soaking through my thick woolen cloak. It had been a wet autumn altogether, wet and dreary and anxious because we didn't quite know how we would manage through the winter. This trip to Farness might be mostly an excuse to Nico, but we really did need the things we hoped to buy there. And if no ships had come in that were willing to trade with us… if things got bad enough, we might end up having to raid Drakan's caravans and coastland fortresses in order not to starve.

"How far is it now?" asked Rose, blowing a raindrop off the tip of her nose. "This is no fun at all!"

I nearly told her that she could have stayed at home, but actually I was pleased that there were three of us keeping an eye on Nico. Besides, she was right—it really wasn't much fun to ride here with every bit of clothing you wore sticking to you like some second clammy layer of numb skin.

"Fair bit yet to go," said Callan.

Falk snorted, shaking his head so that the wet reins slid through my fingers. He didn't like the rain any more than I did.

"Come on, horse," I muttered at him. "We're all wet, and it's not *that* far."

Finally we struggled up the last steep rise. It was a good thing we had two horses pulling the cart—a gray and a black gelding, both of them on loan from Maudi. She wanted her herring barrels home safe.

We could see the sea, now—gray-black like the heavy sky above us. And there, at the end of a long narrow firth, lay Farness. Two hundred houses, perhaps, give or take a couple. I don't know why they made me think of mussels—perhaps because the tarred walls had the same bluish-black color, or perhaps because the houses clung to the rocks much like mussels did. In the harbor were plenty of ships, more ships than houses, almost, or so it seemed at first glance.

We didn't stop to admire the view. Now that we no longer had the mountain between us and the sea, a stiff, briny wind whipped into us, making the rain feel even colder. Rose clucked her tongue encouragingly at the two carthorses, and they began the climb down the long, steep stone slope.

"Remember the brake," I said.

"Oh, yes, thank you *soooo* much, I nearly forgot," said Rose acidly, and it was probably stupid of me to remind her of something that was more or less the first lesson when one learned to drive a cart in the Highlands. But *if* she had forgotten, the heavy cart might plow right into the horses that were supposed to be pulling it, and that could be lethally dangerous. I was really just trying to watch out for her. But… I didn't know how it happened, but we always ended up snarling at each other like a couple of grumpy old watchdogs. In spite of the fact that I actually liked Rose a lot.

Considering that she hadn't been much used to horses at home—she had grown up in Swill Town, the lowest and meanest part of Dunark, where such conveniences were rarely afford-able—it was quite an achievement that she had driven a team of horses all the way from Baur Kensie to Farness without missing a turn. The horses were a fairly placid pair, but still, not much of a city brat anymore, was our Rose.

"Take the North Road," said Callan. "To the Harbormaster's yard. I know the Harbormaster, and if he has no room for us, he'll know who has."

The Harbormaster's place proved to be one of the biggest in the town, four whole wings with a cobbled yard in the middle, with a proper pump and a stone trough for the horses to drink from. Three of the wings were tarred wood, but the fourth was a fine stone house in two stories. The Harbormaster himself came to greet us. He had a broad weather-beaten face and long gray hair held together in a tidy queue at the back of his neck.

"Welcome, Kensie," he said, holding out a hand that was nearly as big as Callan's wide fist. "What takes ye to Farness?"

"Herring," said Callan, shaking his hand warmly. "And nails. And flour. And a couple of other odds and ends. How is trade?"

The Harbormaster made a sound in his throat. "Aye, well, those with goods to sell are happy. Those who need to buy, less so. But herring I can get ye for sure, we catch those ourselves. Come in out of the wet, and we'll sit us down and talk."

The big room the Harbormaster led us into was an odd mixture of office, store, and ale room. There was a constant flow of people, who came to learn news of ships or goods, or to pay their harbor fees—anyone who anchored at Farness had to pay a sort of tax to the Harbormaster, ranging from a few pennies for a small boat up to ten or twelve copper marks for the big trading vessels.

The Harbormaster's wife served something she called toddy, hot and sweet and strong all at once. I'd never had it before, but it was really nice and warmed my chilled body. I wasn't the only one with a taste for it either—most of the Harbormaster's customers stuck around for a drink or two before heading back into the rain.

Callan chatted with the Harbormaster about the goods we needed—what were our chances of getting them, what would we have to pay, would anyone be willing to take Mama's herbs and salves in exchange? Considering that the whole thing was Nico's idea, he didn't participate all that much in the conversation. His gaze wandered around the big room, and every time the door opened, he looked to see who had entered. And while Nico was watching the door, I was watching him. I had no doubts at all—Nico had a plan, and it required him to meet somebody here in Farness.

Suddenly Nico froze. He was no longer looking at the door. Instead, he was staring rigidly at his toddy as if he was afraid that somebody might steal it. I glanced around quickly. Had he finally come, the man Nico was waiting for? Who had been the last person to enter? That had to be the one over there, in the long black cloak and the broad-brimmed felt hat, which he hadn't taken off even though he was now indoors.

I nudged Dina and pointed behind my toddy glass at the man so that no one else would see the gesture. She nodded faintly. She had also noticed how Nico was suddenly so intensely interested in his own toddy.

After a while, Nico got up, accidental-like.

"Where are you going?" I asked.

"Just wanted to stretch my legs."

Oh sure, I thought, but I didn't say anything. I pretended to be interested in what the Harbormaster and Callan were saying to each other instead.

Nico didn't just march over to the table where the man in the felt hat was sitting. He wandered around for a bit, following a card game for a little while, then moving on to listen, apparently, to two men bargaining over the price of some bales of wool. If I hadn't *known* that he was up to something, I might not have noticed what happened when he passed the man with the hat and the black cloak.

But I did see.

As Nico walked by, something passed from one hand to the other. I wasn't even sure if Nico had passed the man a note, or if it was the other way around. I only knew that something had been given, and something received.

I wondered what.

The man in the cloak and hat got to his feet and went out into the rain. I got up as well.

"Where are you going?" asked Nico sharply.

"Just stretching my legs," I said in much the same voice he had used earlier. And before he had time to do or say anything else, I had made my way through the crowd to the door. It was raining so strongly now that the raindrops spattered off the pavement, spraying you from below as well as from above. The man in the black cloak seemed to be in a hurry. I barely got a glimpse of him before he darted through the gate and into the streets of Farness.

I followed. At least the evening dark and the heavy rain would make it harder for him to see me, and if I could discover who he was and where he came from, we would know that much more about Nico's plans.

At first it looked as if the man was headed for the harbor. But then he suddenly changed direction and began to make his way uphill, through one of the narrowest and steepest of Farness's alleys. Rainwater ran in small muddy streams between the houses, and a chorus of barks followed us. I hoped he wouldn't notice that the barking continued for quite a while after he himself had passed by.

Wait. Where did he go? One moment he was there, a dimly seen figure a little ahead of me, and the next… nothing. Just the rain, the darkness, and the alley.

Was there some door I hadn't seen? A corner he could have disappeared behind? I walked faster, even though the alley was so steep that it made my calves ache. Where had he gone?

Something hard and heavy hit me from behind, and I tumbled onto my hands and knees in the middle of one of the muddy rainwater gullies. A second later, something even heavier landed on my back, knocking me flat on my belly, so that I ended up swallowing a mouthful of gritty gutter silt. Euuuch.

"Do you think I'm blind? Or deaf? Or stupid?"

The voice was no more than a whisper, a chill whisper in the dark. I had no trouble hearing it, though. A knife against one's neck sharpens one's concentration wonderfully. I shoved against the pavement and tried to roll to one side, away from the knife, but a warning prick made me stop.

"Lie still, boy. Or you might get hurt."

"Who are you?" I hissed. "What is it you want?"

"None of your business. Didn't your mama teach you not to pry?" Another small jab of the knife stressed his point. "Can you count to a hundred?"

What did he mean?

"What—"

"I asked if you could count to a hundred?" Another prod with the knife, not a deep one, but enough so that I could feel a warm trail of blood running down my neck to mix with the cold rain.

"Yes." Was he some kind of a maniac?

"Then do it. Stay down and count to a hundred before you get up. If you try to follow me again, I'll kill you."

The voice was still only a whisper, but I had a very clear sense that he would do exactly what he said he would do, if necessary.

"Is that clear, boy?"

I tried to raise my head, but the man with the knife shoved my cheek into the stony ground.

"Is that clear?"

"Yes," I muttered, spitting out another mouthful of gutter water. "Let go of me."

"Let me hear you count."

"What?"

"Count. Loudly and clearly, please, so that I know I won't have to put a bolt into your back."

A bolt? Did he have a crossbow? Or was he just bluffing?

"Start counting!"

He had a knife at least; I had felt that clearly enough. Reluctantly, I began to count.

"One, two, three…"

"Go on."

"Four, five…"

The weight was gone from my back.

"Six, seven, eight…"

Steps disappearing into the darkness. I sat up.

Thhhhwappp. Something long and black skittered across the stones of the alley only a few inches from my knee. He did have a crossbow, it seemed, or a partner armed with one. How many of them were there?

"Last warning. Keep counting!"

How far had I got?

"Eight, nine, ten…"

There was a low purr of laughter from the darkness, and a different voice, teasing and soft, quite different from the cold harsh whisper. "Good boy."

A woman, that much I was certain of. That made at least two of them, and one of them had a crossbow. So I sat there in the rain, counting—"twenty-eight, twenty-nine, thirty"—feeling like a complete idiot, and yet too uncertain to get up. Until I had reached sixty-three, and I suddenly heard Nico's voice behind me.

"Davin, anything wrong?"

Oh yes, quite a few things. I was cold, wet, and furious, and I felt like grabbing Nico by the throat to shake the truth out of him. What kind of murderous maniacs had he got himself mixed up with?

"What could possibly be wrong?" I said sourly, getting to my feet. "I'm just sitting here in the rain practicing my counting."

"Davin…"

But I didn't feel like discussing it. "Shouldn't we be going home? Or at least out of the rain?"

Nico looked at me. He was wearing neither hat nor cloak, so he must have followed me as quickly as he was able. His hair was sticking to his forehead in dark, wet spikes.

"That sounds like a good idea," he said. And so we walked back to the Harbormaster's house together, pretending that everything was normal, pretending that there had been no man in a black cloak, no knife, and no crossbow.

I had discovered absolutely nothing. I still didn't know who the man in the cloak was, or what he had given or received from Nico. Of the two of us, only one was the wiser: Nico now knew that we were watching him.

When we got back to the Harbormaster's, there were some people Callan wanted Nico to meet. I got out of it by saying I needed to change into some dry clothes, and the Harbormaster's daughter showed me upstairs, to the room where we were to sleep. Dina and Rose went with us, and the moment the Harbormaster's girl—Maeri, her name was—was out of the door, they pounced on me. Who was the man in the cloak? What had I found out? Unfortunately, the answer to *that* question was nothing much.

"Did he cut you?" Dina eyed me anxiously when she heard about the ambush. "Let me see."

"It's nothing." I wanted to forget the whole episode. I wasn't proud of my belly-dive into the gutter, or of the helplessness I had felt with that knife at my throat. In any case, the cut was small and had already stopped bleeding.

"But I still have no idea where he went. We've nothing to go on."

"Not quite nothing," said Rose.

"What do you mean?"

With a strange, shy-looking shrug, Rose produced a small crumpled up piece of paper.

"What's that?" asked Dina.

"The note Nico got from the stranger."

"But how did you get hold of it?"

Rose blushed and looked at her feet. "It wasn't so hard."

I gave her a sharp glance. "Where did you learn to be such an expert pickpocket?"

"Don't start again!" she said angrily. "I'm no thief!"

"No, but..." I vividly remembered the last time I had suggested that Rose might have a somewhat relaxed attitude to yours and mine. The slap had set my ears ringing, and I had probably deserved it, because Rose hadn't stolen anything. All the same, it was strange how she had managed to get the little note away from Nico without him noticing it.

"It's just not everybody who—"

"Do you want to know what it says or not?"

"Of course I do."

"Then stop asking stupid questions!"

Dina smoothed the crumpled note. "The Sea Wolf, tomorrow before dawn," she read. "I wonder what that means?"

"Has to be a meeting place," I suggested. "An inn, perhaps."

"Or a ship," said Dina. "Are any of the ships in the harbor called *Sea Wolf*?"

"We'll find out," I said. "All we have to—"

Rose flapped her hands in warning.

"Sshh," she hissed. "Give me that. Someone's coming."

She tucked the note into her apron, and not a moment too soon, because just then Nico and Callan pushed through the door.

"Aye, but it is a rude price to ask," Callan growled. He and Nico appeared to be in mid-discussion.

"That's the way of it when goods are scarce," said Nico. "I say we close the deal and count ourselves lucky that we can *get* flour at all."

Callan scratched his neck. "Might be," he said. "But rude all the same!"

A Clip on the Ear

Next morning, the sky was clear, though there was still a great deal of wind. That seemed to be the rule here rather than the exception. In many ways, it was a strange place to put a town—barren and storm-swept, with nothing much to recommend it to anyone who did not love rocks and waves and seagulls. By far the best thing about Farness was the harbor. It was full of life, people and animals and ships, from the huge broad-bottomed trading vessels to the tiny dinghies that splashed their way from ship to pier and back again, or from one vessel to another. There were bleating goats in wooden crates, there were sacks and barrels and chicken cages, coils of rope and cloth for sails, and a briny smell of tar and wood and seawater.

We were searching for the *Sea Wolf*, Dina and I. Rose's task was to keep an eye on Nico, who had gone out with Callan to try to trade for the goods we needed.

"There," said Dina, pulling at my sleeve. "The one with the red sails!"

I ran my eyes over the row of ships along the pier and found one with red sails. Dina was right. The name was painted on a plank up near the bow, along with the black outline of a wolf's head.

I looked curiously at the ship. Was it just a meeting place for Nico and the man in the cloak, or was he planning to sail away right in front of our noses?

"I wonder if I could get aboard," I muttered.

Dina looked frightened. "Davin, no!"

"Why not? It's pretty common, boarding a ship. Look around. People do it all the time."

"But—"

"Might even be rude not to stop by and say hello, seeing as how we're in the neighborhood."

"Davin, you don't know them."

"I know one of them. Sort of…"

"The one who stabbed you with a knife. And told you he'd kill you if you tried to follow him again!"

"It was dark. He probably won't even recognize me in daylight."

"No, Davin. If anyone is going aboard that ship, it has to be me."

"You?"

"Yes. At least they don't know me. They might not stab me on sight."

There was a sort of point to what she said, but there was no way I would stand calmly on the pier and watch my sister walk into danger. Possible danger anyway.

"What would you say to them?"

"Not much," she said evasively. "What is it you want to know?"

"When they sail. Where they're going. Is the Cloaked Man aboard. That kind of thing."

"All right. Wait here."

I never meant to. No way was I letting her do this, what with her being my sister, and a girl, and all that kind of thing. But sometimes, somehow, it's really, really hard to stop Dina when she has her mind set on something. She was already—Wait, where had she gone? She seemed to have disappeared into the crowd without a trace. How can you stop someone you can't even see? So there I was, biting my nails, my eyes glued to that bloody ship. I hadn't seen her board it, but where else would she be?

It took forever. Around me, people were busily loading or unloading their barrels and boxes and whatnot, and I knew I was in the way. This was no place to stand and admire the view. I sat down on a barrel—herring, by the smell of it—but my butt had barely touched the wood before a short, sinewy ship hand told me to be off, this weren't no twopenny show. I was so worried about Dina I couldn't even think of a comeback. Where was she? I could count to twenty, slowly, and if she wasn't back before that… What if the ship sailed?

That thought made my palms sweaty. What would I do? Throw myself off the pier and try to swim after them?

Sixteen, seventeen, eighteen… it was too much like the night before. Was the Cloaked Man there or not? What if he recognized Dina? He might have noticed her at the Harbormaster's. Damn. I had had enough of doing nothing. I was going aboard that ship if it was the last—

"They sail tomorrow morning. But I didn't see the Cloaked Man anywhere."

I think I actually jumped a foot.

"Dina, how the hell do you *do* that? I haven't taken my eyes off that ladder for a second!" Not completely true, of course, but close enough. How could she suddenly be standing right in front of me?

"Do you want to know what they said or not?" She had this oddly wooden expression on her face and wouldn't quite look at me, and all of a sudden I knew why.

"It's something *he* taught you, isn't it? The Puff-Adder."

"Don't call him that!"

"Oh, I do beg your pardon. What would you like me to call him instead? My Lord Blackmaster? Sir Dreamkiller the Brave? The celebrated Colmonte Assassin?"

"How can you say such things when you were *there*, when you saw what he did for us and… and what it cost him. He saved your life, Davin!"

"Don't remind me."

But she just had, hadn't she? And she was right too. I did owe my life to Sezuan and his Blackmaster arts. I just couldn't stand the thought that Dina… that my *sister* was his child, and that she was in any way like him.

"Dina, he was not a good man," I said, as gently as I could.

She looked at me for a long moment, and there were tears in her eyes.

"You don't know anything about him," she finally said, and turned away from me and left me there. And I know she tricked me on purpose. I know it was no coincidence. She *did* something to me, and suddenly, a screaming seagull trapped my eyes, and I had to look at it. And by the time I was able to tear my attention away from the gull and the bay and the wide gray waters, it was too late. Dina was nowhere to be seen.

I was so furious that walking was too slow for me. I ran all the way back to the Harbormaster's house, not caring who I jostled or pushed aside in my hurry. So when Dina turned into the gate, I was already there, waiting.

It wasn't something I calmly decided to do. It was stupid, and afterward I was sorry. But the moment I saw her coming around that corner—practically backward because she was so busy trying to see if I was following her—my hand shot out and caught her on the ear, flat and hard.

"Never do that again. Ever!"

It took her completely by surprise. She hadn't even seen me before I hit her. I saw her tears and her shock, but I was furious.

"Is that what you want to be? A sneaky, belly-crawling *snake* who cheats and lies and deceives everyone?"

She was deathly pale, except for where my hand had hit. Four red fingers showed on her cheek, as clearly as if I had painted them there.

"What if that is who I am?" she said in a hard voice I barely recognized. "I am his daughter too, Davin."

"No, you're not! You're ours. Not his. What would Mama say if she knew about your sneaky little tricks?"

"Shut up." She was trembling all over. "Shut up! If you say one more word about Mama, I'll… I'll—"

"Davin! Dina! What on earth is going on here?"

I spun. Nico stood there. Rose and Callan were coming up the street behind him with the Harbormaster.

"Nothing," said Dina.

"Nothing?" Nico stared at her. "Davin, did you *hit* her?"

Afterward it was very hard to explain. That I had been so furious, I mean. That I hit Dina. *Hit* her. But it was… as if someone had pushed me, or forced me to do something by tying me or holding me. That would be one thing, and bad enough. But what Dina had done was worse. She had pushed me *inside my head*. And that was a different kind of force. More… more like what the Educators had done to me. That was the best explanation I could give.

And I couldn't even tell Nico that much. Because then I would have had to tell him what Dina had done, and then Nico would know that she... maybe he knew already. That Dina could do the same kind of thing that the Puff-Adder had done. But I couldn't make myself say it. And Dina was just as silent. She stood there with those stubborn tears in her eyes and the red marks on her cheek, vivid as a brand.

"What is it with the two of you?" Nico's gaze went from one of us to the other. "Dina, what is going on?"

Dina ducked her head. "Nothing," she muttered once more. She tried to push past him, but he held out a hand to stop her.

"Dina." His voice was very gentle. "Something is wrong, any idiot can see that. But whatever it is, surely it can't be so bad that we can't talk about it."

She looked at him for such a long time that Nico had to look away, even though she wasn't using her Shamer's eyes. Nico would so like to meet her eyes calmly and trustingly, hers and Mama's both, but he was like a horse that had been whipped. He had once been forced to meet the full force of the Shamer's gift, and something inside him could never quite forget the pain.

"You don't know," said Dina. "You just don't know." And when she pushed past him this time, he let her go.

Then it was my turn.

"Why did you hit her?"

His dark blue eyes were cold. I could feel the weight of his gaze, almost like an icy gust of wind. Nico did not have Shamer's eyes, of course, so really there was no need to duck my head. But I felt less than proud of myself right then.

"None of your business," I said and started walking so he

had to step aside or slam into me. "It's a family matter. And last time I checked, your last name was not Tonerre."

I was almost all the way across the cobbled yard before I heard him mutter, "If only it was."

At first I didn't understand what he meant. But then I remembered what he was probably planning. A lonely journey through a hostile land, a journey which would, if he was good and really, really lucky, end in the killing of his own half brother. It might not always be all peach pie and roses, being the Shamer's son and Dina's brother and all that. But I was suddenly glad my name *was* Tonerre and not Ravens.

The Sea Wolf

"The *Sea Wolf*?" said the Harbormaster. "Now, why are ye so keen on that ship? Anyone would think ye were looking to buy her." He laughed gratingly, for people who found it hard to pay two silver marks for a barrel of herring hardly had the means to buy a fully rigged sloop. And that was what the *Sea Wolf* was, I had discovered. A two-masted sloop plying freight from the Magdan Coast to Farness and back again.

"I just want to know who owns it," I said. "Common curiosity is all."

"Common, ye say? Well, your curiosity is uncommonly like to the Young Lord's. What would ye know but he asked me the very same thing."

Did he, now? I wasn't sure whether that was good news or bad. It proved he took an interest in the ship, but then, we knew that already. And if he had been asking questions, at least it meant he didn't intend to leap blindly into the arms of the *Sea Wolf* and her crew.

Dina hadn't come down for lunch. Rose glared at me across the table in a manner that should by rights have left two scorched spots on my woolen jerkin.

"I just thought I saw someone I know board her," I muttered, just to say something.

"Aye well, that might be so. But her owner is not known to me. She comes through here half a dozen times a year, drops her cargo and picks up another, and then is off again. A man they call the Crow pays her harbor fees; that is all I know."

The Crow? Was that the man in the cloak?

"Well, wouldn't he be the owner, then?"

Again, the Harbormaster laughed his grating laugh. "Lad, ye have much to learn about the shipping business. Merchant ships like her are not owned by those who sail in them. No, there is a merchant somewhere, on the Magdan Coast, it might be, getting richer with every voyage she makes. As long as she does not go down, of course, and as long as he buys and sells the right goods." He nodded toward the desk where his wife was selling her toddies. "He is in today, the Crow, with his first mate. Sitting right over there. Ye can ask him yerself, if ye care to."

I scanned the crowd at the desk. The Cloaked Man was not among the people jostling for their drinks.

"Which one is he?"

"The long one," said the Harbormaster.

The long one. No doubt there—one of the guests stood head and shoulders above the rest. And looking at him it wasn't hard to see how he had come by his nickname. His hair was black and smooth like a crow's feathers, and he had the biggest, beakiest nose I had ever seen. It really looked as if he could jab people with it.

"Well?" said the Harbormaster, a glint in his eye. "He does not bite. As far as I know."

"Stay away from him," hissed Rose between her teeth. "Surely you're not that dumb?"

"Maybe later," I told the Harbormaster.

"Aye well, ye know yer own business. No knowing how long he will stay, though."

I could tell he thought I was scared of the man, and that bothered me. But Rose was right. It would be stupid to go up to him openly. Wouldn't it? Or on the other hand…

"I think I'll buy myself a toddy," I said, sliding off the bench. Rose made a grab for my sleeve, but I pretended not to notice. Once I was on my feet, though, it occurred to me that the Crow might have been the ambusher with the crossbow. But by then it would have looked like cowardice to sit down again.

The bar was busy, and Maeri, the Harbormaster's daughter, had to lend a hand with the drinks. She smiled at me.

"Would ye like a toddy, Davin?"

"Please." And then I thought of the shrunken state of our wallet. "A small one."

Maeri threw a quick look over her shoulder. Her mother was busy at the other end of the bar.

"One small toddy, that will be two coppers," she said. But she poured me a full measure and winked at me.

"Thank you." I raised the glass and sniffed at the spicy steam, leaning against the counter to try and hear what the Crow and his mate were talking about.

"… hear the last of it," said the first mate. "Trouble and more trouble, that's what comes of having women aboard."

"Really? You seemed to be having a fine old time," said the Crow drily. "Wasn't it you who lent her the second knife?"

Women aboard? What was a woman with a knife doing aboard a merchant sloop?

"Besides, there's money in it, I tell you."

"Money in it for you, perhaps."

"For all of us. A fortune. As long as I don't have to listen to any more of your yapping!"

Maeri gave me a brilliant smile—I think she thought I lingered at the bar because of her. If only that had been the case. She was dark-haired like her mother and really very nice. But I didn't like what I had heard about the money. Nico didn't have much, not anymore. So how were they planning to make their fortune?

"Drink up," said the Crow. "And go see to that cooper. I need those barrels today."

The mate put down his glass and headed for the door. I followed him with my eyes.

Then I felt a hand on my arm. The Crow's hand.

"Do you like fish, boy?"

I pulled away from him. It wasn't difficult; he wasn't trying to hold on to me.

"Not particularly."

"Then maybe you should keep your ears to yourself. Or someone might invite you to visit with the fish."

What was it about that ship that made everybody tell me to stay away from it?

"Are you saying I was eavesdropping?"

"Yes," he said flatly. "That's exactly what I'm saying."

He slammed a few coins onto the counter and left.

"Now, that was a really clever thing to do," said Rose. "But there might still be one or two people aboard that ship who don't know how curious you are, so maybe you ought to go stand on the pier and shout at them for a while, just to make sure the slow ones get it too."

"You think you're so clever," I said, knowing it wasn't the smartest comeback of all times. "What's your great plan, O Mastermind?"

"How about we get up before dawn so that we can be on the pier to stop Nico from getting on that ship before she sails?"

Well, it wasn't such a bad plan. Although *my* idea was not so much to stop Nico as to be sure he didn't leave without me. But I wasn't going to tell her that, was I?

"All right," I muttered. "Have it your way."

Dina and Rose had it easy. They shared a bedroom with Maeri and her two sisters, and sneaking past three sleeping girls couldn't be that hard. But Callan… Callan had been a caravan guard most of his adult life, and for the past two years he had been my mother's bodyguard. He was used to sleeping with half an eye open, to say nothing of both ears. And what would I say if he woke up? But if Nico could do it, so could I.

Or so I thought.

"Where are ye going, lad?"

"Need to pee," I murmured.

But Callan threw aside his blankets and sat up.

"Use the pot, then."

"No, I'd rather—"

"Listen, now. Ever since we came here, you and the two lasses have been running around with a wasp down yer pants. First one of ye is off, and then the other. Ye cannot sit still for a moment, and now ye cannot even stay in yer bed at night, or piss in a pot like any other man. Something is going on, and ye can damn well tell me what, or else lie back down nice and quiet."

He meant it too. I couldn't see his face—there was only a narrow stripe of moonlight coming through the shutters—but I knew him well enough by now to know that that tone of voice suffered no gainsaying. If I did try to leave, he would do what was necessary to stop me.

Damn. What now?

Nico had not interfered. Not a word, not a move. Was he still asleep? Or even—

"Where is Nico?"

"In his bed," growled Callan. "Like any normal man. And if ye think—"

And then he noticed. There was a roughly human-shaped hump in Nico's side of the bed, but it consisted of a couple of pillows and somebody's cloak. Nico was gone, and so were his saddlebags.

Callan's huge fist closed around my arm like a vise.

"Out with it, boy. What are ye up to?"

Nico was gone. He was probably on his way to the harbor, or already on board. There was no time for talk and explanations. I half-spun in Callan's grasp and jabbed my elbow into his stomach, just below the rib cage.

He had taught me the move himself, but he never expected me to resist, I think. In his eyes I was still the awkward "lad" that he had taken under his wing. Perhaps he was regretting his generosity now. With a hiss like a punctured sheep's bladder he doubled up and went down on one knee. I broke free of his hold and headed for the door. I knew he would follow, but one thing at least my nightly runs had done for me—I was fast, and I could go on forever. Or at least for a very long time.

I took the stairs three at a time, not caring if the racket woke the entire household. I didn't know whether Dina and Rose had made their escape. If not, it was probably all the better. I was not enormously keen on them traipsing around Farness on the wrong side of midnight. Behind me I heard Callan's voice, still breathless from the blow.

"Davin! Stop!"

He was angry. If he caught me, I would feel his fist. But that was not why I ran. What really put the speed of fear in me was the thought of Nico, Nico alone on the *Sea Wolf* with the Crow, who had said there was "money in it." I tore open the door, charged across the cobbles of the yard, and flung myself into the streets of Farness.

The wind had died as much as it ever did here, and the moon shone full and bright through a thin veil of clouds. There had been no time to rummage for my boots, but I was used to running barefoot. Down the steep alley to the harbor, sharp left along the pier… where was the ship?

It had been right—

There.

But there was no ship. Only an empty mooring point.

I stopped. Stared across the black waters of the harbor. And there she was, in a silvery lane of moonlight, her sails still furled. She was waiting, ready to be off, but holding back. A small boat, a dinghy, was on its way out to meet her. They were too far away for me to be sure, but I felt certain one of the two people in the boat was Nico.

I didn't waste my breath shouting. If it was him, he would not stop just because I yelled at him. Instead, I took five long paces and leaped straight in.

Huuuuuuwwwhhhh. Cold, cold, cold. For a moment I could barely breathe, and my arms and legs turned from living, moving limbs into stiff, awkward sticks. I had to force them to get going, urging them on like some recalcitrant horse. Come on. Move. A stroke. Another. Kick, you miserable legs. Come *on*, or we'll never make it!

The boat was already rounding the end of the pier.

Idiot, I hissed at myself. Did you really think you could catch up to a boat rowed by nice long oars when all you have are a couple of frozen arms and even colder legs? It was hopeless.

I kept going anyway. The ship was at anchor and didn't move. If I wasn't able to catch the boat, I might swim all the way out to the *Sea Wolf*.

I battled on through the freezing water, stroke by stroke. Sharp little waves kept slapping me in the face, so that I had to snort the water from my nostrils. How far had I come?

Not far at all. Not even past the pier yet.

I won't make it, I thought. It's too far, the water's too cold. It would be better to turn back now when I still had a bit of strength left to save myself. What good would it do Nico if I drowned from sheer exhaustion between the *Sea Wolf* and the pier?

But Rose was right. I wasn't too smart. I kept swimming.

Splash. A different sort of splash, not the waves this time. *Splash swish, splash swish…* the sound of a rowboat.

"Davin! What on earth are you doing?"

I looked up. Nico was leaning across the gunwale, keeping the boat steady and still with one oar while the other one rested in the oarlock, dripping.

"Swimming," I said between my teeth.

"You can't! It's too far."

"Wanna bet?"

"Turn around!"

I made no answer. I merely reached up one frozen arm to cling to the gunwale.

"And where exactly do you think you're going?" I asked.

I noticed now that the other person in the boat was the Cloaked Man. Same cloak, same hat. But something was missing. What?

The beard. Last time I saw him, he had had a beard. "Hit his fingers," he said.

No. Not he.

Long, red-gold hair beneath the hat. A voice that was not a man's voice. A face too delicate, now that it was not hidden by the beard. And a shape, glimpsed beneath the cloak, that was by no stretch of imagination that of a man. He was a she.

I almost let go in sheer surprise. The Cloaked Man was no man at all!

"Davin, don't be stupid. I'm not letting you into this boat. You might as well go back."

I was still staring at the man who wasn't. I was so freezing cold it was difficult to think, but somewhere in the chilled depth of my brain, an idea stirred.

"It's quite a long way to the pier," I said.

"You'll make it."

"The water's cold."

"You were the one who insisted on jumping in."

"I'm actually quite tired." Not totally wrong.

"You're a strong swimmer. Don't you think I know that?"

I suppose he did, after what happened in the cavern beneath the Sagisburg. Even if he had been the one to find the Educators' fake "golden cup" first.

"My arms are stiffening." Absolutely correct. "I can't feel my legs anymore." Also no lie. "Nico, if you don't let me into that boat, I'll drown."

"Hit his fingers," said the Cloaked Woman once more. "Nicodemus, we have no time for this!"

Nico gauged me with his eyes. Then he did the same thing with the distance and the dark waters between me and the pier. And then, he held out his hand.

"Come on, then," he said. "But I'm putting you ashore. You are *not* coming with me."

"Nicodemus!" objected the woman.

"Carmian, it's no good. It's too far. He really might drown."

He had to haul me aboard like some large and dying fish. I was a bit shaken to discover how much the cold water had weakened me. What I had begun as a trick, might not in fact have been the lie I thought it was.

"Idiot," muttered Nico as I lay gasping in the bottom of the boat. "You'll catch your death of cold."

He stuck both oars back in the water and began to row for the pier. But right then, lights sprang up in the darkness.

"Davin!" It was Callan's voice. "Nico! Come back!"

There was a sound from Nico, a sort of irritable hiss.

"Did you have to wake up the entire town?"

"What did you think? That we were just going to let you sneak off into the night?"

Not that I was all that pleased to see Callan myself, or to see Dina and Rose standing next to him. But I might as well make the most of it.

"What now, Nico? Are you still going to drop me off at the pier? And do you then expect Callan to stand calmly by while you sail off into the moonlight?"

"Throw him overboard," said the woman—what had Nico called her? Carmian? "He'll find his way to shore, or else his fine friends will help him."

Nico watched me for a while. I did everything I could to look at least as worn out and frozen as I felt.

"No," he finally said. "We'll have to take him with us."

Sea Chase

I stood there on the pier, helplessly watching as the ship with the red sails disappeared with my brother and Nico on board. Not again, I thought. Please. Not again. I couldn't bear it if we were to be parted again, if Mama and me and Melli and Rose had to be half crazed with fear all over again because we didn't know what was happening, knowing only that it was dangerous, and that we might never see them again.

"Dina?" Rose touched my arm. "Was he in the boat? Was it him?"

"They were both there," I said. "Davin and Nico."

Callan turned. He took hold of my arm, not hard enough to hurt, but firmly enough for all that.

"I want an explanation," he said. "And nobody is going anywhere until I get it."

Rose and I looked at each other. She gave me a faint nod, and I agreed. There was no longer any reason to keep secrets. At least not the ones that had to do with Davin and Nico.

"Nico is up to something," I said. "Davin thinks he is going to try to kill Drakan. Alone."

Callan cursed under his breath. "And that is why the two of them took off?"

"Yes. Or at least, that's what we think. But it isn't… you see, we think Nico has picked a dangerous ship. Because someone from the crew threatened Davin with a knife, and one of the others said that there was money in it."

"Money? The Young Lord has no money now."

"No. But they might make a great deal of it by selling him to Drakan."

"A hundred gold marks," said Rose. "Drakan has promised a hundred gold marks to anyone who can bring him Nico's head. *That* is a lot of money in anyone's book."

"What is the name of the ship?"

"The *Sea Wolf*."

"The Crow's sloop?"

"Yes. Do you know him?"

Callan didn't answer in so many words. He simply took off at a run in the direction of the Harbormaster's yard.

"Wait," I called, because it seemed to me he was going the wrong way. "We can't just—"

"Stay there," he shouted. "Don't ye dare move! If anyone else is missing when I come back, I'll tan yer hides for ye!"

It was some time before Callan returned. Rose and I stood there, staring across the black waters and watching the sails of the *Sea Wolf* grow smaller and smaller. In the end we couldn't even see the ship itself anymore, just the stern light, shining like a tiny, low star in the middle of all the darkness.

"Why didn't we tell Callan about all this yesterday?" asked Rose after a while.

"Davin wouldn't let us."

"We should have done it anyway."

"Yes."

"We were stupid."

"Yes."

We were both silent for a few moments. Then Rose went on, very quietly, as if she was afraid she might insult me.

"Dina?"

"Yes?"

"Why did he hit you?"

I had almost forgotten about that. But as soon as Rose mentioned it, my cheek stung all over again at the memory, and I remembered the way Davin had looked at me. *Never do that again. Ever*!

"How did you know about that?"

"It showed. And Nico asked. Nico asked me if I knew what was wrong between the two of you."

What is wrong, I thought to myself, what is wrong is that my brother can't stand the fact that Sezuan is my father. *Also, you probably shouldn't have tricked him*, insisted a small inner voice I didn't want to listen to.

"I didn't do anything!"

I hadn't even realized that I had said the words out loud before Rose answered, "I never said you did."

But I had done something. Without thinking. Almost without wanting to. It was just that I wanted Davin to stay on the pier. I wanted him to look the other way while I sneaked aboard the *Sea Wolf*. It wasn't as if I had forced him to look into my eyes and used the Shamer's voice on him, or something like that. I hadn't really *done* anything… and yet I had.

It was a slippery thing, the serpent gift. It didn't wait for you to make up your mind whether or not you wanted it. It didn't even wait for you to decide that you meant to use it. Wanting something was enough.

Wanting. I would have to be careful about that in the future.

I wasn't angry at Davin anymore. I just felt miserable. I would have liked to tell him I was sorry, but that was not exactly possible right now. The *Sea Wolf* had left Farness Bay, and I didn't know whether I would ever see my brother again.

Callan came back with the Harbormaster and two other men at his heels.

"Go back to the yard, girls," he said.

"Why?" I said. "What are you going to do?"

Callan hesitated for a moment.

"We will try to catch them," he said. "The *Sea Wolf* is not slow, but the Master's own ship is faster. We shall catch them, never ye worry."

"I want to come."

"No. Better ye stay here. A ship like this is no place for a lass."

But I was not going to be put off like that. I didn't want to be stuck here, worrying and waiting.

"Callan. *I want to come.*"

Usually, people did what Callan told them to do. Even grown men did as they were bid without a second thought when it was Callan doing the bidding. But when it came to Mama and me, I wasn't sure why, but he seemed to have a soft spot.

He was looking at me now. And more than that. He was letting me have my way.

"Come, then," he said. "If ye must. Rose too. But quick. And stay out of the way of the crew."

I could tell the other men were surprised. One of them grinned.

"Are ye making this a ladies' trip, Kensie? Not so sure I want to come, then."

Callan looked him up and down. "Tell me one thing, Malvin. Can ye stop six hundred fighting men with a word?"

The man looked properly confused. "I cannot say that I can. Why?"

"Because Dina can. So if ye make me choose, Malvin, I take the lass."

Malvin opened his mouth and then closed it again. He looked at me sideways, as if he was trying to work out what was so special about me. But he didn't say anything after that.

"Go below," said Callan. "They have a pretty lead. It will be many hours before we catch up."

"I know that."

"Go below, then. Ye're cold."

I shook my head. Not because I wasn't cold—my teeth were chattering. But down in the cabin I would not be able to see what at least I could see now, despite the darkness and the wildness of the weather: a glimpse, every now and then, of the stern light ahead of us.

A stiff wind blew from the northwest almost straight into our faces, so that we had to cross against the wind. The Harbormaster and his crew were busy, and the *Swallow* leaped and heaved, leaped and heaved, dancing from wave top to wave top.

The light in front of us winked out. It was not the first time I had lost sight of it. The sea was choppy and wild, and sometimes the blackness of a rock spur hid it from view. But this time it didn't reappear. I clutched at the gunwale until my fingers hurt, but still there was nothing to see except dark sea, dark sky, and a few thin slivers of moonlight that escaped the clouds.

"Callan!"

"Aye," he said. "I saw."

"What happened?" What if they had hit a rock? What if they—In my mind's eye, people and wreckage were already floating in the cold water, Davin, Nico…

"They put out the stern light," said Callan. "They know we are chasing them."

I breathed a little easier. But this was bad enough, because how were we supposed to catch a ship we couldn't see?

"Steady as she goes," the Harbormaster called to his helmsman. "If they go on, we'll sight them as soon as the sun comes up. If we do not, there are only two places they can be—Dog Isle or Arlain. They cannot hide in Troll Cove. It is too shallow for the sloop."

"What if they dump their cargo?" asked Malvin. "They would ride higher, then."

The Harbormaster grinned. "That is the Crow's ship ye're talking about, and he is a tightfisted bastard. He will not throw as much as a dishrag overboard, never ye fear."

I hoped he was right. And this time, when Callan told me to go below, I went. But the hours until dawn came were long and restless, and I did not sleep much.

As soon as I woke up, I knew the wind had died down. My hammock was swaying only gently, and although I could still hear the creaking of the boards and rigging, it was nowhere near the racket it had been when I went to bed.

I tumbled clumsily out of the hammock. It was not the sort of bed I was used to, but Callan had said it would be better for me than one of the berths because the hammocks moved with the ship and did not toss you about with every wave.

Rose was still asleep. She had pulled the blanket all the way up to her nose, and all I could see of her was a bit of fair hair, so summer-bleached it almost shone white in the gloom of the cabin. I opened the cabin door as quietly as I could so as not to wake her, crossed the cargo hold almost without teetering, and climbed up the narrow ladder onto the deck.

Behind us, the sea was flame-colored with sunrise. Ahead, the sky was darker, but not so dark that I could fool myself. No sail. No ship. The *Sea Wolf* was nowhere in sight.

"She gave us the slip," said Callan when he caught sight of me. He looked tired, and that was rare. Normally he seemed about as frail as a mountainside or an oak tree. "We'll put in at Arlain to see if they are hiding there."

"And if they're not?"

"We'll try Dog Isle. Never ye worry, lass. We'll find them."

At Arlain—a tiny fishing village, no more than a score of houses—there was no *Sea Wolf*.

"It will be Dog Isle, then," said the Harbormaster, bringing his ship about. But when we cleared the point at Dog Isle, there was no sloop waiting in the shallow bay.

"Could she have returned to Farness?" said the Harbormaster? "She might have run past us in the dark."

"Why would they?" objected Callan. "What use is that to them? Perhaps they've headed out to sea."

"We would have spotted them. The weather is clear enough, and Malvin has been up the mast with the glass four times already."

"That ship has vanished from the face of the sea," said Malvin, and I saw his fingers make the witch sign, just to be safe. "*Poof*! Like magic."

The Harbormaster frowned. "The Crow is sneaky, I grant ye, but he is no magician. They must be here somewhere."

All that talk of magic reminded me.

"Troll Cove," I said. "What about Troll Cove?"

"I told ye, she cannot go in there." The Harbormaster slid me a sideways look, not happy to have his judgment questioned.

"Could we check? Where is it?"

"East. About an hour's sail."

"Please, can we look? Maybe he did dump his cargo."

The Harbormaster shook his head. "The Crow likes his money. Ye trust me now—he does not throw away anything he does not have to."

But I couldn't stop thinking about the words Davin had heard him say: that there was money in it, a fortune.

"How much is his cargo worth?" I asked.

"Mostly wool this time, as I recall, and herring. About sixty silver marks. Or seventy, it might be, with times as they are."

That was a huge amount. More ready money than the whole of the Kensie clan saw in a year. But still nothing to the hundred golden marks Drakan would pay for Nico.

"Go to Troll Cove," I said.

And perhaps Callan's thoughts were like to mine.

"We must," he said. "We cannot afford not to."

Troll Cove

"Well, I'll be damned," said the Harbormaster.

The *Swallow* inched her way forward with the black cliffs of Troll Cove hugging her on both sides, so tall and dark that the water, too, looked entirely black. There were lookouts up the mast and at the stern, and the helmsman looked poised like a hunting dog, ready to act instantly on their calls. This was a narrow, dangerous place, with reefs that could rip and tear like monstrous teeth. But this was not why the Harbormaster cursed.

In the water in front of us, a bale of wool was bobbing. It was low in the water, barely visible. Brine had already started to soak it, and had we arrived half an hour later, we might not have seen it at all.

"I'll be damned," repeated the Harbormaster. "He did dump his cargo!"

Callan smiled. "Yes, and the beauty of it is it does him no good. We have him now."

The *Swallow* moved carefully farther and farther into Troll Cove. At the very bottom, the narrow cove opened up a little, to form a natural harbor. And that was where the *Sea Wolf* was anchored. I knew her at once by the red sails and the wolf's head at her bow.

"Furl sails," called the Harbormaster. "Drop the anchor."

61

"Why?" I whispered to Callan. "Why don't we go all the way in?"

The Harbormaster heard me despite my whispering.

"We have him right where we want him," he said. "This way, we are like the cork in a bottle, and there is no way he can pass us without running aground. And if we want to talk to him, we can always use the dinghy."

"We do want to talk to him," I said. "We want to get Davin and Nico off there."

Callan nodded slowly. "Aye," he said. "If we can."

What did he mean? Of course we could. Hadn't the Harbormaster just said that they couldn't get past us?

The *Swallow*'s small dinghy was lowered into the water, and Malvin dropped the rope ladder down the side of the ship. Callan began the climb, and I moved to follow.

"Not you," he said. "Ye stay here."

"But I can help. Nico listens to me!" I didn't say anything about Davin, because I knew that listening to his little sister was about the last thing he wanted to do right now. But Nico might. He still felt he owed us something, Mama and me.

Callan hesitated. Then he nodded. "Come on, then."

I swung my leg over the gunwale and grabbed the ladder. It was a long way down, longer than I had thought, and when the *Swallow* rocked, so did the ladder. One of the crew held it steady with a boathook, but it still swayed alarmingly. I was quite relieved when I reached the dinghy. Me and boats... we didn't really agree with each other. I'd much rather have a sensible horse.

Rose made no bones about following, and she was clearly more at home with rope ladders and dinghies than I. Callan gave her a grouchy did-I-say-you-could-come look, but he didn't say anything. He and Malvin each took an oar, and the boat slipped across the dark waters toward the *Sea Wolf*.

"Ahoy," called the Harbormaster when we came within hailing distance. "Ahoy, the *Sea Wolf*."

They had already seen us, of course—there was no way two ships that size could be that close without noticing each other—but apparently no one felt like answering. The Harbormaster had to hail them three times before they bothered to reply.

"What do you want?"

It was the Crow himself, leaning across the gunwale of the *Sea Wolf* to look down at us. His narrow face was completely expressionless, and right now he looked more like a hawk than a crow.

"We want to talk. Permission to board?"

"No." That seemed to be all the Crow had to say to that.

"Ye do not have to be rude," said the Harbormaster.

The Crow didn't answer. The waters whispered against the hull, and the silence grew.

"Ye have two passengers aboard," the Harbormaster finally said.

"Really? That's news to me."

"Come on. This is stupid, man. Let us aboard so that we can talk like ordinary, decent people."

The Crow looked no friendlier than before.

"This is Troll Cove," he said. "There's no sheriff here, nor no harbormaster neither. No watch, no port fees to be paid. Here your word means no more than a seagull's cry or the splash of a wave. So turn your ship around and go back where people actually listen to what you say, *Harbormaster*."

And with that, the Crow turned away from the gunwale, and we could no longer see him. It had begun to rain, tiny little cold pinpricks almost like hail. For a while the Harbormaster stood staring up at the *Sea Wolf*, a thunderous look on his face. He did not like being spoken to in that way. Finally he sat down again.

"Go back," he said. And Callan and Malvin turned the dinghy and rowed back to the *Swallow*.

We sought shelter belowdecks.

"What do we do now?" said Callan. "It will not be easy to persuade him."

The Harbormaster growled in his throat. "He is well within his rights. He does not have to let us on board. On the other hand, we are also well within our rights if we simply stay here, riding at anchor. Then we will see who tires of the game first."

Malvin, who apparently doubled as the ship's cook, came in with a pitcher full of hot, spicy wine and half a loaf of dark bread.

"How long d'ye want us to stay here?" he asked. "The larder is a bit understocked, what with leaving so sudden."

"Aye, well, we can manage for a few days, surely," said the Harbormaster. "And I reckon the Crow might be in more of a talking mood by then. He seems to be in a hurry, and he has more mouths to feed than we do."

"A few days, aye," said Malvin. "If ye do not expect a feast."

Callan stirred uneasily. "Maudi's purse might stretch to feeding us," he said, "but we cannot pay the crew wages for many days."

"I know that," said the Harbormaster. "But nearly all my crew are Laclan men, and they will do what serves the clan, with or without wages. Which is more than can be said for the Crow's men."

"Kensie thanks ye," said Callan.

The days passed. We took out the dinghy again, but this time the Crow wouldn't even come to the gunwale, and we had to return once more with our business unfinished and our call unanswered. As the sky grew dark and the sea even darker, I stood staring at the *Sea Wolf*. It was so strange to know that Davin and Nico were so close that they could hear me call if I shouted. But even though I had borrowed the Harbormaster's glass several times, I had seen neither hair nor hide of them. They must be down below, hiding—though I couldn't for the life of me think why. We knew they were there, so what good did hiding do? Perhaps they thought we would give in more quickly if we couldn't see them. But the Harbormaster had a pleasingly implacable look on his face. He wouldn't budge. The Crow's own rudeness had seen to that.

"Get some sleep, lass," said Callan, once the darkness was so complete that the *Sea Wolf* was no more than a vague outline, almost indistinguishable from the black rocks. "You too, Rose. Nothing more will happen tonight."

"Do you think they will try to get past us in the dark?" I asked.

Callan shook his head. "Not unless they are completely daft," he said. "They would end up on the reefs."

Bump. Scrape. Footsteps on the deck above my head.

"Oh, be quiet," I muttered. "Some of us are trying to sleep."

A half-strangled cry, and still more steps.

"What's happening?" said Rose in a sleep-soaked voice.

"I don't know."

I lay for a few moments, listening to the sounds that filled the night. Something was going on up there.

Suddenly Callan's voice cut through the darkness.

"Foes!" he called. "Foes aboard!"

Foes? It could only be…

"The Crow," whispered Rose, her voice thin with fear. "The Crow and his men."

I swung my legs over the side of the hammock and fumbled for the lamp. Then I realized that this might not be the smartest move I could make. I thought of the Crow's cold black eyes, and I suddenly didn't want to do anything that would make it easier for him to see me.

Something touched my arm. I jerked, but it was only Rose, of course.

"Should we go up?" she asked. "Or hide?"

I felt like scuttling under the bed, except there wasn't one. But the *Swallow* was not a big ship, and they would find us sooner or later. I could hear shouts and thumps and tramping feet, and there was clearly fighting going on. If the Crow won that fight—I knew Callan was a strong and cunning fighter, but who knew how many stood against him? Probably there wasn't much two twelve-year-old girls could do, and yet Rose had saved the day before now, once with her knife and once with a frying pan. And I had weapons too, though they were not the kind you could cut and bash with.

"Let's go up," I whispered.

We crept up the ladder, but we were barely halfway there when someone came tumbling the other way. A large body slammed into me, knocking me backward.

"Ouch!" hissed Rose, which was quite understandable. We were all in a pile at the foot of the ladder, me and Rose and the one who had come tumbling.

I didn't say much myself, being winded from the fall. And the idiot who had knocked us down wouldn't move. He lay there across me like a fallen log. I pushed at him, trying to free myself. And got my hands all wet. No, not just wet. Sticky.

He was bleeding.

Rose wormed her way free of me and the wounded man.

"Dina? Dina, are you all right?"

I nodded, but of course she couldn't see that, what with the darkness.

"Yes," I finally managed, still fighting to breathe. "But he's bleeding, Rose."

"Who? Who is it?"

"I don't know. Too dark to tell." I hoped it wasn't Callan. Or the Harbormaster. Or… were Nico and Davin here, too, fighting in the dark?

The man stirred, muttering. I couldn't tell what he was saying, but at least he didn't sound like anyone I knew. It might be someone from the *Sea Wolf*. I managed to wriggle clear and got to my feet.

"I don't think it's anyone we know," I whispered to Rose.

"Should we… should we do something?"

Light the lamp, heat water, clean the wound and bandage it. But not now, not while they were still fighting up there on the deck.

"It will have to wait," I said. "Come on."

But it wasn't easy, up there on the deck, to tell friend from foe. Right next to the hatch, two men were rolling about, trying to strangle each other, and although it was slightly less dark up here under the skies, I still couldn't recognize either of them. Once I had made hundreds of men stop in the middle of battle, in the middle of shouting and fighting and dying and killing each other. Surely I ought to be able to end a simple brawl?

"Stop," I yelled. "Stop that!"

But there was not the least bit of Shamer's edge to my voice, and the brawlers on the deck paid me no notice.

Callan did.

He was all the way up by the bow, surrounded by a pack of *Sea Wolf* men, keeping them off by swinging an oar like a quarterstaff. I recognized him because, well, even in darkness Callan is hard to miss.

"Down!" he yelled. And the order was meant for me and Rose, I knew. He didn't want us here, he wanted us to stay below, crouching in the darkness until it was all over.

But his small shift of attention cost him dearly. One of the sea wolves ducked under the oar and thrust upward with whatever weapon it was he held. And even at this distance, even through the din of stamping feet and grunt and bodies hitting the deck or each other, even in the midst of all that chaos, I heard it—the noise that came from Callan as the thrust went home.

"No!" I screamed, but it was too late, and no one listened anyway. For a moment the sea wolf and Callan stood close together, almost as if they were dancing. Then the oar clattered to the deck, and the pack closed on Callan, so that he disappeared in a whirl of shoulders and feet and flying fists.

I didn't think. I just leaped across the two stranglers, ran across the deck to the bow, and threw myself at them, kicking and yanking and punching, anything, anything to make them stop hitting him.

"Stop it! Stop it!"

If only Mama had been here. She could have stopped them. Any decent Shamer could have stopped them. But not me. Once it would have been easy. It no longer was. Now I was too much my father's daughter, and not enough like my mother.

One of the men jabbed an elbow in my face, hitting me on the chin. My teeth rattled, and there was a searing pain in my jaw. I curled up on the wet planks of the deck, hugging the pain, looking up at the masts that seemed to be swaying much harder than they usually did.

I think I passed out for a few moments. Suddenly, the fight was over, and we hadn't won it. Someone had lit a lantern and hung it on a boom, and the Crow was considering the catch its yellow light revealed: Callan, the Harbormaster, Malvin and six crewmates, and Rose and me. The *Swallow* had fallen to the foe, and now no one knew what would happen to us. Perhaps not even the Crow.

Nico was furious.

"No steel," he said, and his own voice sounded cold and sharp like a blade. "That was the agreement."

"Is that so?" said the Crow. "Perhaps you should have explained that agreement more thoroughly to the *Swallow*. I don't think they quite understood it."

In a way it should have been a relief to see Nico still free to act with some kind of authority. In my mind's eye I had seen him often enough as a chained prisoner deep in the *Sea Wolf*'s belly. But what I felt wasn't relief. More like betrayal.

How could he?

Nico. *Nico* had agreed to the raid on the *Swallow*, Nico had taken part in the planning of it. And now Callan lay on a make-shift mattress of sailcloth with a wound in his side that wouldn't stop bleeding. We didn't even dare try to carry him below. No steel? Look more closely, Nico. That wound wasn't made by a fist.

Nico's face was so pale it was almost the same color as the sails of the *Swallow*. He couldn't even make himself look at Callan. But I felt no pity for him. How could he? How could he let the Crow attack a peaceful ship, how could he agree to men hitting other men, even without "steel"? Hadn't he thought how that might end?

"You can't play patty-cake with people like this," said the Crow. "You don't get a man like Callan Kensie to lie down by patting him gently on the cheek. What did you think?"

Nico glared furiously at the Crow and made no answer. And Davin stood by the railing, staring at Callan with a sick look on his face. Had he been part of the raid too? Probably he had, even though I hadn't seen him. He certainly looked guilty enough.

The *Swallow* crew was sitting or lying on the deck, most of them tied up. Only Callan and Malvin's friend Hector were so badly hurt that the Crow hadn't found it necessary to tether them.

"Row ashore," said the Crow. "We've wasted enough time. Put them ashore, sink the ship, and let's get out of here."

There was a roar from the Harbormaster. In spite of his bound hands, he struggled to his feet.

"Sink her? Would ye sink *my* ship?"

"Sorry," said the Crow. "We haven't enough crew to man them both. And if we left her here how long would it take before you were on our tail again?"

There was a look on the Harbormaster's face that made me cold with fear, although it wasn't even me he was staring at.

"If ye sink the *Swallow*, I'll keep looking till I find ye."

He meant it. He would do it, and when he did, I wouldn't want to be in the Crow's shoes.

The Crow returned the Harbormaster's stare with complete lack of expression.

"Some men think they are kings," he said. "Some men think they are kings because they have been allowed to prince it in a backwater town just a little too long. I'll sink your ship if it pleases me. And if you don't shut your trap, you can join her on her way."

But the Harbormaster was too angry to keep silent.

"If ye so much as touch her, if ye so much as scratch her planks—"

The Crow raised his hand, but Nico caught at his arm.

"No," he said. "The ship, yes. I regret the necessity, but we must. But I am not going to stand here and watch you hit a bound man."

"Close your eyes, then," hissed the Crow. But Nico wouldn't yield. And in the end, the Crow lowered his arm.

"Get them into the dinghy," he said. "We need to get out of the cove before the tide changes."

I was terrified that Callan's wound would tear. He might look like he was built from rock and iron, but no man could bleed as he had done and not be in danger of his life. I had been afraid to let them take him below, and now they were proposing to lower him over the side to the dinghy, bobbing next to the *Swallow*, in order to be rowed across the troubled black waters to the small, bleak, stony beach of Troll Cove.

"Careful," I told the men who were guiding his descent. "Watch out!"

One of them gave me an irritated glare; the other growled, "All right, all right," and continued to let out his rope. Callan didn't make a sound, though I could tell he was still conscious.

When I wasn't holding my breath with terror, I was entertaining murderous thoughts toward the man who had used his blade on Callan. And toward Nico. Well, maybe not murderous, but…

I didn't understand. Nico, who was always so careful to think matters through and do the right thing. Nico, who hated swords and violence. What had happened to him? I had never seen him like this before, so pale and determined, so clenched with purpose. Haunted, almost. As if he was seeing something the rest of us were spared. And whatever it was, it made him do things that were alien to him. Acts I would never have thought he could agree to, let alone commit. The raid. Callan. The plan to sink the *Swallow*. And now this. What did they think would happen to us if they left us stranded here in Troll Cove, where no one lived and the way to the nearest friendly place was treacherous and rocky and several days' long at the best of times? What would we do for heat and food? How could I look after Callan here? Had Nico no thought for that?

The strange thing was, he had. I knew he thought about it, and that it was tearing him apart. He made the Crow part with a tinderbox, some blankets, and what extra food they had. But they still left us there.

But the strangest thing of all happened when they were ready to row back out again. Nico gave a firm nod to two of the sea wolves, and they grabbed hold of Davin.

"What—"

Davin never finished his question. Suddenly he was flying through the air, fighting and yelling, to disappear into the shallow waters just a few paces from dry land.

He came up spitting like a mad tomcat.

"What the hell is that supposed to mean?"

"Discharge," said the Crow, smiling thinly. "Thank you kindly for your services, but this is where you get off."

"Nico!"

But Nico perched in the boat, pale and alien and distant, and would look at neither Davin nor me, and least of all at Callan.

"No," he said. "I won't take you with me."

The men were already running out the oars. Soon it would be too late.

I made my decision.

Whelp

I couldn't believe it. There was Nico, perched in the bow of the dinghy, regarding me calmly while the oarsmen made the boat glide farther and farther away from me, out into the narrow cove.

No, calm might be overstating it. His face might be expressionless, but he was as pale as a sheet. Annoying, superior, unfathomable, yes. But calm he was not.

I yelled at him. I knew it would do no good, but when you stand knee-deep in cold water, dripping wet, while your friend is sailing away from you on his way to—only the gods knew where he was going, and how it would end.

"Nico! You idiot *bastard*. Come back!"

But of course he didn't. All I had for my pains was the sight of the Crow's smile growing wider and more triumphant. Finally I shut my big mouth and waded ashore. There wasn't much else I could do, and this water was *very* cold.

"Take off your wet things," said Rose, handing me a blanket and somebody's sweater. "You'll catch your death, else."

She wasn't kidding. The chill air was nipping at my skin, sucking the warmth out of my body like some alien ghost, and my feet were pale blue with cold. I pulled off my wet shirt and dried myself with the blanket as best I could. Some of the *Swallow*'s crew had already gathered a pile of dry seaweed and were attempting to coax a spark from the tinderbox. But most of the men were standing stock-still, staring out to sea at the dinghy that was even now approaching the bulk of the *Swallow*.

"They'll not do it," said one. "Will they?"

"Oh, they'll do it," said another, spitting as he spoke. "That Crow will kill ye as soon as look at ye."

The Harbormaster said not a word. He just watched, his hands clenched into fists, his arms hanging helplessly.

And then we heard the sound of blows, hammer blows against heavy oak planks. It didn't happen all at once. Very slow, it was, at least at first. The *Swallow* listed a little to one side. Then a little more. And then, clumsy as a calving cow, she keeled over on her side and sank.

"They did it," said the man who hadn't wanted to believe it. "Those evil devils really did it!"

His crewmate made no answer. He merely spun on his heel and hit me flat handed, but so hard that I fell over sideways in the sand. Rolling, I leaped to my feet and swung at him, but the blow was slow and halfhearted, because in a way I understood him better than I liked. In his eyes, I was one of the "devils" who had just sunk his ship, and thanks to Nico, I was right here in front of him. In front of him, and his six crewmates. Not exactly the stuff of wistful dreams. If they really decided to hurt me, there wasn't much I could do.

"Stop that, Malvin," said the Harbormaster. "What good is it? And we'll need all the hands we can get to get us out of this. Even his."

Rose looked as if she thought the Harbormaster was letting me off too lightly.

"Get that fire going," she said. "Some of us must stay here to look after Callan while the rest go for help."

And then she suddenly seemed to miss something. She looked around. And looked around again. Then she leaped to her feet.

"Davin," she said, "where is Dina?"

"Dina! Diiiiina."

I called. Rose called. But I think we both knew we would get no answer. Dina was no longer at Troll Cove.

"I'll kill her!" hissed Rose. "If she disappears on me again or gets hurt or dies or something, I'll bloody well kill her!"

"Strictly speaking, she hasn't disappeared," I said. "I mean, we both know where she is, don't we?"

Rose bit her lip. "With Nico."

"Yes. What I can't quite figure out is why."

Rose shook her head. "Why is easy. But how? How did she do it? When Nico wouldn't even take you?"

"He didn't see her," I said.

"Didn't see her? Come on. It's broad daylight! And that dinghy is not much bigger than a bathtub."

I didn't answer. I felt very tired, and not at all like explaining to Rose about Sezuan and the serpent gift. Couldn't she work it out for herself? She had heard it as often as I had, the bit about "only seeing Sezuan when he wants to be seen." That my little sister was just like him—that wasn't something I really felt like talking about.

"What do you mean, 'why is easy'?" I asked instead.

Rose looked at me gaugingly. "Surely you've worked that out."

"If I had, would I ask?"

Her lips tightened. I couldn't tell if it was a smile or a grimace. I often felt like that with Rose.

"If you don't know, then I won't tell tales."

"Rose!"

"Yes?" She gazed at me so innocent-sweet it nearly made my teeth ache. I gave up.

"If you don't want to tell me, then don't. I'll work it out."

"I'm sure you will. Sooner or later."

This time it was definitely a smile. And definitely, the joke was on me. Nothing new in that, and nothing I could do about it. And much, much better than that cold it's-all-your-fault glare. But why was I such a constant source of secret amusement to girls and women? Carmian had laughed at me too.

Carmian. Nico had thrown me overboard, but her he had kept. Did he really think she was more use to him than me? Granted, I had never seen a woman handle a knife as well as she did, not even Rose. But still.

Unless he just wanted her to himself? Perhaps it wasn't her knife he was really interested in.

"The idiot," I muttered.

"Who?" asked Rose.

"Nico." She had very long hair, had Carmian. And even though she usually wore trousers, I couldn't for the life of me understand how I had once believed that she was a man.

"What are you thinking?"

I shot her a quick look. Maybe it would be best not to mention Carmian. Rose took offense at the funniest things sometimes. But at least Dina would not be the only female aboard the *Sea Wolf*.

"Oh, nothing much."

Carmian had called me sweet. But she had said it in the way one would talk of a kitten or a little boy.

"Dina will manage, Davin. She… she is good at so many things."

I nodded. Rose was right, but Dina was also…. Most people thought she was strong and maybe even dangerous because of the powers she had, but she was also just a little girl sometimes, a girl that needed looking after. I didn't like to think of her aboard the same ship as the Crow. And I could hardly bear to remember that almost the last thing that had passed between us was the slap I had given her.

We walked back to the beach. The fire had caught at last, and the seaweed was burning rapidly, with loud pops every time the bladders burst. It smelled terrible, but we needed the heat. Callan most of all.

Callan. That was another thing I could hardly bear to remember. But there was nowhere to hide, and no way I could run, so in the end I crouched next to him, staring at my hands.

"Sorry," I said.

His eyes were ice.

"Where is your sister?"

It wasn't that he didn't know. I think he had figured it out even before I did. So at first I didn't answer, but he wasn't about to let me off the hook.

"Where is your sister?"

And so I had to answer.

"Gone. With Nico."

He nodded—once, and a very small nod only. I didn't think he had much strength left right then.

"This time, boy. This time *you* can tell yer mother."

That was all he said. It was more than enough.

◆　　◆　　◆

Troll Cove really was a backwater. The cove was too narrow for bigger vessels, and very few of the smaller ones ever came here. Why should they? There was nothing here. Only rocks and seaweed and two small freshwater springs.

"It will take at least three days to reach Arlain over land," said the Harbormaster. "Then one more day before a ship can get here. Four days. Might be five, even."

He looked at Callan and, though he didn't say it out loud, we all knew what he was thinking. Would Callan be alive five days from now? With no shelter, hardly any food, and only our poor stinking seaweed fire to keep him warm?

"We didn't know it would take that long," I said. "Nico and I. We didn't know that." And we hadn't thought that anyone would get seriously hurt.

The Harbormaster gave me a cold glare.

"The Crow knew."

"Then he didn't say." A small defiance had crept into my voice. Did they have to paint us blacker than we really were? Did they think I had *wanted* anyone to get hurt?

"Shut yer face, whelp," said the one who had struck me, balling his fists once more. "Better not smartmouth the master, or—"

The Harbormaster suddenly looked even taller and more commanding.

"Pipe down, Malvin," he said. "There'll not be fighting here. And as for you, whelp"—he stuck his finger almost in my face—"I'll not hear another peep out of ye. You and yer folly lost me a good ship already, I'll not lose a good—" He glanced down at Callan and bit back the words he had meant to say. "I'll not lose more. D'ye hear me?"

My defiance melted away. I just nodded, miserable and dispirited. Callan lay in a sort of seaweed nest now, swaddled in every bit of blanket we had. Even his head was blanket-hooded, and the little you could see of his face was pale and shiny with the kind of sweat that has nothing to do with feeling hot. Pain sweat. I knew it well enough myself. And I felt sick to the bone to see Callan like that, knowing part of the blame was on my head. Me and my folly, just like the Harbormaster said.

"Aye well," said Malvin. "The whelp needs a lesson, right enough, and he can count himself lucky we have not the time for such teaching. Someone had better be going."

The Harbormaster nodded. "You know the way," he said. "Best if there are two of ye, though."

"Take me."

I heard the words, and I knew I had said them, but I hardly believed it myself. Three or four days in the company of Malvin, who wanted nothing better than to finish what he had started? Yet that was what I wanted. Better to walk and run than to sit still and wait. Better to strain until the body reached its limits than to look at Callan and be sick to the soul.

Malvin was not thrilled by my offer.

"I need someone I can trust," he said.

I felt like hitting him. So he didn't think he could trust me? I would show him.

"I'm fast," I said. "Faster than any of you. I might save us a whole day, even." And time mattered now.

Malvin ignored me.

"Tristan," he said. "Will ye come with me?"

One of the other men nodded, getting to his feet. But then Callan cleared his throat.

"The lad can run," he said. "Runs every night, nearly."

How did he know? The only other person who knew about it was my mother. Had the two of them been talking about me? Did Mama tell Callan things like that?

And then it hit me, like a slow sort of lightning bolt. A flickering pain through my body. Mama and Callan. Suddenly a thousand little things made sense. Glances, movements. The way he touched the small of her back when he helped her dismount. The evenings he sat in our kitchen, instead of going home while there was still light to ride by. When had it begun? This summer, when we came home from Sagisloc? Or earlier still, back when we thought we had lost Dina, perhaps. I knew something had shifted, then. That he was no longer looking after us because Maudi Kensie told him to. That he had begun to look at us, and especially at Mama, in a different way. Like family, or clan. Someone who had a claim. Someone who belonged to him. Callan. Callan and Mama.

"Are you getting married?" I burst out. The Harbormaster looked at me as if he was now quite sure I had lost my mind. But Callan knew what I meant.

"Mind yer own business, lad," he said. "And run like ye mean it."

Don't die. I only just managed not to say it out loud. Bad enough if I had to tell Mama that Dina had gone missing once more, along with Nico. If I also had to tell her that…

Run like ye mean it. Oh yes.

"Tristan," said the Harbormaster. "Lend him yer boots. The lad cannot run all the way to Arlain barefooted."

Tristan took off his boots and handed them to me. I put them on and did up the laces. They were only a little big.

"Let's go," I told Malvin. "Which way?"

And this time Malvin made no more objections. He pointed up a steep gully, more or less due east.

"That way," he said. "I hope ye can climb as well as run."

The Way to Arlain

We didn't bring much in the way of supplies. Most of it, food and blankets and so on, stayed with the crew at Troll Cove. We would reach shelter long before they did, and it was best for us if we didn't have much to carry.

In the beginning it was a relief to get away from the sight of Callan and from the reproachful looks of the *Swallow*'s crew. Malvin might not love me, but at least he was too busy watching for handholds and footholds to give me much in the way of angry glares. The first part of the way to Arlain called less for the skills of a racehorse and more for those of a mountain goat. But when we had been climbing for about an hour and noon was approaching, Malvin stopped for a breather. We were well up into the black rocks by then and could only see the ocean as a sudden green glint in the distance now and then.

Malvin sat down on a boulder, rubbing his calves. I was too ill at ease for that. Once we stopped, I discovered that I had not escaped Callan. Whenever I wasn't walking or climbing, he was there, inside my head, like a ghost that wouldn't go away.

"Sit down, whelp," said Malvin. "Rest awhile. Drink some water. We have a long way to go."

I didn't want to rest. I wanted to move on. But I took the water skin and had a few long swallows.

"Shouldn't we be going?"

Malvin looked at me sourly. "There's no call to kill yerself."

"Callan can't wait."

"And whose fault is that?"

I clenched my fists, but though I felt like taking a swing at him, I knew that getting into a fight with him was just about the worst thing I could do right now. Besides he was right. More or less.

Malvin was still breathing heavily, I could see. The last rise had been a steep one. But he got to his feet all the same, and started walking.

That night, we slept very little. Only enough so that our weary bodies could rest a bit. It was cold, hoarfrost cold, and I could not stop thinking about Callan and the rest of them and their pitiful seaweed fire. When I finally did fall asleep, the Whisperers were waiting, and now they had fine new weapons to use against me.

… your name is murderer…

… your fault…

Callan's pale face, bloodless and dead.

… your fault…

I sat up with a jerk. My body wanted to run. It was so tired it hurt all over, but I couldn't bear to lie still.

"Malvin."

No answer.

"Malvin, wake up. I want to move on."

He woke only slowly and reluctantly.

"Bloody hell, lad. It's the middle of the night!"

"No, it isn't."

A vague paleness colored the sky, the merest hint of a false dawn.

"Ye cannot see the hand in front of yer face!"

I didn't answer. I just began to roll up my blanket and tie the laces of my borrowed boots. And grumpy old Malvin sighed and rose with a sound like the grunt of a tired horse leaning into the harness once more, though it barely has the strength for it.

"Here." He passed me a couple of the ship biscuits which had been part of the provisions on the *Swallow*. "Ye'll be sick if ye do not eat first."

Surprised, I accepted the biscuits. When had Malvin started to care about my health? But perhaps it was Callan's health he was thinking of.

Climbing and walking, climbing and walking. It was past midday the second day before we got to the first stretch of even ground, and an actual road.

Malvin sank to the ground as though someone had cut his legs in half. His skin was sallow, and his thin reddish beard and hair looked sticky with sweat. He seemed to have aged ten years in two days.

"Malvin, we can't stop now!"

He looked up at me. His eyes were veined with red.

"This is as far as I go," he grated. "Follow the road, lad. Not even a no-sense whelp like yerself can get lost now."

"But…" He really looked completely done for. Even the way he said "whelp" was toothless and pale compared to his earlier efforts. Could I leave him here on his own?

"Off with ye, lad. Run, if ye still have the strength."

Strange. Even though I was very tired myself, the thought of running somehow felt encouraging. My body had so longed for it, because it was the only thing that completely erased the gnawing pain inside. The only thing that would rid me of Callan's face, bloodless and pale… run. *The lad can run*, Callan had said. The time had come to prove it.

I gave Malvin my blanket and the rest of my provisions. All I kept was the water bottle. I thought for a bit. Then I took off my heavy sweater and Tristan's boots.

"Are ye sure, lad?" said Malvin when he saw what I was doing. "If ye have to stop—"

I knew what he meant. If I had to stop, I would get cold. Freezing cold, too cold, perhaps, to survive it. But I was not going to stop, was I?

"I'll not stop," I said. "Not till I get there."

He looked at me. Then he nodded.

"Good luck then," he said, "whelp."

Two sandy ruts and a narrow hump of grass in the middle. That was the road. It cut through heather hills like those familiar to me at home. Heather and shrubs and long, withered grasses, wet and winter yellow. The sun was low in the sky now, but this late in the year no birds were singing. The only sound I heard was the *slap-slap-slap* of my running feet and the noise of my own breathing.

At first, it was pure relief. Finally to run, finally to be free of any thought but the thought of the road. The soles of my feet hit the sandy trail with a muffled sound, and my breathing had a rhythm of its own, not exactly quiet, but all the same, there was a certain strange calm in the middle of all the motion because of the sameness of it. *Slap-slap-slap*, one foot in front of the other, breathe in, breathe out—it was perfectly simple. Easy, almost.

At first.

The sun dropped lower. The road went on, weaving through the hills. And still no houses were in sight. How far to go? Three days, the Harbormaster had said, and Malvin and I had walked almost through the night also, so how far could it be?

Breathe in, breathe out. It was becoming harder. There was a pain deep in my side, and my legs were starting to hurt. But surely I had to be nearly there. Surely!

Uphill. My thighs were practically screaming at me now, but I wouldn't listen. I couldn't slow to a walk now, to say nothing of resting. On. And on. One foot in front of the other.

The sky was charcoal gray. The sun nestled among the hills now, glowing like hot coal. A wind swept through the heather, a cold breath against my sweat-soaked body. And then it began to rain. Heavy, cold drops spattering the sand, striking my shoulders so that it almost felt as if someone were prodding me with a finger.

I thought of Malvin—had he found somewhere to hole up?—and of Rose and Callan and the others. I wanted to run faster, but I couldn't. My legs felt weird, heavy and burning all at once, and my chest and stomach were hurting now with a steady throbbing pain. If that town didn't show up pretty soon…

Rain and sweat ran down my neck. My shirt was clinging to me like an extra skin.

I can't go on.

It was almost like a voice saying it aloud, but the voice was inside me, inside my head.

"Have to."

Like I was scolding some sulky child who had had enough. Won't! Well, you just have to. One foot in front of the other. Just a little bit longer.

I could smell the ocean now. Arlain was a fishing village. Did this mean I was near now?

And then a light shone out through the gathering dusk. The trail dipped, and the light disappeared again, and stayed gone so long that I grew afraid I hadn't truly seen it, but yes, there it was once more, like a tiny star at the end of the road.

I stared at it so hard that I forgot to look where I was going. I staggered sideways, tripped over the grassy verge, and fell. It wasn't that I really hurt myself. I was just unable to breathe for a few moments. I lay there with the raindrops drumming against my back and thighs, and I could easily have gone on lying there. No problem at all, and never mind the rain. The really difficult thing was getting up.

Come on. Get up.

Won't!

Have to.

Can't.

"Up!"

Callan's bloodless face.

I got up.

It was full dark before I reached the first house, and when I tried to stop, I weaved and staggered so badly that I hit the wet stone wall with a thump and dropped to my knees.

Up. Get up.

But this time, my legs really couldn't, and I hadn't enough breath left to yell. I had to crawl on all fours up to the door, hitting it with the flat of my hand.

"Open up!"

Nothing happened. Surely they couldn't be abed already? I thumped the door once more, as hard as I was able. Come on, then!

"Open up, damn it!"

Finally there was a rattle of bolts being drawn, and the door opened. A frightened child peeked out.

"Papa isn't home," she said. "Go away."

I had to be careful not to frighten her even more, I thought. She looked quite scared enough already, and it probably didn't help that I was sitting there on the muddy ground rather than standing upright the way grown-ups usually did.

"Please go get your father," I said as calmly as I could, though I was still heaving for breath. "Tell him a ship has been wrecked in Troll Cove, and that there are wounded people there. They need help, and they need it quickly."

But she just stood there as if she had been turned to stone. She was no longer looking at me, but beyond me, over my shoulder.

"Who has been wounded?" asked a male voice behind me.

I was so relieved to hear a sensible and adult voice that I could have wept.

"Callan," I said. "Callan Kensie. If there is a fee, the Kensie clan will pay it."

"Kensie, you say? We will have to try and get there, then. And who might you be? Not Kensie, by the look of you."

"I'm Davin Tonerre."

I made a last attempt to gain my feet, but failed. My legs had completely lost their strength. But at least I managed to flail around so that I was able to see my rescuer.

It was only then that I discovered he was wearing the black uniform of Drakan's Dragon army.

Stowaway

Nico saw me first.

The *Sea Wolf* leaped and sprang, her sails billowing in the wind, and the Crow and his crew were busy with ropes and booms and the like. I had found a hiding place of sorts behind a water barrel, and I no longer needed to play my father's flute to make them not notice me. It was enough to sit quietly and not be in the way and perhaps to blow a few notes if someone happened to be looking my way.

It had been so easy. Much, much too easy. How had I become so good at it? Before I met Sezuan, I hadn't even known that such a thing as the serpent gift existed. I had never learned to use it, unless you could call the short journey from Sagisloc to the Sagisburg the term of my apprenticeship. It was certainly the only time I had ever really spent with my father, and back then I would much rather have been spared his company. Now... now I no longer knew up from down. I had the serpent gift; I could make other people's eyes and ears lie to them. Lie, or dream. Or maybe both. But I couldn't lie to myself. And in the end, it turned out I couldn't keep lying to Nico either.

I wasn't quite sure how it happened. I was cold, and I felt sick, and I was heartbroken to have left Davin and Rose on that beach with Callan, not knowing whether he would live or die, not knowing if help would reach them in time. But I was tired too. I hadn't had much sleep the last several nights. Perhaps I dozed for a moment. At any rate, Nico was suddenly standing right in front of me, staring at me.

"Dina!"

He looked as if he half expected me to be a ghostly vision. Quickly I raised the flute, but not quickly enough. Nico's hand shot out and seized the shiny black shaft. I knew he recognized it. He had seen Sezuan playing it; he had seen him open gates and locked doors with it the night we entered the Sagisburg and freed its many prisoners.

And now he had seen it in my hands.

He didn't even ask how I had come aboard. I think he knew the moment he saw my father's flute.

"Why?" was all he asked.

"Because I don't want you to get killed."

"So you think that's your decision, now, do you?"

"If I'm with you, you have to be more careful," I said stubbornly.

He closed his eyes for a moment.

"Are you never going to let me go?" he said. "You and your mother. And your stiff-neck brother. Have you any idea how cold that water was? He could have drowned. Any reasonable person would have given up. But, oh no. The Tonerres cling to me like I'm a prize sheep they want to herd back into its proper field."

His eyes were red-rimmed, and there was a smell of beer on his breath. One could say as much for many men, or women too, for that matter. If one was none too sure of the water, it was as good a way of quenching one's thirst as any. But with Nico… with Nico it was a bad sign. He was a poor drinker. And once he got going, he didn't stop. Beer, wine, spirits, anything would do.

I didn't mention it. He already looked… I wasn't sure. As if he was hurt somewhere but had decided not to show it. And at the same time, the very first time I saw him, I had been told that he had killed three people—an old man, a woman, and a child. Only my mother believed in his innocence. Yet I hadn't been afraid of him. Not really. Now something had happened. And this new Nico, him I might fear.

"Let go," he said. "Give me that flute."

"Why?"

"You've boarded this ship without permission," he said. "That's what they call a stowaway. And the first thing you do when you discover stowaways, Dina, you disarm them."

"It's just a flute!"

"You and I both know that flute is a weapon. In the hands of someone who knows how to use it, at least. And it seems you do."

I had to force my fingers to let go. It was almost as if my hands loved the flute better than the rest of me did.

"Now get up."

I looked at him uncertainly. "What are you going to do?"

"What one does with stowaways."

"Which is?"

"Lock them in a safe place to make sure they make no trouble. This way, Medamina."

He took my arm, not roughly; Nico was never rough. But all the same his hand was firm enough that I knew he meant to make sure of me. And the flute… he held it as if it really was a weapon that could stab or cut. Cautiously, with respect. And out of my reach.

◆　　　◆　　　◆

The Crow regarded me with displeasure.

"What kind of witchling have you caught us now?"

"Dina Tonerre," said Nico briefly. "Davin's sister."

"Yes, I can see that. But what the devil is she doing here? We left her on the beach with the others, didn't we?"

I could feel Nico's hesitation.

"It seems not," he said, and failed to mention my father and the serpent gift.

The Crow glared at me. His eyes were like lumps of coal.

"How did you get aboard?"

If only I could make him think of something else, if only I could make him look away for a moment… but Nico had the flute, and he had not let go of my arm.

I stood there without speaking because I couldn't think of a single explanation that wouldn't sound like lies or witchcraft or both.

"Well?"

"I just climbed the rope ladder."

"The rope ladder. But that is no longer—" He glanced quickly down the side of the ship. And there it was, right enough, the ladder they themselves had used as they climbed aboard.

"Enoch," shouted the Crow. "What is this?"

One of the sailors put down his mug to come and see what the Crow meant. He stared at the ladder swaying gently with the motions of the ship, dipping into the brine every time the *Sea Wolf* listed to port.

"Sorry, Skipper," he muttered, looking puzzled. "I must have forgot."

The Crow's hand shot out, fetching the man a thumping blow across the back of the neck.

"You must have forgot. I see. And at home, do you leave the door open to every man and his brother? Look what your forgetfulness brought us." He pointed at me with a sharp, accusing finger.

It was as if the sailor hadn't noticed me before.

"That's a girl!" he said.

"Damn right, it's a girl. We only just got rid of the brother, and here's the sister come to haunt us. Now, get that ladder up before the rest of the family decides to join us!"

"Aye aye, Skipper." The sailor began hauling on the wet ladder right away. He looked confused, and small wonder. I was too busy feeling sorry for myself to spare any pity for him, otherwise I might have felt a twinge of bad conscience. If not for me and my father's flute, he would never have "forgot" the ladder.

But I had my own worries. The deck was moving queasily beneath my feet. And the Crow was looking at me as if he was thinking that dumping me over the side might be the easiest way to solve his problem.

"What do you want here?" he said.

I wasn't sure I could explain it to him. I shrugged, staring at the deck.

"I just wanted to come," I muttered.

"You just wanted to come," repeated the Crow in a disbelieving tone of voice. "What the hell do you think this is, girl? A picnic?"

I kept my mouth shut.

"Is she worth anything?" The Crow glanced at Nico.

"What do you mean?"

"You know what I mean. Is she good for anything? Or can we sell her to anyone?"

Nico's face stiffened. "We do not sell people," he said flatly. "It hasn't yet come to that." And then he added in a peculiarly harsh voice: "Or at least, we do not sell people who haven't asked to be sold."

It was my turn to frown. What did he mean by that? Surely no one asked to be sold?

"Now, you listen," said the Crow. "I just dumped cargo worth nearly seventy silver marks because of you. So if I can get a bit of ransom for this lassie, I will. Whether or not His Over-Righteousness approves."

Nico stood stock-still for a little while. I could feel the anger in him. It made him tense as a bowstring. But he did not release it.

"Yes," he said slowly. "She is worth something. Quite a lot, actually. So much, in fact, that if you try anything like that, anything at all, then our agreement ends right here, right now. See if you can figure out how much *that* would cost you."

The Crow narrowed his eyes. "Is that the way of it?"

"I said so, didn't I?"

"The Young Lord owes me a considerable sum by now. *Quite* considerable."

"You'll get your money."

The Crow slowly nodded. "That I will. One way or the other."

I glanced uneasily from one to the other. All this talk of money. The Crow was a man who counted everything in silver, that I knew already. And Nico had none. So what would he do when the Crow demanded his pay?

Nico shrugged as if that was of no importance.

"One way or the other," he said, with a short, sharp nod. "Those were the terms, yes. But until then—"

"Very well, then. If she really means so much to you. But keep her belowdecks and see to it that she makes no trouble."

"Carmian can keep an eye on her. She won't get past *her* in a hurry."

The Crow gave an unexpected bark of laughter.

"No. I'll grant you that."

Carmian? Who on earth was Carmian?

Carmian

There was only a rough drape across the entryway, no proper door, but Nico knocked politely anyway by tapping his knuckles against the low ceiling.

"Carmian?"

We had to wait awhile for an answer.

"What do you want?"

"I just want to talk to you."

"Oh, so we are now on speaking terms again?"

"Carmian, please. I have no time for these games. I want you to do something for me."

The drape was jerked aside. In the doorway stood a woman who—Well, the first thing you noticed was the hair. Copper gold, like the autumn leaves when they were at their finest, and long and ripply like—Of course I'd never actually seen a mermaid, but I felt sure they had hair just like Carmian's.

The next thing I noticed were the trousers.

It wasn't that I had never seen a woman wearing trousers before. Sometimes, when there was hard work or hard riding to be done, the Highland women borrowed a pair off their men-folk. But those were usually rough work trousers so big they had to be held up by a belt or a bit of string.

Carmian's pair had clearly been made for her. And they weren't the least bit big on her. They fitted smoothly along her slim legs and hips and ended at the top in a sort of bodicelike lacing that came nearly up to her breasts. And those breasts showed quite a bit, because she hadn't laced up her shirt very tightly.

She leaned against the doorframe, crossing her arms.

"And how may I serve the honored gentleman?" she said. But it was clear from her tone that she didn't honor him at all. On the contrary, she was mad at him. So mad that her gray-green eyes were as narrow as a spitting cat's.

Nico looked at her for a moment. He could hardly miss her anger, but he chose to pretend there was nothing wrong.

"This is Dina. She has embarked on a career as a stowaway, so you'll have to share the cabin with her. And I'd like you to keep an eye on her. Keep her belowdecks. The Crow doesn't want her getting in the way."

Carmian gave me the same narrow-eyed stare she had just nailed Nico with.

"Oh, so now I'm a nursemaid?"

Her voice was venomous, but again Nico appeared not to notice.

"Yes, please," was all he said. "It's only for a day or two." He turned to me. "Do as Carmian tells you, Dina. Stay with her. I don't want to see your face above deck, is that clear?"

No. Actually not much was clear to me. Who were these people Nico had chosen to befriend? The Crow and his men who had wounded Callan so that I wasn't sure he would survive. And now Carmian, in her trousers that weren't men's trousers, with her mermaid hair and those breasts that she clearly wanted Nico to look at, even though she was furious with him.

I looked straight at Nico.

"What will you do if Callan dies?" I said. And I could see that the blow went home, straight to the heart, as if I had stabbed him with a knife, even though I had neither Shamer's eyes nor Shamer's voice at the moment.

But Nico hardly ever hit back. Not even when he was like this, alien and miserable-looking all at once, and smelling as if he had drunk more than he ought to.

"Take care of her," he said. "Keep her here, even if you have to tie her up like a dog. I don't want anything to happen to her." He gave me a small shove so that I ended up closer to Carmian than I liked. And then he went away—and took my father's flute with him.

Carmian looked at me with a mixture of irritation and curiosity.

"Dina," she said. "Davin's sister, I presume. And what manner of beast are you? Why is it that he cares so much?"

All of a sudden I felt so exhausted my legs would hardly hold me up. The rolling motion of the ship made me nauseated, and if I didn't get some sleep soon, real sleep, then I thought I might be sick.

"I don't know," I said. "Is there somewhere I can lie down?"

All day I lay in Carmian's quarters, but I felt so sick I couldn't sleep. Carmian gave me a cool, measuring look and fetched a bucket, which she placed next to the bunk. She wasn't wrong. I soon had to use it.

"I hope for your sake that it's worth it," she said when I puked up my insides for the third time.

"What do you mean?" I muttered tiredly.

"Whatever it is you think you'll get out of this."

"I'm not getting anything out of it." At least, not in the way she probably meant. If Nico was alive and more or less himself when this was all over, then I would be satisfied. But achieving that seemed a mountain of a task right now.

Once more she gave me that look, as if she noticed everything and measured it all and calculated the results until she knew exactly where she was with me.

"There has to be a reason why you cling to him like some kind of climbing plant," she said. "People always have their reasons."

"How about if you simply happen to like somebody?" I asked. "Doesn't that count?"

"In my experience, not very often," she said. "Not so you'd notice. And usually not for very long."

Actually, she wasn't beautiful, I thought. Not ugly either, not by a long shot, just a little sharp-featured, a little too much nose. It was just that at first one didn't notice that because of the hair and the breasts and… and her ability to make you *think* she was beautiful even though she wasn't. It was a trick almost worthy of a Blackmaster.

"I don't have a reason," I said. "Or at least, not a reason that someone like you would understand."

Her eyes narrowed. "Watch the claws, little darling," she said. "I don't mind a catfight, but I don't think you would like it."

Probably not. Right now raising my arms seemed too much effort.

"I'm not looking for a fight," I said.

"Smart girl," she said. With a couple of quick tugs on the lacings, she closed her shirt a bit more so that the breasts were less noticeable. Then she stuck her head through the door and called up through the hatch. "Mats!"

It wasn't long before a sailor appeared in the door, a young man with fair hair and beard and curious blue eyes. Even though she had closed her shirt, there was little doubt what he was curious about.

"Take the bucket," she said. "Empty it over the side and rinse it properly. The whole place stinks of child puke."

"At your service," he said and tried a wide grin on her. A bit of one front tooth was missing.

Carmian didn't return his smile. Yet he still took the bucket uncomplainingly, disappeared up the ladder, and brought back the clean and empty bucket a little later.

"As requested," he said, and even bowed, saints help us.

"Thank you," she said. And then, when he showed no signs of leaving on his own, "That will be all, Mats."

He left, looking a little browbeaten.

It did clear the air a bit. The ship's movements seemed gentler now too. I closed my eyes for a minute. And slept.

When I woke up, the whole day had passed. What sky I could see through the porthole was gold and pink with sunset, and Carmian's hair was glowing so much that it almost seemed to be on fire.

What was she doing?

She was standing with her back to me, on one leg, one hand resting lightly against the doorframe for balance. The other leg stretched out behind her as straight as was possible in the narrow confines of the cabin. Slowly she sank down until she was squatting on one leg, the other still stretched behind her, then just as slowly she rose to stand again. It looked extremely strenuous, and her neck and shoulders were damp with sweat. When she had repeated the exercise a couple of times, she switched legs.

And then she lay down on her stomach and did push-ups, just like Davin sometimes did.

I had never seen a woman act like that before. She was training! Davin did it because he wanted to be strong and good with a sword. But why did Carmian do it? She didn't carry a sword, did she? Or maybe she did? She certainly wasn't like any other woman I had ever seen.

"Where are we going?" I asked, even though I was afraid I knew the answer already.

She jerked a little. I suppose she had forgotten I was there. "Dunark."

This was what I had expected. All the same, a sharp jolt of fear went through my stomach. If there was one place in the world more dangerous to Nico than all the others put together, it was Dunark. Dangerous to me, too, come to think of it.

"Why? What are we going to do when we get there?"

There was a glint in her gray-green eyes, and she pushed a damp lock of hair off her forehead.

"What do you think?"

"But it's dangerous to Nico!"

"Is that so, little darling? Perhaps you'd better run and tell him, he may have forgotten."

Easy for her to mock. She wasn't the one lying here with a lump of ice where her belly used to be. Probably she didn't care one way or the other. If she had a lump of ice anywhere, it was where her heart should have been.

"When—" I had to stop and clear my throat. "When will we get there?"

"Tomorrow. Just before noon, probably."

Tomorrow. My heart missed a beat. Tomorrow. And here I was, flat on my back, having slept the day away when I ought to have been—

"Where is Nico?" I struggled upright and swung my feet over the side of the bunk.

"Somewhere above," she said. "But where do you think you're going?"

"I have to talk to him."

"No you don't. You're not going anywhere."

"But—"

"You heard him, little darling. Even if I have to tie you up like a dog."

There wasn't much I could do. She was probably stronger than me, and a fight would only mean that the Crow or some of his men would come running. And even though I tried, I couldn't make her not see me. Not without the flute, and Nico had taken the flute away from me. To disarm me, like he said. And it seemed to work, at least where Carmian was concerned. I thought she might be hard to fool in any case.

She was deaf to other pleas. I said I thought I would be sick again if I didn't get some fresh air, and she said that was tough, but we had been through that already, hadn't we? I said I needed to pee, and she said do it in the bucket. No, Nico was right. It wasn't easy to get past Carmian.

In the end, Nico came below. As it grew darker and darker, I was lying on the bunk trying not to fall asleep, because sleep would eat up all the time we had left in one gulp; when I woke up again, it would be the next day, and Dunark would be in sight, and everything would be almost too late.

There was a quiet knocking on the other side of the drape.

"Carmian?"

"Yes."

"May I come in?"

"If you must."

This time she did not arrange her shirt one way or the other. She merely stretched and shook back the mermaid hair so that it cascaded down her back like a… no, not a waterfall; a firefall, perhaps.

"Is she asleep?" he asked, low-voiced.

"No," I said. "She isn't."

He looked at me. The light from our lone lantern fell unevenly across his face, making him look older. Like an old man, almost.

"It would be better if you could sleep," he said quietly.

"Yes, well, I can't. Is that so strange? We'll be in Dunark tomorrow, or so I've heard."

He nodded. "That's the plan."

"The plan? Nico, do you even have one? Except to… to let the nearest Dragon soldier kill you?"

"Dina. I'm not a complete idiot."

No, he wasn't. But neither was he quite himself, and I was cold with fear that he might be too desperate for his own good.

"Carmian, I want to talk to you," he said.

"Talk away."

He shook his head. "Not here. Come up with me. Dina, you stay here."

"But I have to—"

"No. Stay here. Promise."

He held my gaze longer than he usually did. Nico could never forget that I had once had Shamer's eyes and still felt the gift sometimes at unpredictable moments. It was natural, I supposed. A man who had once in his life been under a Shamer's long and thorough scrutiny, the way my mother had scrutinized Nico… it was not something anyone would easily forget.

"Promise," he repeated.

I nodded. "All right. I'll stay here."

Arms crossed, Carmian watched us. "Are you sure you don't want me to tie her up, just to be sure?" she said, and I couldn't tell whether she meant it for a joke or not. She had not enjoyed being my nursemaid and keeper all day, that much was certain.

"When Dina gives her word, she keeps it. Don't you?"

"I suppose so."

And I did. At least for five whole minutes, or as long as it took them to reach the deck and forget about me.

Not that it was easy for me to break a promise. With a mother like mine, I hadn't exactly been raised to lie and cheat. But I told myself it was for Nico's own good. My father wouldn't have hesitated for a moment.

They were standing to the lee of the cabin, perhaps twelve paces from the open hatch. Up here there was still a bit of sunlight left, just a sliver of gold between sea and sky. They were talking, or at least, Nico was. But to hear what he was saying, I had to get closer.

It would have been easier with the flute. But even without it…

Look at the waves, I thought. *Look at the seagull diving at the dark water.*

If you tell someone "Don't look at me," of course they do. My father taught me that that is not how you hide. You can't forbid them to look at you. But most people can't look at more than one thing at a time, not really, and so, if Nico and Carmian looked at something else, they wouldn't be looking at me. Quite simple, really.

The flute worked because it caught people's attention without them noticing it. It filled eyes and ears with thoughts and dreams, until the eyes no longer saw what the Blackmaster wanted to hide. So like I said, it was easier with the flute. But not impossible without it….

Look at the sunset. Look at the light dancing on the waves. Look at Carmian's hair dancing in the wind.

And don't see me.

They didn't. I kept low, all the same, and crept a little closer on all fours.

"It's important," said Nico. "When I leave this ship tomorrow, she stays. And whatever else happens, she is going home to the Highlands."

"And just how do you imagine that will happen?" she said. "She's not exactly easy to deal with. She is hell-bent on looking after you, and she is stubborn as they come."

"You don't say. But, Carmian, in the old days. Back when you… back when you and Tip-Toe were running that little scam of yours—"

"Nico, you promised you wouldn't—"

"And I won't. I don't tell tales."

"A bunch of old rich fools who barely knew what to do with their miserly hoard. Did they come to any harm if we unburdened them of a fraction of their wealth? They had their money's worth in entertainment, I can tell you."

"Probably. But that isn't—"

"And they hanged him, Nico. Did you know that? He never hurt a fly. He never mugged people, or threatened anyone. And still they hanged him. Is that justice?"

"No. No, it is not justice."

"Perhaps you think I should have bedded them instead? Because where I come from, Young Lord, there aren't many other ways for a girl to make her living."

"Carmian, I said I wouldn't tell anyone. But I just thought… how did you make sure that your—what did you call them, your old rich fools?—how did you make sure that they didn't wake at the wrong moment?"

"Bit of poppy in their wine."

"And that's not dangerous, is it?"

"No one ever complained. Not about that, anyhow."

"Do you still have some? In that box of yours?"

There was a pause.

"I might have," she finally said.

"So, a little poppy in Dina's water, perhaps a little wine to disguise the flavor. And when she wakes, it'll all be over. One way or the other. Isn't that possible?"

Carmian stood still for a very long time. I couldn't see her face properly, but her shoulders looked high and tense.

"Why do you care so much about her?" she said. "She shows up out of the blue, sneaks aboard ship uninvited—and how she did that is a bloody mystery. It's not your fault she got mixed up in this."

"I just don't want her getting in the way."

"Come on, Nico. I know you. It's more than that. The men don't like her being here. Enoch swore she had to be some kind of witchling to sneak aboard without him seeing her. But Mats said you practically bit off the Crow's head when he began to talk about a ransom. What is she, your secret half sister, or something?"

"Of course not. I just owe her family, quite a lot. Life, limb, and whatever shreds of honor I retain, just to mention the first things that come to mind."

She snorted. "Honor. That is for those who can afford it. And you were never one to go charging off on your high horse, waving the family coat of arms."

"Honor can be more than that. Self-respect, for instance. And I think even the lowliest beggar in Swill Town possesses his own sense of honor. I know you have yours, or I would never have written you that letter or put my life in your hands."

Oh no, I moaned to myself. Don't. Don't trust her so. Trusting someone like Carmian can kill you.

She straightened and turned away from him abruptly, as if she no longer wanted to look him in the eyes.

"You and your fancy notions," she said, her voice low and hoarse. "Not all of us can afford them, you know."

"Carmian—"

"No. Don't look at me with those eyes. Not when you don't mean it. That little miss down there, her you would wrap up in cotton wool to keep her away from harm. Not me. With me it doesn't matter so much, does it?"

"You're a big girl now. Isn't that what you usually tell me? You are better at looking after yourself than most people. But I'm not forcing you. If you would rather stay here tomorrow—"

"No. No, that's not what I'm saying."

"What *are* you saying, then?"

"You know very well what I mean. Ever since Farness… you haven't even touched me once."

Nico hesitated. Then he put a hand on her shoulder.

She spun and struck it away with a furious movement.

"Not now!" she snapped. "Not like I'm some dog you have to remember to pet!"

"But—"

"If you can't work it out for yourself, it really doesn't matter. But once, Nico, once, you knew where my bed was. Am I so ugly now that you won't even touch me?"

I closed my eyes and felt like closing my ears too. I didn't want to hear this. It might not be a huge surprise; I knew Nico had had more than one girl back when he still lived in Dunark and was the youngest son of the Castellan and in unrequited love with his brother's wife. I had seen everything in his eyes that night in the dungeon when it all started, that night two years ago when I met him for the first time. And Carmian—just the way she laced her shirt, or rather, didn't lace it—no, it was no surprise.

Why, then, did it hurt? Two years ago it had meant nothing to me, Nico and his girls.

"You're not ugly," he said, and something in his voice made me open my eyes. "You are as beautiful as you ever were." He reached out to touch a lock of her hair, and this time she let him do it. "You are strong," he went on. "If the world kicks you when you're down, you get up and kick back. That strength, it's part of your beauty. And that is why I don't wrap you in cotton wool. You wouldn't like it."

"What do you know about it?" she said, but for the first time since I'd known her, she didn't sound angry. She even put her hand on top of his and pressed it against her neck.

I had had enough. Maybe I should just drink his damn poppy, I thought, and leave him to Carmian and the Crow and their callous plans. I slipped down the ladder and ducked behind the drape. The lamp was just a guttering spark by now, and in the dimness I knocked into the bucket. It made a fearful racket, but there was no one but me to hear. I rubbed my shinbone and slowly and clearly repeated the ten worst curses I knew. It helped a little, so I did it again.

When Carmian came down, I pretended to be asleep. Whether she believed in the act, I didn't know. She moved about in the dim light, hanging another hammock. Then she turned the wick of the oil lamp all the way down, and the darkness became total. There was a creaking from the beams and the ropes as she swung into the hammock, then those sounds died down as well. Was she asleep? It wouldn't surprise me. Nico had called her strong, but I just thought she was cold. Cold, heartless, and false. And she was the one Nico had chosen to trust? Out of all the people in the whole wide world. *I have put my life in your hands*, he had said.

I stared into the darkness.

If he absolutely had to put his life in someone's hands, why not mine?

The Dragon Is Not at Home

One couldn't sail all the way to Dunark. The closest a ship like the *Sea Wolf* could get was the small port town of Dunbara, which lay at one end of North Cove, just below the Dun Rock. But Dunbara had grown lately, and Dunark had spilled across its old boundaries too, so that now there were people living at the foot of the castle rock, in what was called Netherton. There was only a narrow stretch of mud flats between Netherton and Dunbara, so it was probably only a matter of time before the two towns merged completely.

The harbor was busy with more ships than I could readily count, and on the pier was a lively traffic of people and goods, barrels and crates being carried one way or the other by sweating sailors or by little donkeys that could climb the narrow planks of the gangways without tripping, even with what looked to my eyes like quite unreasonable burdens on their woolly backs.

"Enough of that, little darling. Get below. Now."

I turned. A moment ago, Carmian had been sleeping soundly in her hammock, but not anymore, it seemed. For a brief moment I actually considered whether it would be better to jump onto the railing and leap into the sea. But the water was cold, and there was still a fair bit of distance to the pier. Davin might have managed it. Not me.

"I just wanted to see the town."

"Great. You've seen it. But if you can see the town, the town can see you. Get your posh little tail below, and I might think about getting you some breakfast."

Breakfast. Oh, yes. With wine and poppy.

"I'm not hungry."

"You think I care?"

Did this mean no poppy after all? No, better not count on it. Carmian took my arm.

"I can walk," I said, tearing free of her grasp.

"Then pray do so, Your Ladyship."

I didn't want her to touch me. I didn't want her hands on me. As a matter of fact, I wished violently that she and I were very far apart—like at opposite ends of the world—instead of sharing a space no larger than three paces by four paces, if you didn't stretch your legs too much when you paced.

"Weren't you getting breakfast?" I said.

She measured me with her cool gray-green eyes.

"I thought you weren't hungry?"

We glared at each other. If I had still had my Shamer's eyes, she wouldn't be so full of herself, I thought. Or would she?

"I'm not," I said.

Maybe she was like Drakan, completely unmoved by the Shamer's gaze because he had no more shame than a beast. Nico had said she had her own sense of honor. But his judgment didn't count where Carmian was concerned. *Once, you knew where my bed was*, she had said.

In the end she did get the breakfast, having told Mats to keep an eye on me meanwhile. She obviously didn't trust me. Mats I might have tricked into not seeing me, but what good would it have done? Even if I did find Nico and manage to talk to him alone, I was by now pretty certain he wouldn't listen to me. He was set on a plan that included Carmian and the Crow but not me.

Carmian returned with two bowls of porridge and two beakers of toddy. I looked at the beaker with the steaming hot red-gold liquid. There it was, I thought. If she had used the poppy, it would be in there.

"Eat," she said. "You may or may not be hungry, but you had nothing at all yesterday, and no one here has the time or the leisure to nurse sick kiddies."

I considered it. I was as good as certain that the porridge was safe. And she was right. If I didn't eat, I might regret it later. I tried a spoonful. It was too salty for my taste, but other than that there seemed to be nothing wrong with it.

Carmian noticed my caution, and her lips tightened.

"It's the same porridge everyone else gets," she said. "But perhaps Her Ladyship is used to finer things?"

"No," I muttered, taking another spoonful. "Nothing wrong with porridge."

At first she didn't mention the toddy. But as it became more and more obvious that I wasn't touching it, she raised her eyebrows.

"So you don't like toddy either?"

I shrugged. "I'm not so used to wine."

"I should have guessed," she said in a condescending tone. "Your mama won't let you, I suppose. She's right. It's not a child's drink."

"I'm no child."

"No? You're sure you wouldn't like some nice hot milk instead? We could heat a bottle for you."

Her condescension rankled, but I wasn't quite stupid enough to drink her poppy juice just to prove what a big girl I was. And so, when the ship finally bumped against the pier at Dunbara and we could hear the shouts and movements of landing, I was still awake. And Nico was furious.

"She wouldn't drink it," said Carmian, completely unruffled by his anger. "What did you expect me to do, hold her nose and force it down her throat?"

"You promised—"

"I promised to see what I could do. It's hardly my fault that Her Ladyship is sly as well as stubborn."

Nico regarded me with an expression of fury and a strange despair. His dark blue eyes looked nearly black right now.

"I don't want you here," he said. "You weren't supposed... I didn't want..."

It was so rare for Nico to stumble like that. He was usually so precise. But here he was, searching and struggling just like Davin sometimes did, as if there *were* no words to fit what he wanted to say.

"The Harbormaster will be here any minute," said Carmian, watching him coolly. "So unless you want them to take you here and now, uselessly, I suggest you make for the hole. And decide what you want us to do with Her Ladyship meanwhile."

She didn't mean it as a compliment, the Ladyship bit, and I wished she would stop it. But it was perhaps a slight improvement on the "little darling" she had used to begin with. And in any case, it seemed to me that the cleverest thing to do right now would be to keep my big mouth shut.

Nico kept that nearly-black-looking gaze on my face.

"She'll have to come with me," he said. "For now, at least. We can't let them see her either, they want her almost as badly as they want me. It'll have to be the hole."

"If there's room for both of you."

"There has to be."

She shrugged. "If that's the way you want it. Come along, then. We haven't got all day."

The hole in question was a narrow space between the hull and some floor planks in the cargo hold where the ballast—the heavy rocks that kept the *Sea Wolf* from capsizing when the wind filled her sails—was normally kept. The Crow, however, had moved some of the stones and created a tiny boxlike room. I don't think he normally smuggled people in it, though there was no doubt that he smuggled something there, but there was just enough room for Nico and me, as long as we didn't breathe too deeply or try to move.

He was still angry with me, and it was odd to lie so close to someone so furious. I was half on my side, with my face against his shoulder, so that I could feel the edge of his collar against my cheek. He was so angry that he wouldn't put his arms around me, though that would probably have been more comfortable for both of us. He couldn't avoid touching me, what with us having to lie practically on top of each other, but he made it clear he only did it because he must.

"Nico, please," I said. "Please don't trust the Crow."

"I don't trust the Crow in the least."

"But why, then…"

"I trust his greed and his nose for money. That is all."

"But Nico, they'll pay him a hundred gold marks to betray you."

"Yes."

"I don't understand."

"Dina. Stay *out* of it. You will do as I tell you and stay here until someone can take you back to Farness. Do you hear me?"

I didn't answer. I didn't want to break any more promises to him.

"Where is the flute?" I asked instead.

"The Crow has it."

"The Crow?" I was outraged. "You gave my father's flute to the *Crow*?"

"It's his ship," said Nico curtly. "Who else would I give it to? One of his men?"

The very idea of any of them holding it, touching its black smoothness, their heavy fingers on its slender neck, their fat lips—No. It didn't bear thinking about. My outrage boiled so hotly that for a moment it almost matched Nico's fury.

"That flute is irreplaceable."

"You shouldn't have taken it with you, then, should you, back when you decided to play the stowaway."

But without it I couldn't have got aboard at all, and he knew that.

There were steps in the hold, and I felt Nico hold his breath. He didn't even dare to shush me, but then, that wasn't necessary. I was no more interested in getting caught than he was.

Footsteps. More than one man. Four or five, perhaps. And voices.

"Where the devil is the cargo?" asked an unknown voice.

"We sold most of it at our last port of call."

"And where was that?"

"Pottersville."

"In Loclain? You didn't stop at Farness, then?"

"We thought it best to stay clear of the Highlands."

"Wise man. If you are telling the truth. Traveling with empty holds is not your style, Cador."

Cador was the Crow's real name. Not many people called him Crow to his face.

"It's no crime."

"No, just very strange. And not your usual profit-making habit. Hallan. Bosca. Take this poor excuse for a ship apart at the seams. I'm betting he does have a cargo somewhere that he has just forgotten to tell us about. Meanwhile Mesire Cador will do me the favor of accompanying me to my offices so that I can run through some new regulations with him. This way, Mesire, if it pleases you."

The Crow clearly wasn't pleased at all, but he managed a barely civil reply. And the men began their search.

It reminded me of the time I had been hiding beneath the boards in Master Maunus's bed in Dunark Castle while Drakan and his men took the place apart looking for me and Nico. Did Nico think of that time too? I had been so scared. Almost too scared to breathe.

I was frightened now too. But back then, all I could do was lie there, waiting to see if they found me. Now... now, there was perhaps something I could do. I couldn't see the men up there, could only hear them rummage around, knocking on boards to test for hollows, prying into nooks and crannies. They were looking for exactly such a space as the one we were in right now, and if they kept looking, they would find it. Now the Crow had two reasons to curse the decision to dump his cargo at Troll Cove. Dunbara's Harbormaster might not have been quite so thorough if his suspicions hadn't been aroused by the empty hold.

"Yeecch!" There was a sudden exclamation of disgust from one of the men.

"What is it?"

"A rat. A rat the size of a dog!"

Normally, I wasn't crazy about rats. But right then, I could have kissed the beast.

Rats are disgusting, I thought, as loudly as I could. *And where there's one, there are more. Filthy creatures, spreading disease. If they bite you, you can die.*

Nico stirred uneasily. It wasn't his head I wanted to fill with pictures of rats, but since I was lying practically on top of him, he was bound to catch it too.

"There's another one!"

"Lord, what a biggun. Did you see the size of him?"

"Yanus Roper was bitten once," said one of the men, revulsion in his voice. "His hand swelled up so badly the fingers were nearly black. All but did him in."

"Disgusting creatures."

"Yes. You done at your end?"

"Yup. Nothing there."

"I think the master is off on a wild goose chase. There's nothing to find here except rats."

We heard them tramp up the ladder, and then the cargo hold grew quiet except for the creaking of the hull and a scuttling that might or might not be a rat.

"I'm not afraid of rats!" said Nico suddenly, rather loudly.

"Nico—"

"You did that, didn't you? You made us think of rats!"

He said it so accusingly that I ended up having to defend myself.

"Would you rather have them find you? Perhaps you would have liked for them to haul you out of your hole and drag you to Dunark so that your beloved half brother could finally cut off your head? I think he is quite bothered that he didn't get the chance last time."

"It *was* you!"

"What if it was?"

"Make it stop now!" he said, and his voice trembled. "I want those rats *out* of my head. I want the darkness out! And the smell of blood."

The smell of blood? That was none of my doing.

And suddenly I knew what had happened. It wasn't Master Maunus's cozy workshop Nico was thinking of, lying here in the darkness. It was the dungeon cell where they had made him sit with his dead family's blood on his hands for one whole night and one whole day. There had been rats there too.

"Nico, please, this isn't—"

His whole body shuddered, head to foot. His breath came in gasps, as if he were choking.

"Nico, nothing happened. We're safe!"

"Make them go away," he said between clenched teeth. "Make them go away *now.*"

But that was no easy thing. You can't make people *not* think of something. The more you try, the worse it gets.

"Nico, think of something else."

"Think of something *else*? Is that all you can say?"

"I mean it. Think of something nice. Something you like. Your horse, Nico. The Highlands. Master Maunus." But he was still shaking, more so than before, and I was running out of ideas. "Oh, hell. Think of Carmian, if that's what it takes."

Apparently, that helped. His breathing eased, and the worst of the shudders stopped.

"You two don't like each other much, do you?" he finally said.

"No. I don't suppose we do."

"That's a shame."

"Why?"

"Because you are both remarkable."

I had to mull that one over a bit. I wasn't sure I liked being compared to Carmian, but I knew he meant well. After all, he did like her. Enough to… I might not like to think of it, but that didn't change the facts. Enough so that she had once been his girl. Or whatever one called it, in Nico's old world where princes could do pretty much as they liked, as long as they didn't get funny ideas about marrying girls like Carmian.

"Do you think we might get out?" I asked.

"No," he said.

"They're gone now."

"Yes, but we have to wait for Carmian to let us out. We can't open this ourselves."

I hoped she would come soon. One leg had gone all pins-and-needles, and even though I was not afraid of rats or darkness or had nightmares quite like Nico's, still I would have liked some light, and some air that had not been breathed in and out a couple of times by someone else, and space to move without crushing another person. Even if that other person was Nico.

"Why did you write to her?" I finally asked.

"I had to do something. I couldn't just keep on waiting while other people died. Every day, Dina. Every single day."

"Yes, but why Carmian?"

"She knows people. People who will do dangerous things for money."

"People like the Crow, you mean."

"Yes. Like the Crow."

"But Nico, you know plenty of people who will do dangerous things *without* getting paid." The Weapons Master and the Widow and all their followers. Master Maunus, Davin. Me, for that matter. We would all do just about anything he asked us to do if there was a chance of ending Drakan's rule.

"I know that," he said, almost as if he could hear what I was thinking. "But they are people whose lives I'm not willing to risk."

I could see how it might be easier for him to put the Crow's life at risk. But Carmian's?

"But Carmian's life, you would risk her?"

It came out more harshly than I had intended. But Nico's answer surprised me.

"Carmian isn't like other women. Or like very many men, for that matter. She thinks she does these things because people pay her. But Carmian was born for danger, I think. Or perhaps she grew accustomed to it very early in her life. If she didn't risk her life for me, she would be off risking it somewhere else. She can't help herself."

Was he right? He knew her better than I did, of course. But I remembered what she had said the night before, as they stood together by the railing. *Her you would wrap up in cotton wool to keep her away from harm. Not me. With me it doesn't matter so much, does it?* And I was fairly sure that the envy in her voice had been real. Maybe even girls like Carmian liked to be cotton-wrapped every so often. Especially if it was Nico doing the wrapping.

◆　　◆　　◆

In the end, Carmian did come to let us out.

"He isn't here," she said.

At first I wasn't sure who she meant, but apparently Nico was.

"Where, then? When will he be back?"

"He's gone off with the Dragon Force somewhere. And no, we don't know where or for how long."

Drakan. It was Drakan they meant.

Nico cursed quietly, but I breathed a huge sigh of relief. More time. That was all it meant to me at first. More time before Nico could get on with his dangerous plans.

"We shall have to wait, then," he said.

"Well," said Carmian, "that's one way of going about it. If you think the Crow's patience will last."

"What do you mean?"

"You know what I mean. If it becomes a bit too hard or a bit too risky, well, then, the Crow has an easy way of making a modest but very nice little fortune. He can sell you to Drakan's people—even if Drakan himself isn't in Dunark."

"He will get more by waiting and doing as I tell him."

"Only if you succeed. If you get caught without his assistance, at best he can kiss his fortune good-bye. At worst, he will face trial for hiding and abetting an outlaw. The penalty for that is death, particularly when the outlaw is you."

Nico cursed again, more loudly this time.

"How long do you think—" Nico broke off, but Carmian was not afraid of calling a spade a spade.

"Before he betrays you? Is that what you mean?"

"I suppose so."

"Only the Crow can tell you that. But I wouldn't leave it too long if I were you."

I felt sick, almost as if I was about to be seasick again. But the *Sea Wolf* was riding at anchor and moving only gently up and down, and it wasn't her motions that made my stomach contract.

"Is he back yet?"

"No. Still at the Harbormaster's."

"Nico." I spoke softly. "Perhaps we should get away from the ship."

Carmian looked at me attentively. "Your little friend could have a point," she said. "It might not be wise to tempt the Crow too far."

"Where would we go? All Dunark is a death trap."

Did you only just realize that? I thought, but I didn't say it out loud.

"We could go ashore, move on, try to find the Dragon Force and Drakan," said Carmian persuasively. "I… there are some people I know. People who might help. Surely anything is better than being stuck here like rats in a trap."

Nico thought about it. Then he shook his head.

"No. We stay. I'll talk to the Crow."

Carmian looked angry. "Nico. Don't you get it? Anything you can promise the Crow depends on your success. If he no longer thinks you have a decent chance, you can promise him the sun, the moon, and the stars, and he will still turn around and betray you the minute your back is turned."

"No. We have a deal. And surely even the Crow has some sense of decency."

Carmian looked at him darkly.

"I wouldn't count on it if I were you," she said.

One Girl, Ordered
and Paid For

"Wake up, girl."

Someone was shaking me by the shoulder, and not very gently either. I opened my eyes—and looked straight into the sharp, dark features of the Crow.

"What—"

"Come on. Move. Someone wants to meet you."

"Meet—"

He practically hauled me out of the bunk.

"Yes. Come on. Save the talk for later."

I was muddled with sleep, and my head hurt from the heavy air in the cabin. But his grip on my arm was a no-nonsense one, and before I was fully awake, he had dragged me up the ladder, up on deck. But when he tried to get me down the gangway too, I balked.

"Wait. Where are we going? Where is Nico?"

"Waiting for us. Come along, girl."

I wasn't buying it.

"What do you want with me?" I said, remembering only too clearly all his talk of ransoms. Had he found someone he could sell me to?

The Crow looked at me for a moment with no expression whatsoever. Then he suddenly jerked his head. Just one brief, sharp movement, but apparently that was a signal they had arranged, because all of a sudden I was blinded by a blanket that someone threw over my head, and although I waggled and fought and tried to call out, it didn't amount to much. The blanket muffled everything. They spun me around and wrapped me up like a parcel someone had ordered and paid for.

Where was Nico? Where, for that matter, was Carmian? She hadn't been in the other bed.

I was lifted and carried and handed from one man to the next. My hip bumped against something hard—it might have been the gunwale—and then there was a drop, so sudden I was afraid for a second that they had simply dumped me over the side. But rough hands caught me, and I ended up head down over someone's shoulder. Not the Crow, I thought, but one of his men.

"Nico!" I shouted, as loudly as I could. "Where are you?"

"Quiet," hissed the man who was carrying me—it sounded like the one called Enoch. "Do you want the guards to hear us?"

The guards? For a moment I considered yelling even more loudly. But no, probably not a good idea. If we weren't actually headed into Drakan's arms, there was no reason to ask for it. But if it wasn't Drakan they expected to sell me to, who then? And what had they done with Nico? I couldn't believe he had agreed to this.

"Put me down," I said. "I'll walk."

"Captain? She says—"

"No," said the Crow curtly. "You never know with a witchling like that one. See to it that you keep a good grip on her."

Enoch tightened his hold on my legs. What did he think I was going to do? Fly away?

A dog barked loudly and angrily quite close by, and at once, six or seven others took up the chorus.

"Damn mutt," growled Enoch. "Wake the whole town, why don't you?"

"Hurry," said the Crow. "The sooner we get off the streets, the better."

I hated not being able to see. Being scared was bad enough without being blinded into the bargain. I tried to worm one arm free of the rope, but sailors don't tie the kind of knots that come undone with a bit of wriggling. I could hear the footsteps of the men, first on boards and then on gravel and pavement. I could also feel how Enoch's breath grew shorter and shorter, burdened as he was with me. But I could see nothing but blanket.

"Can't you carry her for a bit?" he groaned to one of the others.

"Is she too much for you? Slip of a girl like that," came the teasing answer.

"Quiet," hissed the Crow. "We're there. Keep your gobs shut and let me do the talking. These aren't ordinary folk."

There was a gentle knocking, and then the sound of a bolt being drawn.

"Inside," whispered a low voice.

The men obeyed. And I could hear the door closing behind us, and the rattle of a lock.

"Put her down," said the Crow.

Enoch did as he was told. I was so dizzy that I could barely stand. People weren't meant to hang head down like bats.

"Let me see her." A new voice, both strange and yet familiar.

The rope was loosened, and the hateful blanket was finally removed. I saw a small, low-ceilinged room almost without furniture. A table, a bench, a fireplace. And by the fireplace…

My heart clenched. It couldn't be.

But—

"Papa?"

The word slipped out of me unasked. But then he moved. And I knew that miracles did not happen. It wasn't him. He looked like him, so much so that it made my chest ache to see it. But though the hands held the flute knowledgeably, they weren't my father's hands, and there were other things too—the set of the mouth, something about his nose and chin. It wasn't him. He was dead. I knew this, and yet it felt as if he had just died all over again.

"My name is Azuan," he said. "And you must be my brother's daughter."

His eyes were as green as mine. As green as my father's. He had no serpent earring, but the pin that held his cloak together had the same shape—a silver snake, with tiny green gemstones for eyes. It had to be true. He was my uncle. My father's brother.

"You say nothing?"

"What do you want me to say?" It came out more defiant than I felt. I wasn't defiant. I just felt as if someone had hit me over the head with something heavy.

"You might start by telling me your name."

That had been the first thing my father had said to me. *What is your name? I mean you no harm. I just want to know your name.*

He *had* done me harm. But also good, whatever other people said about him.

"Her name is Dina," said the Crow, apparently thinking me too slow and unresponsive. "Dina Tonerre. She is the Shamer's daughter."

"Yes," said Azuan. "The rebellious Melussina. We remember her well."

There was something about that "we" that caused a shiver down my back. As if his whole family were there behind him, watching over his shoulder. My father had never talked like that, even though it was clear that he never forgot who he was or where he came from.

I think it was then that Azuan began to scare me.

My mother had fled head over heels, from my father, yes, but most of all from his family. And there was a… a greed in the way Azuan looked at me. As if I belonged to him. No, not to him. To them. The Family. I might have escaped them once while still in my mother's belly. But now they wanted me back. And they were probably willing to pay handsomely for it. Enough to satisfy even a soul as grasping as that of the Crow.

Would he simply buy me and take me to… to Colmonte, or wherever it was, far away, in any case, whether I wanted to come or not? I looked at him. At the face that was so like my father's and yet was not his. Azuan didn't love me. Not the least little bit.

"That is my father's flute," I said, to buy time.

"Yes," said Azuan, simply.

"May I have it back?"

"Did he give it to you?" Again this glimpse of… not just interest, more like a greedy sort of attention. Like a cat looking at a mouse.

I nodded. "It's mine now."

He considered. Then he held it out toward me.

"Let me hear you."

He meant it as a test; I was well aware of that. He wanted to know whether I had the serpent gift or not. But what he held out to me was also a weapon, and I meant to use it. I brought it to my lips and blew.

At first it sounded terrible. My mouth was dry, and I couldn't quite purse my lips the right way. The Crow gave a sharp bark of laughter.

"Some musician," he said. "If you are buying her because of her music, the price is too steep."

I could feel a hot flush rising in my cheeks even though I knew the last thing in the world I had to worry about right now was the Crow's opinion of my playing. Then I rallied. I had this one chance. I could not afford to waste it.

I pursed my lips the way my father had taught me. And started playing.

It was not a tune. More like the hiss of the wind in the chimney. The crackle of the fire. *Nice and warm*, said the flute. *A good place to rest.*

The Crow sat down on the bench. One of the men yawned.

It is late, said the flute. *The middle of the night. How nice it would be to lie in one's bed.*

Enoch leaned back against the whitewashed wall. His chin came down to rest on his chest.

I let the notes become heavier, slower, softer. Like the body becomes heavier, like the heart becomes slower, like the breath comes more softly as you fall asleep.

And the men slept. One by one they crumpled slowly where they sat or stood, and sleep took them. I backed slowly out of the room. I felt like running, but that was not how it was done.

So I walked, quietly, still playing my heavy sleep notes one by one, like the last drops of rain in a shower.

Down the dark hallway. Toward the door and freedom. I played on with one hand only while I fumbled at the handle with the other.

No good. The door was locked.

"You are very good," said Azuan. "He trained you well."

A frightened, off-key squeal from the flute. I spun. He was right behind me, and he looked very much awake. In one hand he held the key.

"Where is he?" he asked.

Azuan had not fallen asleep. Perhaps that was not so very strange if he himself had the serpent gift. But what did he mean by...

"Who?" I whispered.

"You are not stupid. Do not try to pretend that you are. Sezuan, Dina. Your father. Where is he?"

And then I realized. He did not know that Sezuan was dead.

I opened my mouth to tell him.

"He—"

And then something stopped me. Not something as well thought out as a plan, or even an idea. Just a feeling, a feeling that the less I told Azuan, the better.

"I don't know," I said. "I haven't seen him for a really long time."

"How long?"

"Months."

"Where? Where did you see him?"

I threw a nervous look down the hall, but as yet no one was stirring.

"I'm sorry, but shouldn't we get out of here?" I said. "Before they wake up? At the very least it might save you a great deal of money."

He actually laughed, a laugh that seemed to startle him.

"You really *are* clever," he said. "Your father's daughter, as one might say. And you are right. It is so much cheaper this way."

He smiled at me. But he also took a solid hold on my arm before he turned the key and let us out and locked up the Crow and his men.

Hoarfrost

It was cold outside, and I began to shake almost at once. The thatched roofs of the little cottages were white with hoarfrost and glistened in the moonlight, and there was a thin glaze of ice on the puddles. Azuan seemed not to notice the cold, but then he had a nice warm-looking cloak, while I didn't even have my shawl, which still hung beside my bunk aboard the *Sea Wolf*.

"Come on," he said when I had trouble keeping up with his long, rapid strides. "They won't sleep forever."

Probably not. But where was he going in such a hurry? It dawned on me that he was headed not toward the harbor and the ships there, but inland, toward Dunark.

"Where are we going?"

"Just hurry up."

We turned a corner, and that was the end of the Dunbara. Ahead of us stretched a strip of marshy flats, with ditches and little brackish tide pools glittering through the mists whenever the moon peaked through the clouds. On the other side of that the Dun Rock towered, tall and dark, with crenellated castle walls and a few lights dotted here and there. Between Dunbara and Dunark ran a road wide enough for two carts to pass each other and raised above the flats almost like a bridge. We were somewhere near the middle of it when a shout rang out behind us.

"There they are!"

Four men appeared from the narrow alleys of Dunbara, and even at that distance the tall, angular shape of the Crow was easily recognizable. They must have broken down the door to get out, and now they had found us. They started down the road at a run.

"Don't just stand there," hissed Azuan. "Use the flute."

I didn't think I could. It was one thing to let the notes sneak up on people when they were standing still, unsuspecting. But stopping the four men running toward us now at full speed...

"I don't think I can." Perhaps Papa might have done it. Not me.

The same thing must have occurred to Azuan.

"Run, then," he said.

When he saw me still hesitating, he grabbed my wrist and hauled me down the road. But my legs were shorter than his, and shorter than those of the Crow too. Our lead soon shrank. Azuan threw a quick look over his shoulder and cursed at what he saw.

"Go on," he said, giving me a small shove. "I'll try to stop them myself."

Stop them? How? He had no weapon that I could see. But perhaps he had a better grasp of the serpent gift than I.

I knew there was only one thing I could do if I wanted to avoid the greedy claws of the Crow. I veered sharply to one side and jumped into the ditch. The thin crust of ice broke like glass, and the icy water soaked me to mid-thigh, but I had no time to curse at inconveniences. I struggled up the far bank of the ditch on all fours, clutching the flute one-handed, and began to run across the marsh as quickly as it might be done. I hopped from tussock to tussock when I could and waded through black mud when I couldn't. It was slower progress than on the road, but it would be no faster for them if they tried to follow.

The Crow was in no mood to go mud hopping. "Enoch, Keo, you catch the girl. The rest of us will deal with the foreigner."

I glanced across my shoulder. Enoch was balancing on the edge of the road, not looking as if he greatly fancied getting his feet wet. But he didn't dare disobey the Crow either, it seemed. At any rate, he leaped, trying to clear the ditch in one bound. He didn't quite succeed. For a moment he struggled to keep his balance on the other side, arms flapping like he was trying to take off and fly. Then he slid down the bank again and disappeared from view.

There was no time to enjoy the sight. Keo, the other sailor, had been luckier with his leap, and now he was hopping from tussock to tussock just like me.

In the middle of everything, a sudden clear memory came into my head: a summer afternoon back home in Birches and a toad race that Davin and the Miller's boys had come up with. They had each caught a big toad, but the toads didn't take to racing and had to be goaded back in line after each hop, so that their progress toward the finish was a strange and zigzagging affair. The race Keo and I were having was the same. Charging forward in a straight line would have had us mired in mud within minutes; we had to hop left, hop right, wherever there seemed to be an inch of firmish ground to stand on.

It wasn't easy to gauge one's footing. A damp hoary mist hugged the marsh, like mold on a loaf of bread. My legs were numb with cold, and my skirt clung to my legs like an extra coating of mud. Yet at the same time runnels of sweat were trickling down my back under my blouse, and I was beginning to pant like a thirsty dog.

Back on the road, someone was shouting, but I couldn't see what was going on. The mist was dense and white, and I had to keep my eyes on where I was going, and on Keo. Was he gaining on me? Yes, definitely. He leaped adroitly from one tussock to the next and didn't seem to put a foot wrong. Was the man half toad?

My own leaps grew shorter and shorter, and more awkward. My cold dead legs were on the point of failing me. My tired body sent treacherous messages to my brain: Might it not be easier just to stop? Just to let them catch me? At least they would have to find me somewhere warm and dry, somewhere to rest for a little while… a fireplace, a blanket, perhaps even a hot drink.

My foot slipped. I waved my arms and fell, and the flute flew from my fingers. It floated in a lazy arc through the air, turned once end over end, and tumbled into a tide pool and was lost from sight.

No!

All thoughts of fireplaces and warm blankets evaporated from my head. The flute. The flute! I dropped to my knees by the side of the pool and pushed both hands into the dark water. Where was it? I couldn't see anything. The surface was smooth as a mirror, a moonlit mirror, and I couldn't see through it into the hidden ground below. I rummaged blindly among slimy reeds and mud and stones, but there was nothing.

No, wait. There. My finger closed on a familiar smoothness. I snatched it to me, not caring that the water dripped all over the parts of my blouse that weren't already soaked. Had it been damaged? Would it ever—

A sound behind me. A splash and a grunt.

I spun.

Keo was only a few tussocks away. Another leap or two and he would—

"*Stop.*"

I wasn't sure where it came from, the Shamer's voice. I didn't mean to use it. But suddenly that one word came out of me with that precise edge, that precise tone that made people stop and listen. Even Keo.

He paused almost in midleap and stood there for a moment, teetering on one leg like a stork, while the mists rubbed against his legs like a begging cat.

"If you take one more step," I said in a weird, cold voice I barely recognized as my own, "I'll turn you to stone."

He hesitated. His eyes gleamed whitely in the moonlight, and his mouth was a dark O in the middle of his face. I could hear his strained breath, *huff, puff, huff, puff,* like Rikert's bellows back in the smithy in Birches.

"You don't scare me," he said.

But I could hear the lie in his voice. I had already scared him. This was why he had stopped. They all knew I was the Shamer's daughter, and I had listened while they talked up there on the deck when they thought I couldn't hear them. The witchling, they called me, or worse things: devil's spawn, witch's brat. Oh yes, I knew all the names. I could almost see how the thoughts chased one another around his head. If a girl could make a grown man fall asleep with a flute, could she turn him into stone as well? He didn't know. But he wasn't certain that I *couldn't* do it.

I raised the flute.

"Go back," I said. "Tell them you couldn't find me. Tell them I fell into a tide pool and drowned. Tell them anything you like, but go your way and let me go mine."

"They can see us," he said.

"Not anymore."

I meant simply that we were now so far away that the darkness and the mist hid us from their eyes. But he took it differently. He turned around and looked back. And if he had been scared before, he was terrified now. The hoar mist lay like a heavy white blanket across the marshes, and the moon had disappeared behind a cloud. The road was gone. It was there, of course, somewhere in the dark, but we could no longer see it. It was as if we were suddenly the only people in the world, him and me.

Still, he hesitated.

I raised the flute a little higher.

Reflexively, his hands clenched into fists. Then he turned and ran, no longer smoothly and cleverly from tussock to tussock. This was sheer panic, a heedless blundering through pools and ditches and black mud, like a sheep with a wolf on its tail. Long after the mists had swallowed him and the darkness hid him from sight, I could still hear him run and fall, run and fall, with no other purpose than to get as far away from me as possible.

I sat by that tide pool for a long time, hugging my wet flute to my chest. I was shaking all over from the chill and from exhaustion, and the longer I sat there, the colder I got. At some point there were voices in the mist, raised in anger—one of them was the Crow's. But they never came anywhere near. I had escaped from all of them, from the Crow and his men as well as from Azuan, at least for the time being. And that was good, of course. That was fine. If only I had had some idea where to go from here.

The Spinner's Web

In the fog, the *Sea Wolf* lay like all the other ships anchored at Dunbara's piers, a dark island with masts for trees, swaying gently every time a tidal ripple rolled on past.

It wasn't an island I wanted to return to. Carmian's cabin had been a prison, even if it lacked a proper door. Nor was I keen to be anywhere near the Crow again. A distance of a couple of hundred miles would have suited me just fine. But I had to find Nico, and I didn't know where else to start looking.

Right now there was no sign of life aboard. I didn't think they would all be sleeping. Probably most of them were out looking for me. But what about Nico? He would never have permitted the Crow to trade me to Azuan like that, not if he knew about it and was able to object. I was terribly afraid that the Crow had sold him off first—he was, after all, worth a lot more in gold than I was.

You'll have to go up there, I told myself in my sternest inner voice. You have to know whether they have him chained up in the hold or something like that. I raised the flute and made my stiff fingers move. The notes crept through the fog on gray cat's paws, almost soundlessly. I played until I felt sure even the rats were asleep, and then I made ready to enter the *Sea Wolf* one last time.

They had pulled up the gangway, but I found a ladder I could use instead. I had had quite enough soakings for one evening.

I had had to steal a sweater and a pair of boy's trousers from a cottage on the way, or I would have frozen to death. I had left my own wet clothes as payment of sorts; I didn't know if they had any girls in the family, of course, but if not, they could sell them, or at least they might once they had washed out the mud. The knitted sweater was much too big and smelled strongly of fish, but at least it was warm. And the trousers would stay up—just—if I tightened my belt a little more than I usually did. I wasn't quite sure what I looked like to other people. If anyone saw me, I hoped that at first glance, they would take me for a fisherman's son wearing his older brother's castoffs. And perhaps not give me more than that first glance.

I crept across the ladder onto the ship and then flipped it back so that it landed with a clatter on the stone pier. A passerby might wonder what a ladder was doing there, but not half as much as he would wonder if he saw it leaning against the side of the ship, a clear sign that uninvited visitors had come calling.

The deck rose and fell slowly. The tide was coming in one long, soft swell after the other. I stood there for a moment, poised to flee if the flute's music had failed me. But there was no one in sight, not even the guard I was positive the Crow had posted somewhere. The hatch to the cargo hold was neither bolted nor locked, but this meant nothing. If Nico was down there, they would have tied him up in any case. But even though it was unlocked, it wouldn't budge when I pulled at it. I had to put down the flute, wedge my heels against the edge, and heave for all I was worth. Come on, I swore silently. Come on, you blasted thing!

There was a yawning creak that could be heard several ships away, and I stumbled back and fell down with the hatch on top of me. I froze, listening. If anyone came…

But no one did. I stuck the flute into my belt and climbed through the hatch into the empty cargo hold.

It was dark and silent down there. The hull creaked with each tidal swell, but other than that, I could hear nothing, not even the scuttling of rats. Perhaps I really had managed to put the beasties to sleep? It would be nice to think so.

I couldn't see a thing. How on earth was I supposed to find Nico? Fumble my way along the floorboards? And if I didn't find him, would it be because he wasn't here, or because I had missed him in the dark?

"Nico?"

No answer. But then again, if everyone else was asleep, so presumably was he. This was hopeless. I needed a light. But how? I didn't have a handy candle in my pocket.

The lamp in Carmian's cabin. That would do very nicely.

I fumbled my way back to the ladder and climbed out. I hesitated a bit on the last rung, like a fieldmouse before leaving its hole. But there was still no sign of movement. The dogs in Dunbara were barking at something again, but aboard the *Sea Wolf* everything seemed serene and peaceful.

I darted across the deck to the cabin steps. And then I heard it: a snore. A heavy, clotted snoring from behind the drape. It didn't sound like Nico. I couldn't recall if I had ever heard Nico snore, but this was certainly not how I thought it should sound. To my ears, this had to be an older, heavier man. And then I noticed the soles of his feet. They poked out from beneath the drape along with ten dirty bare toes. Definitely not Nico's, I thought. A lot of the sailors went barefooted, though, even this late in the year, because it let them climb the rigging more easily.

Whoever it was did not seem to be on the point of waking. It sounded as if he was uncommonly soundly asleep even if he had found an odd spot to lie down in. Cautiously, I eased the drape aside and picked my way past him. He was lying on his stomach with his head on one arm, and he took up almost all the floor space in the cabin. It was one of the Crow's helmsmen, a man the others called Gorgo. What was he doing here? If the flute had made him fall asleep, it had come upon him rather suddenly. He looked as if he had dropped where he stood.

The lamp was lit, but the wick had been turned almost all the way down. Unfortunately it was hanging from a hook in the ceiling directly above him. But if I climbed into the bunk and stretched a bit—

"Gorgo! Mats!"

I was so startled I nearly spilled from the bunk. I made a wild snatch at the lamp, which tilted. Burning hot oil ran across my hand and splashed onto the back of Gorgo's neck.

"Whah," he grunted thickly, "whah the devil?"

I blew out the lamp. From the pier outside, the Crow's voice sounded once more.

"Damn it, Gorgo. Will you run out the damn gangway!"

I didn't know what Gorgo thought had happened. Possibly he wasn't thinking much at all. He seemed a bit groggy. I cowered down in the bunk and tried to be invisible. Right then I didn't even dare use the flute.

He got to his feet, cursing like the sailor he was. Then he clambered up the ladder without taking any note of his surroundings.

"Coming, Cap'n," he called.

There was a clatter and more curses.

"Where is Mats?" asked the Crow.

"Dunno, Cap'n." Gorgo still sounded as if clear thinking was at a minimum. "Not here."

"What happened? Where's the woman? And Liam? Damn you for a pack of useless dogs, can't I turn my back for even one moment without—" and then he broke off. When he spoke again, his voice was different, cold and sharp as a blade. "Where is His Righteousness?"

"In… in the hold. Wasn't that what the Cap'n—"

But the Crow interrupted him. "Why, then, is the hatch open?"

Because I hadn't closed it. I breathed a few of the words I had just heard Gorgo use.

"Keo. Pass me that lantern."

Why hadn't I searched better? Why had I wasted precious time on snores and lanterns and the like? Now it was too late. Now I would never be able to get Nico out of the hold without—

"Cap'n. He's gone!"

"I can see that, Keo."

Gone?

How?

"Treacherous bitch," said the Crow in the coldest voice ever. "When I catch her, she can wave her fine good looks good-bye."

For one brief moment I thought he meant me. But me he usually called the witchling or just "girl," and I didn't think he considered I had any good looks to lose. It wasn't me he was cursing at. It was Carmian.

Carmian. Who must have escaped with Nico—possibly even before the Crow dragged me off to sell to Azuan? Or while we were gone? Yes, that was probably more likely. While the Crow was gone from the ship.

How could Nico do that? How could he run off and leave me behind? And run off with *Carmian* too. I would never forgive him for that. Never. I pressed my face against the rough cloth of the mattress, trying to smother the sniffles that I couldn't quite stop. Right now it didn't seem so important, though, if they found me or not. Maybe the serpent side of the family was where I really belonged. No one else seemed to want me.

They didn't search the ship. Why should they? Nico and Carmian were no doubt running as fast as they could away from the *Sea Wolf*. I realized that I was probably safer here in the Crow's own nest than anywhere on land. The Crow had all his men out searching for Nico and Carmian, and the Dunbara dogs had a busy night, barking and howling at one intrusion after the other. For now, this was the best place. But for how long?

I sneaked off the ship in the earliest hour of the dawn. It was still freezing cold, and the rigging was so rimed with frost that the ropes were thick as cats' tails with it. My footprints showed clearly on the gangway and the pier, but I hoped no one would realize they were mine. Crouching behind a barrel, I peered up the nearest alley. I didn't have a clear plan; I just didn't want to be captured by the Crow, or by Azuan, or by Drakan's men. That seemed enough to be going on with. More definite plans could wait.

At the moment the alley was deserted, so I scuttled across the pier and dived into the narrow passage between the houses.

Phew, what a stench. Puke and pee and unwashed clothing. Compared to that, my sweater's fishy smell was the sweetest of perfumes, and I would have liked to turn back. But I could not afford such delicate sensibilities. Up through the alley, and then—

"Dina."

The soft whisper made me leap like a startled cat. Who—

"Sit down before someone sees you."

Leaning against the wall, half shielded by some rotten old planks and other rubbish, sat an old woman wrapped up in layers of filthy old shawls, with rags around her hands and feet. She was the source of the stench.

But how did she know me?

"Dina. Sit. Or do you want them to catch you again?"

It was only then I realized. This was no old woman. This was Carmian.

I was so taken aback that the sitting down happened almost without my doing it.

"What—"

"Be quiet. Wrap this around your head."

"This" was one of her disgusting filthy shawls.

"It stinks."

"I certainly hope so. Now, do as I say!"

There were footsteps and voices at the end of the alley. I quickly wrapped the stinking shawl around my head and huddled up next to Carmian.

"… disappeared off the face of the earth," said a man's voice.

"The Crow is spitting mad," said the other.

"No wonder. He reckoned on making a pretty penny on those deals. What with both golden geese gone in one night—God, what a stench. Did we search that alley?"

"Yeah. Nothing. Just some drunken old hag smelling as if she's been dead for three days."

They passed on. We sat very still for some time after they had gone. Then Carmian slowly got to her feet.

"Come on," she said. "Best we get out of here before the whole town wakes up."

"Carmian, what... where..." I could barely make head or tail of all the questions I wanted to ask her.

"He wouldn't come without you." Her voice held no hint of friendliness. It seemed colder, in fact, than the frost that whitened the thatched roofs of the cottages around us. "First he doesn't want you along, then suddenly he won't leave without you. Men. Impossible to please!"

"But how did you know that I would—"

"That you would return to the *Sea Wolf* like one of its very own rats? I didn't. But I heard them saying you had done a runner, and you are about as pitifully stuck to him as he is to you. It's enough to make a thinking woman sick."

We walked in silence for a while. Suddenly Carmian hunkered down and signed for me to do the same thing. A moment later two men turned the corner with a handcart. They weren't the Crow's men, and they didn't give us a second glance. As soon as they had disappeared around the next corner, Carmian got up again.

"Why did we have to sit down?" I asked. My bottom was all wet now from the frost on the cobbles.

"I'm a little tall for the poor-old-woman bit," she said. "And your boots are too good. Pull the shawl forward so that it hides more of your face."

I did as she said, but I didn't enjoy it.

"Does it have to stink like this?"

"Yes," she said.

"Why?"

She threw me a cold glance. "Do you always gab so much when you have someone after you?"

"I just want to know if—"

"It keeps people at a distance. They don't even want to look at something that smells like this. We're practically invisible. And shut your face now. I think I hear someone."

I shut up. And I saw what she meant. The stench was almost as good as the flute, in a different way. But phew!

We left Dunbara behind. But Carmian didn't take the nice straight road to Dunark. Instead she turned west, following a twisted little path that wound its way through the marshes like a very long snake. It wasn't always easy to spot, and sometimes we had to do a bit of tussock hopping like Keo and I had done earlier. Farther and farther into the marsh we went, until the mists closed around us like a hand.

And then the trail disappeared into a bog. Still black waters glittered among the weeds, and there seemed no end to it. The other bank, if there was one, was lost from sight in the fog.

Carmian showed no signs of stopping. But I wasn't having any.

"Carmian—"

"Walk right behind me," she said. "Put your feet where I put mine."

And then she strolled right into the bog. I stood there gaping. Because she didn't sink. The black waters barely reached her ankles.

"We haven't got all day," she said, when she noticed I hadn't followed. "Use your eyes—does it look as if I'm drowning?"

I stared at the shiny dark water. If I hadn't seen her standing there almost as if she could skim along the surface like a pond skater, I would have thought this was a bottomless hole. I took a cautious step forward. And then another. And then I realized why she wasn't sinking. Someone had built a bridge here, but *under* the water, so that it would be invisible to anyone who didn't know it.

It was slippery, and you had to be careful, and I still couldn't see how Carmian could tell precisely where it was. She seemed to be very sure of her way, though, and as long as I followed close on her heels, probably it was safe enough. But I still heaved a sigh of relief when we reached the other side and I could put my feet on more ordinary firm ground.

The sun was rising above the marshlands, and the fog shimmered white and gold and pretty. I trembled with cold, though. The fishy sweater might be warm, but cold wet feet sucked the heat right out of you.

"How far is it?" I asked, and then bit my lip, wishing I hadn't said anything. I didn't expect sympathy from Carmian.

But actually she didn't snarl at me this time.

"Not far now," she said, moving on.

I was quite surprised to avoid some nasty comment along the lines of "Perhaps Her Ladyship is unused to walking on her own two feet." But perhaps she was beginning to feel a little cold and a little tired herself.

When the settlement appeared, it looked at first like a grove of willow and elm, like a sort of island in the middle of the marsh. But when we came closer, I could see that the trees grew on a mound of earth. It wasn't until we climbed the mound and could look down on the houses it encircled that I could tell this was a place where people lived.

"What is this place?" I asked.

"A Geltertown."

"A… a what?"

She gave me one of her razor looks. "Before the Magdans came, this was Gelterland. They are still here, the Gelts, living in the marshlands. They have no love for the Magdans, nor for the House of Ravens. But they like Drakan even less."

A young man was standing in front of us. I started, because I hadn't seen him coming at all. It was almost as if he had shot up out of the marshy ground.

"Is this the girl?" he said, pointing at me.

"Yes."

"Then come. The Spinner wants to see her."

He was very slender and not very tall. If it hadn't been for his long silky mustache, I might have thought him not much older than myself. The Spinner, he had said. Who was that?

He led us into the settlement. It wasn't very large, no more than fifteen houses all told, and some of those had to be for livestock rather than people. The houses crowded together in the narrow space behind the earthworks, but despite the lack of space, they kept both goats and chickens *and* pigs, I noticed. A young woman was milking a goat, having to push away a large kid that appeared to think the milk in those teats belonged exclusively to *him*.

In the exact center of the settlement stood a large old ash. The leaves were long gone, but even in the summer I doubted it had sported very many. It looked more dead than alive. Why had no one cut it down? Perhaps to avoid damaging the cottage nestled next to it. The man with the mustache pointed at the doorway.

"The Spinner's house," he said. "Please enter."

He himself was apparently planning to stay outside.

"Isn't he coming with us?" I whispered to Carmian.

"He can't," she said curtly. "He's a man."

And men couldn't come here? What sort of creature was this Spinner?

The room was rather gloomy after the brightness of the frosted landscape outside. And it wasn't very big. One wall was strangely curved, unplanned, and full of strange growths that had been left untrimmed. And then I realized this wasn't simply sloppy carpentry. The house didn't just lean against the ash tree; the trunk of the tree *was* the gable of the Spinner's cottage.

A woman—the Spinner?—sat weaving. How she could see what she was doing in the gloom was beyond me, but the shuttle flew busily from one end of the weft to the other, and she didn't even pause in her work as we entered.

"Sit down," she said. "And, Carmian, please leave those rags outside."

There was only one place to sit—a low bench next to the door. There was no fireplace, I suddenly noticed. And yet it seemed much warmer than outside. I returned my borrowed shawl to Carmian, who was obediently unwrapping herself from the smelly old rags she had worn.

The Spinner was my mother's age, just about. Neither young nor old. And what you noticed first was the eyes. Or rather, what was around the eyes. It looked as if she was wearing a mask, but when I looked more closely I could see that it was her skin that was blackened, dyed, or even tattooed, in a wide strip from ear to ear, across the bridge of her nose.

"Your mother is a Shamer," she said. "And so were you, once."

I nodded. I supposed Nico must have told her. The last bit stung. She made it sound so final, as if I would never get back the gift my mother had given me.

"You are something else as well," she continued. "You have the dreamer's gift."

The dreamer's gift? I had never heard anyone call it that, but it wasn't such a bad name, so I nodded once more.

The shuttle darted this way and that. There was a strange whispery music to it, as if she was playing a harp with very muted strings.

Carmian had rid herself of her rags. She tossed them out the open door and came to sit beside me.

"At this time you do not know what you are," said the Spinner suddenly. "And neither does Carmian—she knows her own heart so poorly."

Carmian snorted. "I have no heart. You know that."

The Spinner paid no attention to the interruption. But her words struck me to my soul. *You do not know what you are.* Not who—what. Like I was some creature that was barely human. I shuddered, and it wasn't because of cold.

"You. Shamer's daughter with the dreamer's gift. You face a choice. The thread has twained, but you cannot be two. Choose— before both threads are severed."

All the little hairs at the back of my neck stood up. It wasn't just the words, it was the way she said it. Like she was certain. Like she could see things that weren't visible to the rest of us. A little like my mother and yet... not at all.

"Are you a fortune-teller?" I whispered.

The white in her eyes showed very pale against the black strip across her face. She shook her head. "No. I am the Spinner."

Carmian stirred uneasily. "Not to be rude," she said. "But we do have quite a lot to do—"

The black-and-white gaze of the Spinner left me and grabbed Carmian instead. "You are too much in haste," she said. "You always were."

I felt a tingling of childish glee, as if I were five years old and Davin was being told off and not me. And the Spinner seemed to note that too.

"You really don't like each other very much, do you?" she said with a smile that looked suddenly very human.

Carmian shrugged. "She's no favorite of mine," she said, as if I wasn't in the room at all. "Spoiled and stuck-up little Miss Know-It-All."

I didn't think I was spoiled or stuck-up. And the charming words did not make me like Carmian any better. I could have returned her compliments—calculating, cold, and… well, not shameless, not quite, but near enough. But though I didn't say any of it out loud, I had the same see-through sensation I sometimes got when my mother looked at me. I was very certain that the Spinner could tell, almost word for word, what I was thinking.

"Nevertheless, your threads run together in the weave," said the Spinner. "And you will do each other much harm and much good. And now you may go, seeing that you are in such a hurry."

Carmian immediately rose. I took a bit longer.

"What is a Spinner?" I asked. She was no Shamer, though there was a likeness. Nor was she a Blackmaster.

The Spinner shook her head. "At the moment, just a woman who weaves. And sometimes catches a glimpse of a greater pattern."

My stomach prickled. Was it human destinies she wove? Right here in this hut?

"What do you weave?" I asked, and could not keep my voice from trembling.

She turned her black-and-white gaze on me again, as if she could see straight into my head.

"A shirt for my cousin," she said drily. "The old one is worn through."

A Better Deal

"Are you Gelt?" I asked Carmian outside in the square.

"No," she said. "But I knew someone who was."

It came to me like a whiplash, unexpected and painful. A voice I had to hear whether I wanted to or not.

I told you to be careful. I told you and told you. But oh no, you could easily do it alone. Until they caught you. Until they—

"The one they hanged?" I said without thinking, or at least without thinking any thoughts other than hers.

"It wasn't my fault!" she burst out. "I told him not to try it alone, but he—" and then she broke off. "How did you know?"

I couldn't tell her. Some of it I had seen in her thoughts because the Shamer's gift had suddenly come upon me. The rest I knew because I had eavesdropped on her conversation with Nico, that night on the deck. I didn't think either explanation would please her.

She shoved me so hard I tumbled backward.

"Get off me!" she shouted. "Don't you pry and poke and… and sniff around my life. What is in here"—she pointed at herself—"is *mine*. Do you understand? *No one* has the right to see that."

She was right.

"I didn't do it on purpose," I said tiredly. "Sometimes it just—"

"I don't care if it was on purpose or not. Just stay away from me!"

"If I can," I said. "I can't always control it."

"Then *learn*, damn it! The Spinner doesn't go around attacking people with what she knows. If you enter her house, yes, then she will tell you what she sees. You know that. And if you don't want to listen, you can just stay away. But you, what does a person have to do to get rid of you?"

I got up slowly. A suspicion had entered my head.

"Did you get the Crow to sell me to Azuan? To get rid of me?"

"No," she said. "Not you. Just the flute. I thought we could make a bit of money off it. And when the man from Colmonte saw it, he became very keen to know where we got it."

I wasn't sure I believed her. Nico had said she had her own sense of honor, but all I had seen so far was her sense of a good deal. I didn't think she had very many human feelings at all. Except… there was that glimpse of her I had just had. She had had feelings for him, the Gelt they had hanged.

"Who was he?" I asked. "Your friend the Gelt?"

I hadn't truly expected her to answer. But she did.

"His name was Jaerin. He was the Spinner's brother."

The Spinner's brother? From what I had heard on the *Sea Wolf*—what had Nico called him, Tip-Toe?—it sounded as if Carmian's friend had been a confidence man or a clever burglar or something like that. Hard to imagine *that* about a brother to the wise Spinner. And hard to imagine that the Spinner and her people would take so kindly to Carmian, who must have been his partner in crime. But apparently they did. There had to be something there I didn't understand, but I didn't think she would tell me.

"Where is Nico?" I asked instead.

"In the guesthouse," said Carmian. "Over there."

I looked where she pointed. It was not the meanest of the

cottages, far from it. The gables had been carved to resemble herons, and the whole door, too, had been carved into a picture: ducks on the water, geese in the sky, yet another pair of herons stalking fish among reeds and rushes. If this was the guesthouse, hospitality was clearly a virtue here. Why, then, was there a man posted on either side of the pretty door, each with a long and dangerous-looking spear?

"Guesthouse?" I said. "Why the guards?"

"It's not every day of the week that a prince of the House of Ravens sleeps in that house," said Carmian in a dry tone, and I couldn't tell whether she considered the men to be jailers or guards of honor. Perhaps even the Gelts themselves weren't quite sure? In any event, the guards let us pass without any trouble. One of them even gave Carmian a friendly nod.

There was a fireplace at one end, and on either side stood a chair made from skins on a frame of… bones? Whalebone, even? In one chair sat a gray-haired, gray-bearded Gelt. In the other sat Nico.

He certainly didn't look like a prisoner. He had bathed—his dark hair was still damp—and the Gelts had given him a long woolen robe embroidered with herons. And he had shaved off his beard. I didn't like to see that. The beard had not suited him, but it had been his way of hiding. Without it, he looked more handsome, it was true, but also more like the son of a prince. Did this mean he thought he was done with hiding?

He rose when he saw me.

"Dina. Is… everything well with you?"

Actually I would have liked a hug. I needed one, and badly. But at least he didn't seem to be furious with me anymore, and the worry in his dark blue eyes was unmistakable.

"Well enough," I said. Which was almost true. I certainly felt better now than I had a couple of hours ago, and being frightened and worried had become almost a habit.

"Welcome," said the Gelt, who had also risen. "The Spinner says you have more than one gift. And that you have come like the geese in spring to tell us that change is upon us. A harbinger of storms, perhaps?"

He may have meant well, but the fancy imagery made me ill at ease. I was no harbinger. I was a girl, a human girl. And I didn't know what to answer. Had the Spinner known all this about me before she had even met me? She was either a very gifted seer or else Nico had told tales.

Perhaps the Gelt felt my discomfort, or maybe he merely got tired of waiting for an answer.

"My name is Ethlas," he said. "I am the chieftain this year."

"And last year, and the year before that, and the year before that," murmured Carmian. "They never elect anyone else."

He looked at her sharply, but chose to smile.

"True. I have been this town's chieftain for seventeen years now. But one must never take one's rank for granted, Carmian."

"The Gelts elect their chieftains," said Nico, as if this was very interesting and very important. "It's not a position you are born to."

I just thought it sounded weird.

"I'm Dina," I said, making a sort of small bow.

"Yes. Welcome, Dina. Are you hungry?"

I was about to say no, because my stomach felt like one big, cold, heavy knot. But then my nostrils caught the scent of frying fish, and I changed my mind.

"Yes," I said. "I think I am."

"Carmian, will you ask Imma to prepare a little breakfast for our guest?"

I glanced at Carmian. She might not be too thrilled at being asked to wait on me like that. But for some reason she merely nodded and did as he asked.

She was different here, I realized. To the Spinner and to Ethlas. Not so belligerent. Not so sharp.

She returned within moments with a clay platter that held some baked roots and two small fried fish. There was neither bread nor porridge, the way there would have been at home, but a mug of warm goat's milk. Carmian put it all on the long table in the middle of the room.

"Breakfast is served, Your Ladyship."

I wish she wouldn't call me that. But I didn't say anything. I just sat down and began to eat. And finished everything, except for the bones.

I was so busy eating that I paid little attention to what Nico and Ethlas were talking about. Nico seemed to be asking a lot of questions about how they elected their chieftains. It sounded very boring. But then, in the middle of the second fish, I realized why Nico was so concerned. He had never asked to be the son of the castellan. And if someone suddenly had the idea that people should *elect* who should be castellan, rather than just having to live with whoever was next in line to the throne, well, one thing was certain—Nico would never run of his own free will for such an election.

Ethlas answered willingly enough, but it seemed to me there were other things he would rather discuss. Something about taxes and land rights and fishing rights. I didn't quite understand it, but it seemed the Magdans had once taken something away from the Gelts.

"But the worst thing is the children," said Ethlas, and there was now a sharp emotion in his voice that made me put down my knife and listen. In its own way, that voice could be as commanding as a Shamer's. "We cannot live with that fear. How can our children grow up to be free and strong when we must keep hiding them from Drakan's men? Six of them. Six we have already lost to his so-called *Dragon schools*." Ethlas practically spat the word into the fire. "And now we no longer dare to have our young ones with us here, where they belong."

"Where are they, then?" asked Nico, and I saw how he straightened and tensed like a coiled spring. He was thinking of the Educators; one didn't have to be the Spinner to guess that much. Was Drakan doing the same thing his grandfather Prince Arthos had done? The thought made my skin crawl.

"I will not tell you," said Ethlas firmly. "No Gelt would. If they find the children's village and take the ones that remain to us, what future will we have? How, then, shall we live?"

"But they are safe?"

"What is safety? Drakan has not found them yet. That is as much as I can say."

Nico rose.

"Land rights and fishing rights," he said. "On those issues you may have my word on parchment, but I cannot guarantee that I will ever be able to back it up with real power. But the children, that must stop. That I swear, even if it costs me my life: He shall not take your children. Or any children at all, ever again."

There was a sudden silence in the guesthouse. Carmian, who had been drumming her fingers absently against one thigh, stopped abruptly. And I slowly put down my mug of goat's milk.

Even if it costs me my life.

I had no doubt he meant it. Lately, Nico set a lower price on his life than I thought he should. But when you knew what the Educators could do to children, well, perhaps I understood him.

"Then we understand each other," said Ethlas. "We will aid your cause to the best of our ability. And I speak for all Gelts in this." He poured a golden liquid into two silver cups. "Here."

"What is it?"

"Geltermead. Brewed from honey and fermented goat's milk. This is how we seal an agreement. We have no need of parchment."

"Thank you," said Nico. "But to seal it with the rest of the world, we had better have parchment as well."

"What about me?" Carmian had risen too.

"You?" said Nico. "I thought you were the one who wanted this."

"Why would you think that?"

"Oh, I don't know," said Nico. "Possibly because you had me drugged, rolled up in a blanket, and carried here before I woke up."

I straightened. Oh, so that was how it had happened… Carmian's poppy juice. Some of the chill in my stomach eased a little. Nico had not willingly abandoned me.

"I'm risking my life for you," said Carmian. "What do you think the Crow will do if he ever sees me again? How many Dragon soldiers do you think are hunting for me now? I am as dead as Jaerin if they catch me."

She can wave her fine good looks good-bye, the Crow had promised. And she was probably right about the Dragon soldiers too.

"I'm not denying it," said Nico. "But you did rather force my hand, didn't you? I would have chosen to protect you better."

"I don't want you to protect me. I want you to pay me."

"Pay you?"

"Yes. Seeing that you are so busy settling rights and putting things on parchment, I want something too."

"What, then?"

"A marriage contract."

I think we all gasped. I know I did. Marriage? To Nico? But he was…

"Such matters are not dealt with like this," said Ethlas quietly. "Surely you know that."

"Princes don't marry for love," said Carmian in a voice as cold as steel. "He doesn't have to love me. I just want to *be* somebody. I want to get up so high no one can ever step on me again."

For once, Nico looked completely out of his depth. "You mean you… you want… you want to be the castellaine?"

"Yes."

"And that is your price?"

"Yes. Is it so very different from settling the fishing rights or the land rights? If your father had been alive, he would have negotiated a marriage for you sooner or later."

"Don't bring my father into this," said Nico somewhat tensely.

"Why not? I know he would never have agreed to let you marry someone like me. He would have chosen some noble family he wanted something from. There would have been councils and negotiations and documents on dowry and inheritance and titles and the like, but in the end he would have decided who to sell you to—oh, sorry—who to marry you to. Isn't that how it's done in your family?"

Nico could not deny it. It was part of being a prince.

"Very well, then," said Carmian. "Matters have changed slightly. Your father is dead, the House of Ravens is somewhat down on its luck, and the noble families aren't lining up their marriage candidates on your doorstep. But I have something you want. My help, and that of the Gelts. You don't even have to pay up here and now. Only if we succeed. We can write that it only comes into effect upon Drakan's death."

"Carmian, is this really what you want?"

"Yes."

"And feelings just don't matter?"

"Love is for wide-eyed schoolgirls. A bit of mutual respect, Nico. That should be enough. With some noble heiress you wouldn't even be sure of that much. And I am not stupid, Nico. I may not have been born to wear silks, but I learn quickly."

I could see that Nico was actually giving this some consideration. Serious consideration. I felt like shouting and yelling at both of them. At Carmian for being so mercenary—castellaine? Someone like her who had certainly not been born to silks. Born to dirt and squalor, more like, if my guess was correct. And at Nico, who… who surely couldn't be that *stupid*. Could he?

"Ethlas?" He looked at the chieftain questioningly. "What is your word in this matter?"

Ethlas looked less than pleased at the way things were turning.

"We owe Carmian a great deal. For this and past favors. But, Carmian, did you talk to the Spinner about any of this?"

"Yes. She… she wouldn't forbid it."

"Carmian, the Spinner never forbids us anything. She thinks we have a sacred right to cast ourselves into whatever morass of folly we choose. You know this. What else did she say?"

"Only that I knew my own heart badly." Carmian looked as if it cost her blood to say it. But she spoke the truth, and that in itself was surprising enough. I had heard the Spinner say those very words.

"But you know your will? You know that this is what you want?"

"Yes!" She looked at him almost angrily, as if questioning her judgment was a crime. "I know my own mind!"

Ethlas shook his head gently, but he asked her no more questions.

"If she is determined, we must support her in this," he said. "We owe her that."

Nico bent his head for a moment, as if to hide his expression. Then he straightened, and if there had been emotion on his face, now it was well hidden.

"Let us finish this business, then," he said in a peculiarly harsh voice. "Fishing rights, land rights, and marriage rights. Ethlas, I think you are getting a better deal than she is."

Carmian merely stared at him in silent defiance.

I got up.

"Dina?" said Nico. "Where are you going?"

"Nowhere," I said. "Just out."

The mist was letting go at last. The sky was clear and blue for the first time in days, an ill match for my mood, which was pitch-black. Carmian. I wish I had never met her. I wished even more that *Nico* had never met her. Damn her and her mermaid hair and the calculating brain underneath all that hair. Castellaine. As if someone like her could… as if they would ever allow…

Hot tears were creeping down my cheeks. Angrily, I wiped them away. I didn't want to cry now. And if I absolutely had to cry, couldn't it be over something else? Something more important than Carmian. Like Drakan. Like the children of the Gelts, the ones he had taken and the ones who had to hide in the marsh and couldn't live free and ordinary lives with their families. But no. It was Carmian who made the tears come, Carmian and her hateful calculations and contracts and… and…

"Dina?"

It was Nico, of course. I didn't dare turn around, didn't want him to see the stupid tears.

"Dina, what is it?"

He had noticed anyway. He was good at things like that.

I couldn't talk. My throat was one big lump, and even if I had been able to talk, I wouldn't have known what to say.

Cautiously, he touched my shoulder. And suddenly I could hold nothing back, and it was no longer just Carmian I cried over, it was everything. That everything had to be so hard. That Drakan existed. That my father was dead and my mother didn't like what he had given me. That we had to be scared all the time, that Callan was wounded and might die, that we all might die. *And* that Carmian had long, golden mermaid curls, while I was small and square and had hair like a horse. Everything at once.

He put his arms around me, and I hid my face against the heron gown and sobbed. And for once he kept his mouth shut and asked no more questions. He didn't tell me to stop crying. He didn't say that everything would be all right and that it would all look much better in the morning. He just held me.

After a while, the tears stopped. I was exhausted, and my head hurt from crying so hard. Yet somehow, I felt a little better.

"That sweater smells awfully fishy," said Nico, as if there was nothing out of the ordinary about my soaking his borrowed robes in tears. "Don't you think the Gelts can lend you something slightly more fitting, and slightly less smelly? A bath might help too."

"Do I smell *that* bad?"

He laughed. "No, I meant—to help make you feel better. About everything."

"Nico, are you still mad that I followed you?"

"No," he said. "Not mad. Only I wish you hadn't. If it had been at all possible, I would have done this completely on my own. Just me and Drakan. But I had to have a ship, and that meant bringing Carmian in on it. And then Davin—and the minute I got rid of him, there you were, and you just wouldn't go away. And now… now it seems I've gone and recruited an entire people."

"The Gelts?"

"Yes. I knew they were here, even though my father pretty much discounted them as an unruly pack of smugglers, unreliable and impossible to govern. But there are many more of them than I thought. Some have left the settlements and live in the coastland towns and villages like ordinary people, but they have not forgotten they are Gelts, says Ethlas. When they hear of the bargain we have struck, they will give us aid. And a people who has lived in hiding for centuries, well, they know a lot of secret ways and hiding places. They will find out for us where Drakan is now, and they can help me get to him."

I pulled away just far enough to see his face. Where the beard had been, the skin was slightly paler.

"Nico, are you sure—I mean, you… you don't even like swords. And Drakan, do you really think you *can* kill him?"

The muscles round his eyes tensed to hear me put it so bluntly.

"It seems to be my task," he said. "And I will make certain I don't fumble it this time."

"Nico, you hate such things."

"Yes."

"But are you any good at it? All that sword stuff, I mean." I knew he had been taught swordplay as a child, and that he and Davin had been training together lately. But Drakan had been far superior that day in the Arsenal Court, and it had only been because of Rose that Nico hadn't been killed there and then.

"Many are better," said Nico.

"Then why not let one of them do it?"

If only he would. I was so afraid he wouldn't be able to see it through. And even more afraid that he would die trying, and uselessly. But he shook his head stubbornly.

"I have been hiding for more than two years now. And throughout that time things have become steadily worse. All the time, more deaths, more destruction. None of it would have happened if I hadn't hesitated when I had the chance. Enough is enough. I want an end to it now. Not a grand war that will kill even more people. Just one quiet murder. If I can do it."

"Nico!"

"There is no reason to call it by a prettier name. I have no intention of challenging him to an honorable duel. I just want him dead so there will be an end to it."

It was the second time he used those words, and I wondered whether it was only Drakan's death he wanted.

"Nico, you will do what you can to survive this, won't you?"

"Of course. I don't want to die."

I didn't quite believe him. Someone like Nico—could he kill another human being, even a human being like Drakan, and live on afterward? Like nothing had happened?

"When do you think we will hear news?"

"In a couple of days, I hope. It would not be wise to stay here much longer than that. The Crow will do what he can to find us on his own, but if he fails, he will try and earn his reward by selling what knowledge he has. And once the Dragon soldiers start searching the marshes, well, I would rather not make the Gelts face such troubles. They may come to count our bargain a costly one."

"Not much time, then." And somewhere out there was also Azuan. I didn't think he was the type to quit and go home.

"Dina."

I waited, but at first no more words came from him, only a strange hunted look.

"Yes," I prompted.

"Will you please stay here?"

"Here?"

"Yes. It would be so awful… I wouldn't know what to do if you—" He broke off again.

I stepped back even farther and set my hands on my hips. "Are you planning to run out on me again?"

"No."

"Or drug me with poppy?"

"No. That didn't really work, did it?"

"But you would rather I stayed behind?"

"Yes. The Spinner said I mustn't force you. That I had to let you make your own choices. But please will you stay here? It would feel so good to know you were safe."

"Are you taking Carmian?"

"Carmian? Yes, I—"

"Then I'm coming too."

"Dina, it isn't a good—"

"If you think I am going to let you go traipsing off with that scheming female, think again. Castellaine, my eye. If she gets a better offer, do you think she would hesitate to sell you to the highest bidder, like a farmer sells a cow that doesn't yield enough milk anymore?"

"Actually, yes. She wouldn't do that."

"You trust her?"

"Yes."

I shook my head. "Well, that does it, then."

"Dina—"

"No. If she comes, I come."

He looked so miserable that I nearly felt sorry for him. But I was in no mood to back down, and I think he could see that. He spun on his heel and went back to the guesthouse. The rest of the day he steadily drank one glass of Geltermead after the other and grew more and more irritable and silent. When Carmian asked if he didn't think he had had enough, he slammed down the metal cup and walked out without a single word.

Two days passed. Two strange days of living in the guesthouse, Nico, Carmian, and I, trying not to fight too much. After that first day, Nico stayed off the mead, but it still wasn't easy, and a little past noon the second day I reached the point where I had to go outside, despite the chilling winds that howled through the marshes, simply because I was so fed up with Carmian that I couldn't stay under the same roof as her. It was as Nico and the Spinner had said—the two of us really didn't like each other much.

I did see Ethlas go into the guesthouse, but I was not yet ready to come inside. I pretended that I wasn't cold at all and was in any case terribly interested in watching two half-grown goat kids tussle with each other, each trying to ram the other with its budding horns.

In a while, Nico came out.

"Dina?"

I raised an arm in a hesitant wave. His voice sounded all wrong, and there was something about the way he moved… The chill crept into my chest and centered on my heart. Something had happened. Even at this distance, I could tell as much.

"What is it?" I said. "What has happened?"

He stopped while he was still a few paces away.

"Drakan has moved into the Highlands," he said.

I stared at him. "But it's winter," I said tonelessly. "Or nearly so. He can't do that. Not now." That he would do it one day was something we all knew. But seeing that autumn had passed without an attack, we thought… "It's not spring yet!"

"I'm sorry."

"Where? *Where* has he attacked?" Not Baur Kensie, I silently prayed. Not Kensie.

"Baur Laclan. But he has taken more than half the Dragon Force with him, they say. Dina, it's only a matter of time."

"Can't they stop him?" I whispered. "Laclan is a big clan. Powerful. Surely they can…"

The pity in Nico's gaze took my voice away. He knew so much more about armies and soldiers than I did, so much more about how war was waged.

"Perhaps," he said, but I could tell he didn't believe it.

"Why not?" I asked.

"Dina, Drakan has more than eight thousand men. How many do you think Laclan can muster? Two thousand? Three thousand, if they let the old men fight?"

"But if the other clans help—"

"Yes. A big if. The clans like to mind their own business, and some of them might even be shortsighted enough to delight in Laclan's misfortune. And even the ones that are willing, will they get there in time? No one thought he would attack now."

"Callan will unite them and make them help. Callan can lead—" And then I realized what I had forgotten in the heat of the moment. Callan was not at Baur Kensie, and he couldn't at the moment lead anything or unite anybody. He might not even... might not even be alive anymore.

Nico didn't say anything. His guilt at Callan's fate made him look at the ground, so that all I could see of his head at the moment was his dark hair.

Something cold and wet touched my face. I brushed it away.

"We leave in a couple of hours," he said. "If we hurry—Luckily there aren't that many Dragon soldiers left in the coastlands, and the ones that are still here are busy just staying in control. We can travel more openly than we would otherwise have dared."

"To Baur Laclan?" I asked.

"No," said Nico. "No matter how fast we travel, Dina, Baur Laclan will have fallen long before we get there."

Helena Laclan, who had given me Silky. Tavis and his mother. Ivain, who had fought against Davin in the Ring of Iron and spared his life. Baur Laclan was a city, by Highland standards. Could it really be true that... that all those people... Ugly sights crowded together in my head. Burning thatch. Panicked children and animals, wounded men, and people dying. I tried to blink them away and would rather look at Nico. What was that in his hair?

Snowflakes. Tiny white crystals that melted almost right away. But when I stared up at the sky, I could see that more were coming.

The young goats stopped their fight to stare at the strange new fluffiness whirling among the houses.

"Look," I said. "Nico, it's snowing. Do you think there is snow in the Highlands too?"

"Possibly. The winter comes earlier up there in the high places."

"Then he has to turn back. Surely, he has to turn back."

Nico shook his head. "No. If he hadn't decided that this would be a winter war, he wouldn't have left in the first place. I don't think we can count on a couple of snowflakes to stop him."

Stupid snowflakes. I stared at them as if it was all their fault. Couldn't they have arrived a little earlier? Couldn't there have been more of them, many more, so that Drakan would have been forced to give up his miserable war before it had even started? Now it was all too late.

DAVIN

Soldiers

Was it better to be saved by the Dragon Force than not to be saved at all? I didn't know. Without aid Callan would die—but a helping hand from a Dragon soldier? I didn't think Callan would thank me for my efforts, especially not if it meant that Rose, the Harbormaster, and all the rest would fall into Dragon hands as well. But I had already said far, far too much.

"The boy came tearing into town like the devil himself was at his heels," said the Dragon soldier who had first seen me. "Something about a shipwreck, he said, and a Kensie."

His superior looked up from the report he was making. His face was full of tiny scars where the beard didn't cover it. They looked white against his weather-beaten skin.

"Was he alone?"

"Looks like it."

"What's your name, boy?"

"Damian," I said in a last-ditch attempt not to reveal too much.

"Damian?" said the first soldier. "I thought you said Davin?"

"No. Damian."

The two men exchanged a look, and I saw the soldier shake his head.

"No, My Lord Knight," he said. "He said Davin. I'm sure of it."

My Lord Knight? So this was one of Drakan's dreaded Dragon knights? Except for the scars, he looked quite ordinary.

"Lying to me isn't wise," he said in a flat voice. "It makes me suspicious. Which ship was it?"

I opened my mouth, then shut it again. I had already messed up once. No, twice, actually. I wasn't a great actor at the best of times, and right now I could barely stay upright. I was shaking with fatigue, and my body was going from hot to cold so quickly that it was making me dizzy and sick. Keeping track of a lot of half-lies and half-truths… no, I was better off saying nothing at all.

"Please," I murmured, "may I have some water?"

"Answer me. Which ship?"

I hung my head. "I'm thirsty. Please can I have a little water?"

If only the other one would—

Yes. The blow hit me across the back of the neck, not all that hard, but hard enough. I let myself drop. The soldier attempted to haul me back on my feet, but I wasn't having any. I *was* close to not being able to stand, so it was not particularly hard to pretend it was impossible.

"Not his head, Balain. How often do I have to tell you?" said the knight.

"But I didn't hit him very hard," said the soldier defensively.

"Then hit him not very hard somewhere else. We can't interrogate an unconscious prisoner."

Exactly. That had been my thought too.

The soldier kicked me in the side, a little tentatively. But I was no blank-back. I had taken my turn in the Whipping Yard of the Sagisburg, and it would take more than a measly kick to make me yelp.

"Well?"

"Sorry, sir."

"Is he gone?"

"I think so, sir."

The gravel crunched next to my ear. Out of the corner of my eye I could see his boot, and this gave me a second's warning before he grabbed me by the hair with one hand and raised my head off the ground. A blade flashed, and for a second I thought he simply meant to cut my throat there and then. But it wasn't my throat he was aiming for. The point of the knife broke the skin just below my left eye.

My eye. He was going to take out my eye.

There was no time for thought. I twisted to one side and knocked away his knife hand with my arm. Not my eyes, please no, I didn't want to be blind, couldn't let him—

He let go of my hair and shoved me with one boot so that I flopped onto my back. As I lay there, I felt a thin thread of blood run down my cheek, almost like a tear.

"Not quite gone after all, it seems," said the knight drily.

"Sneaky bastard," muttered the soldier, and looked like he wanted to kick me again.

"Did he say where the shipwreck was?"

"Someplace called Troll Cove. A half-day by boat, the Arlainfolks say."

"Very well. Take a couple of the fishermen and one boat—the others you may burn—and go to this Troll Cove. Since he is trying so hard not to tell us anything, I'm sure it will be worth our while. I can spare you... hmmmm... ten men. That ought to be enough."

"Sir, might it be a trap, do you think?"

The knight hesitated only for a moment. Then he shook his head. "No. He's not that clever."

The soldier gave me a venomous look. "What about the boy?" he said. "Do we take him as well?"

"No. Leave him to me. I may be wrong, but I have a feeling the Dragon Lord will be pleased to see him."

I fell down three times during the first half mile of the walk.

"The lad is all in," said one of the fishermen from Arlain, who had been trying to keep me upright the last bit of the way. "Surely ye can see it is no good. He cannot go on."

"He'll have to learn, then," said the nearest Dragon soldier. "We can't drag our heels just because he has decided to be delicate."

"It is hard on the little ones too." The fisherman was not easy to shut up, it seemed. "Dragging them all over the countryside in the middle of the night!"

The Dragon soldier rode his horse very close to the fisherman.

"What's your name?" he asked.

"Obain."

"Listen, Obain. The next time you open your big mouth without being asked, I'll take your ear off."

The stubborn fisherman glared at the soldier. He took a deep breath, and I thought he might be about to speak again despite the threat.

"Don't," I said. "He means it."

The fisherman—Obain—still glared, but at least he glared in silence. Satisfied, the Dragon soldier nodded briefly and moved on down the long line of people straggling through the night.

There were perhaps forty of us all told. Every grown man in Arlain except for those who had been ordered to take the boat out to Troll Cove. And a child from every single house.

The youngest wasn't even a year old—a small girl riding in a rucksack at her father's back, and probably the only prisoner in the long line who was not afraid.

The women remained behind. But how were they to survive when the men were gone and the boats burned? It was hard to see how they would manage. In less than eight hours the Dragon soldiers had torn everything in their lives apart and had changed everything in the little village for always.

"Devils," muttered Obain, as if he could hear my thoughts. "Damned devils."

My legs felt as if they were on fire, while the rest of me was shaking continuously from cold and exhaustion. The muscles of my stomach felt like wood, and my back was screaming at me. There didn't seem to be a single part of me that didn't hurt. Back when I still had enough breath left to speak, I had asked Obain if he knew where we were going.

"Baur Laclan, I think. But it's more than a day's journey. And with the little ones…"

Baur Laclan. More than a day. We would have to rest then, I thought, at some point. Sleep. Oh, sweet Lady, sleep. But it seemed the Dragon soldiers had no plans to let us rest while there was any strength left in us at all. What was the hurry?

Maybe there *was* no hurry. Maybe it was just because exhausted men are easier to control.

When I fell down for the fifth time, even the Dragon soldiers could see it was no use. One of them prodded me with his sword, and I made one last effort to rise. I got no farther than my knees, then my midriff cramped so badly that I collapsed completely.

"My Lord Knight!"

The Dragon knight rode up. "What is it now?"

"We can't get him up."

The knight halted his big gray horse and looked down on me. "I see," he said. "And is his faintness real this time?"

The soldier raised his sword. "Do you want me to—"

"No." The gray horse snorted, and the knight rested a calming hand on its neck. "I have reason to believe the Dragon Lord wants to see this one. Throw him across one of the packhorses. And see to it that you tie the knots properly. We don't want to lose him on the way, do we now?"

When I woke, I thought for a moment that I was back at the Sagisburg, in the Gullet with Mascha and the rest. I think it was because everything hurt, and I was so very tired, and because my foot was stuck to something, just like when they used to chain us up at night.

My head hurt so badly it felt as if it might burst any minute. I hadn't had enough to drink, and right now my throat felt as if it had been hung out to dry for months, like a split cod.

Water. Wasn't there water somewhere?

I sat up with some difficulty. I didn't remember how I had come to be here, in this large dark room that seemed to be a barn of some kind. There was straw underneath me, and above some long narrow... not quite windows, but slits, at any rate. I could just make out a patch of sky, sky that had begun to lighten.

I was about to try and get up when I remembered the chained-up feeling. I fumbled in the dark. Around one ankle I found a sort of wooden shackle with a thin metal chain attached to it. Lightweight irons. How practical, I thought bitterly. This way you could shackle a whole town without dragging around several tons of metal.

I closed my eyes for a moment. If only my head would stop hurting. And the rest of me too, for that matter. I couldn't even think.

"Oh, so ye're awake, then?"

The man next to me had noticed me stirring, it seemed.

"Yes. Do we have any water?"

"No. They gave the rest of us a drink before turning in, but you were out cold."

I squinted at him and tried to make out his features in the dark.

"Obain?"

"Aye, lad. And thank ye, by the way. You were right, the devil would have done it."

At first I couldn't remember what he was talking about. The throbbing in my head was about all I could think of. But then it came back to me—the Dragon soldier and his threats.

"You probably look better with two ears," I said. "And if one has to bleed a little, it had better be for something worth bleeding for."

"Ye're no Highlander."

"No." The way I talked gave me away immediately, I knew.

"What is yer name then, laddie?"

"Davin. Davin Tonerre."

"Oh, aye, the Shamer's son, what lives with Kensie?"

I nodded, but then realized he wouldn't be able to see it in the dark.

"Yes. But it would be nice if you didn't mention that to the Dragon knight."

He snorted. "Never ye fear. I'll not say a word to that bastard before I can spit on his grave."

Obain seemed to be a fairly belligerent man. Now, at any rate. What he had been like before the Dragon Force took his town and dragged him away from house, home, and family, I couldn't tell.

Family…

"Do you have any children?"

"Three," he said. "Those devils took my oldest girl, Maeri. The lass is only eight."

Maeri. That was the name of the Harbormaster's daughter too, the one who had smiled at me and given me a full cup of toddy though I had only paid for the smallest measure. Right now I would cheerfully swap all the toddies in the world for one long drink of cold water.

"Where are the children?" I couldn't see them or hear them anywhere.

"They'll not tell us. They have them somewhere, and if we give them any trouble—" He spat instead of finishing the sentence. "Devils. If only I had my good, keen flensing knife."

The sun had barely risen before they came to herd us back onto the road. My bruised and weary body complained violently at being told to move, but I was almost past caring. All that mattered right now was that I was finally able to drink. Three whole cupfuls I managed to down before I was shoved away from the water barrel.

My feet were still bare, and they were not a pretty sight. Bloody and swollen and full of cuts I had not even noticed getting. Some of my toes felt completely dead, and I knew this might mean frostbite and eventually even gangrene and death. Callan had preached at us often enough, and Mama too. In the Highlands, the cold could kill you.

I didn't even have a couple of rags to wrap them in. My poor, ragged shirt was already a meager shield against the chill.

"How far are we from Baur Laclan?" I asked Obain.

"The better part of a day," he said. "Here, lad. Take my socks. I can line my clogs with straw."

I was so tired this was nearly enough to make me cry like a girl. The man was offering to give me his socks. It was the best and kindest thing anybody had done for me since… since I couldn't remember when.

"Thank you," I said. "I'll not forget that."

He growled something—the only word that stood out clearly was "devils." Normally it might have taken years before a man like Obain would have been willing to see me as anything other than a no-account Lowlander. But for making friends quickly, there is nothing like a common enemy.

Baur Laclan was nestled in its wide valley like always. But around it…

There were thousands of them. Thousands of men, thousands of tents and little fires, wagons and horses and weapons.

"Have they taken the town?" asked Obain. "Lad, can ye see if they have taken the town and the castle?"

"I don't know."

But there were no sounds of battle, and when you looked down at the anthill multitude of Dragon soldiers, it didn't seem possible that Laclan could have held out against such an over-powering force.

Our little column, led by the scarred Dragon knight, passed unchallenged not only through the camp but also into the town, and from there right through the castle gates and into the yard where I had once faced Ivain Laclan in the Ring of Iron because I thought he had ambushed Mama and shot her with an arrow.

There we stopped, not because anyone barred us from entering but because the foremost children suddenly started screaming and tried to run away.

"What is it?" called Obain. "Maeri, what is wrong?"

He pushed on through the throng and dodged a spear shaft meant to bring him down.

"Obain, wait…"

But he didn't listen to me; all that mattered to him was that he had heard his daughter scream. Nor was he the only disorderly prisoner. The Dragon soldiers cursed and snapped angry commands, laying about them with spear shafts and swords. I hoped they were using the flats.

I said a few curses myself. I could no longer see Obain; nor could I leave him to the Dragon soldiers' untender mercies. The man had given me his socks. I pressed on through the heaving crowd myself, edging past the rear end of a frightened horse, past a Dragon man with his back turned, and on to—

"Back!" shouted another soldier, and lashed out at me with his spear shaft. I took the blow on my forearm and kept going, dodging him too.

"Obain!"

A terrified little boy cannoned into me. I caught him before he ended up under the horses' hooves and settled him on my hip like I might have done with my little sister, Melli.

"Easy there," I said. "Take it easy, now."

He was heaving and sobbing with fright.

"Monster," he keened. "T'sa monster!"

Monster? Where?

There. In the middle of the castle courtyard. Torchlight fell on gleaming scales, on a huge body taller than that of a horse and longer than… longer than a river, it seemed to me at first, but there was after all a beginning and an end to the creature, a head and a tail. And a wide stinking maw filled with needle-sharp teeth.

I knew well what it was, because this was not the first time I had seen such a monster.

It was one of Drakan's dragons.

Monster

A dragon. In Helena Laclan's courtyard. How could that be true? It was like seeing a whale in a garden pond, or perhaps rather a snake in a henhouse, wrong and dangerous and somehow completely inappropriate.

The boy clung to me like a leech and tried to hide his face in my armpit.

"Monster," he sobbed once more. "Monster."

"It's just a dragon," I said and then realized how stupid that sounded. "Look. It's all tied up."

And it was. A fat chain tethered it to one of the thick upright poles that made up the Ring of Iron. It hissed at us and did not look very friendly, but at the moment it couldn't harm us.

I could still barely believe it. How had it come here, all the way from Dunark? And why?

"Give me that kid," yelled a Dragon soldier into my face, so that the boy grew even more frightened and started bawling his head off. "And get back into line, cur!"

My hold on the boy tightened all by itself. But at that moment, the Dragon knight rode his gray gelding in front of the dragon, so that he was between the monster and the heaving mass of frightened children, half-panicked horses, and fishermen struggling to reach their terrified offspring. The gelding didn't like any of it, but the knight kept it under control with a firm hand.

"Order!" he called in a bellow that rolled among the castle walls like thunder. "The dragon is chained. It will not harm you, as long as you obey!"

A semblance of order did spread through the crowd. There were still whimperings and sniffles from the children, and two fishermen lay on the cobbles, one with a leg wound that bled copiously, the other apparently unconscious, hit by a spear butt or kicked by a horse, probably.

"We have only one use for people who do not obey," said the knight. "Dragon fodder. But each man who serves us faithfully and well—he has his place in the Order of the Dragon. And that place may well be a high one, as high as mine, perhaps. Think about it!"

Nobody said anything. One of the fishermen spat on the ground and got a warning whack from a spear butt for his pains. But to me there was something chillingly familiar about that refrain. It reminded me of the Sagisburg and the Educators. Obedience was all. If you were obedient, you might end up at the Prince's own table. If not, it was the filth and darkness of the Gullet and the knowledge that if you died there, you would indeed be dragon fodder. Oh yes, Drakan had learned a lesson or two from his grandfather.

"The children will have their own quarters. The first meal is the gift of the Dragon Lord. After that you will have to earn their food. The child whose father or brother or uncle does not serve the Lord, that child will cry itself to sleep on hungry nights."

The fishermen were listening. The one who had spat now looked as if he regretted it. I had a glimpse of Obain's face, and even he looked tense rather than belligerent. Had Drakan done

183

this every time he conquered a new town? Then it was no wonder the Dragon Force had grown to such numbers so quickly.

"I can tell you are already more obedient," said the knight. "Very wise of you. You will now let go of the children and follow Balain here quietly and promptly. He will show you where you are to sleep and eat during your first days here."

Still, it took a little time. The smallest of the children clung to their relatives—fathers and brothers in most cases—but the fishermen had understood the message all right. And if they had a little trouble remembering, the dragon lay coiled behind the knight like a scaled and fanged reminder of what might happen to them if they did not do as they were bid. So Obain gently explained to Maeri that he had to leave her now and that she had to go along with the Dragon men and do as they told her to do. And that the dragon wouldn't hurt her as long as she was being a good girl. Most of the fishermen took pains to hide their own anger so as not to alarm the children, and I too loosened the little boy's tight hold on my neck, put him down, and sent him off toward the other children with a gentle push. I had hated Drakan before this, but now my hatred settled in to become a deep, abiding thing.

"This way," said Balain. "Down the steps here."

The men went. Two of them were supporting the one whose leg was bleeding; two others lifted the unconscious man as gently as possible. The children made no move to follow. The older ones held the younger by the hand, and a girl of Dina's age clutched the baby in her arms like a doll.

"No, not you," said the knight when I moved to go with the others. "You're staying here."

I stopped.

"Me?"

"Yes, you. The stupid boy who tried to cheat me and to lie to me. Did you think I had forgotten?"

They chained me next to the dragon, to one of the metal posts of the Ring of Iron. The dragon was inside the ring, I was outside. Between us was a length of rusty chain so low a child could step over it. Could a dragon?

I didn't *think* it could reach me. They were probably only trying to scare me. The knight had said that Drakan wanted to see me, and that would be fairly difficult if the dragon had eaten me. It stood to reason that they had not in fact shackled me so that the dragon could get at me. Right?

At first it seemed completely uninterested in any case. It was cold, and like all reptiles it was slow and dumb with chill. Lying here as it did, in the middle of the castle courtyard, it had to be used to people and horses passing by all the time, and it must have learned that they weren't all dragon food. But gradually it seemed to occur to the beast that one of the people wasn't going away. That he couldn't go away. Slowly, it raised its head.

I stood still, barely breathing. If I didn't move at all, perhaps the dragon would lose interest in me.

No such luck. With a heave it rose and waddled a couple of steps closer on fat, short legs. I could hear the claws scrape against the gravel. It halted for a moment when it reached the rusty chain of the Ring. Then it simply flopped down on its belly and began to slither under it. I tried to take one more step backward, but the chain tethering me was taut now. If I wanted to move farther away, it would be without my left foot.

Could the dragon really pass under the Ring chain?

185

No. Not quite. Its shoulders were too high.

I let go of a long breath I had been hanging on to for quite a while. No. It couldn't get at me.

The dragon wasn't pleased. It opened its maw and hissed at me and seemed to think that anything that stood where I was standing and did not go away *ought* to be dragon food. Its pale yellow eyes were staring at me, and I could smell the stench of rotting meat surrounding it.

Once before I had been this close to a dragon. That was back when Mascha and I had to save Gerik in the dragon pit of the Sagisburg. But it had all been so quick, and it had been Gerik standing there, shackled and helpless, not me.

This was different, I told myself. Gerik's dragon had not been chained. It would have devoured him in three gulps. My dragon couldn't do that. It lay there, belly flat against the ground, stretching its neck as far as it would go, and it still couldn't reach me.

"You can't get at me," I told it, and perhaps I was telling myself as well, with as much certainty as I could muster.

Suddenly it braced its thick legs and tried to rise. The rusty Ring chain went taut across its shoulders, and there was a creak of metal joints and a groan from the heavy posts. I could see the dragon's muscles bulge with power under the scaly skin, and I lost some of my hard-won certainty. It couldn't really burst the chain—could it?

No. It couldn't. But at the dragon's second attempt I saw one of the poles move, like a tree being uprooted. The dragon felt it too, and it threw itself forward like a horse straining against its harness. And with a drawn-out shriek like the sound of a rusty old iron gate opening, the post tore free of its hole. The dragon shook itself once, like a dog shaking water from its fur, and the chain slid down its jagged spine. The beast was clear of the Ring.

I remembered Gerik's scream at the end, no words in it at all, just pure terror.

"The dragon is loose!" somebody was shouting, but it wasn't me. I watched, dumb with fear, as the monster waddled one step closer, one step more, one more… and then stopped.

It wasn't entirely free. There was still the chain around its neck, like the one that shackled me. But it had managed to uproot one Ring post like that; it might easily do the same to the one it was tethered to. It leaned into the chain like a dog straining at its collar, digging in its claws for a stronger pull. I looked around wildly for a weapon—a spear, a sharp stick, a rock, anything.

There was nothing.

A couple of uniformed men had come running into the courtyard. They stared at the dragon, and at me.

"It's torn up the bloody post," said one. "A good strong cast-iron post like that!"

"Get the dragon keeper," said the other. "This is for him to deal with."

The other nodded and disappeared back into the castle at a run.

The remaining Dragon soldier was watching me with a strange expression—almost hungrily, I thought.

"Are you scared?" he asked.

Of course I was scared. What did he think? I gave him a single nasty glare and returned my attention to the dragon. It was only a short distance away—seven or eight paces, had it been free. But it wasn't. It turned its head and snapped at the chain in irritation. But even dragon jaws can't snap a steel chain in half.

The Dragon soldier came closer.

"It looks like the post will hold," he said. "Almost a pity, don't you think? Seeing that it wants you so badly."

"Are you *cheering* it?" I snarled. "Anyone would think you were rooting for the dragon."

"Oh, I am," he said. "Always."

Something about the way he said it made me take another look at him. He wasn't just an ordinary soldier, I noticed. His uniform was that of a Dragon knight, with the dragon edged in red and gold on his breastplate and on both shoulders, and his cloak and trousers looked oddly scaly, as if they might have been made from dragon hide. Who knows? Maybe they were. Dina had told me that Drakan himself had a dragonhide cloak, so maybe his knights did too.

"You enjoy watching people get eaten?" I asked.

He regarded me with complete calm, a cool, dark blue gaze. "You eat meat yourself, don't you?" he said. "They're not so different from us."

This was what Master Maunus would call a question of philosophy: Wherein is man different from the animals? But I had no taste for philosophy at the best of times, and this was far from the best of times. At that moment, there was a jerk on my chain so strong that my leg went out from under me and I tumbled down on one side.

What...?

It was the dragon. Instead of snapping at its own chain, it now had hold of mine. It stood there with its head lowered and the chain in its jaws, and I am not sure it had even discovered yet that there was a fish at the other end of the line. It twisted its powerful neck and gave another tug on the chain, and I slithered a few feet closer, despite my best efforts to get up and stand firm. The monster stared at me, and at the chain stretched between us, and I swear it almost grinned. It tugged at the chain again.

I scrabbled in the dirt with arms and legs and fought as hard as I could, but the dragon's strength made a joke of my poor human efforts. It pulled at the chain the way a cat tugs at the loose end of a ball of yarn, and the only thing that saved me was the fact that it couldn't hold the chain in its mouth and bite me at the same time. It had to let go of the chain, and I flung myself backward and escaped the darting head by inches. The dragon's angry hiss was a hot wind in my face, but it wasn't about to give up. Once more it grabbed the chain and jerked, dragging me close. And this time it planted a heavy foot on the chain before spitting it out. It opened its mouth and struck at me like a snake does, fangs glinting in the gray daylight. Its jaw snapped shut less than an arm's length from my leg.

"*Do* something!" I yelled at the Dragon knight, who was watching everything like it was the best entertainment he had had in years. He had a sword, didn't he? And he couldn't really mean it about being on the dragon's side, could he?

"Sly beast," he said almost lovingly. "They get cleverer and cleverer, I've noticed."

There were more people in the courtyard now, but none of them seemed to want to interfere. I tried not to think about what it would feel like if the dragon caught my foot next time. They were needle sharp, those fangs. And venomous. When Dina was bitten by a dragon, her arm went numb almost right away, she had told me.

The next jerk was so ferocious that I almost flew across the gravel and ended up right between the front feet of the beast.

189

There was only one thing I could think to do. I snatched up the chain and flung a loop of it around the dragon's snout, trying to keep its jaws shut. It snorted in surprise and batted at me with one foot. Two of the claws drew long bloody furrows down my arm, but if I let go, I had had it. If I could keep the chain taut, at least it couldn't open its jaws. If it couldn't open its jaws, at least it couldn't—

It flung up its head like a wild horse, tossing me into the air like I weighed nothing at all. I lost my grip on the chain, and went sailing across its neck until a sharp wrench of my ankle brought an end to my brief flight. I came down like a sack of potatoes, on top of the dragon's scaly gray-blue back, with a dim view of its long tail. I dug my fingers into the scales and tried to hang on to its shoulder blades, but they were rough and bumpy, those scales, like plates of bone, and it was hard to find a grip. Another vicious jerk at my ankle, and I slid along the neck, toward the head and a set of jaws that would not remain closed for much longer.

The head.

The eyes.

I could see one of them, matte gold and furious, right beside me. I clenched my hand into a fist and punched it as hard as I could into the dragon's yellow eye.

A hiss came from the dragon, a hiss so thin it was almost a scream. It forgot all about being clever. It flung itself from side to side, tossing its head, batting at me with first one leg, then the other. I couldn't hold on, couldn't do anything, not anymore. A last jerk of its head hurled me forward, to be flipped head over heels as the chain tightened once more, and I landed flat on my back with an impact that blacked out everything for a moment.

I couldn't move my arms. I couldn't move my legs. If the beast wanted to reel me in again and eat me, it could do so. There was no more resistance in me.

Somebody was bending over me. I slowly opened my eyes. It was the Dragon knight, the one with the cool, very dark blue eyes. They reminded me of someone, those eyes, reminded me of…

"Can you hear me?"

I nodded faintly. I had no breath for talking.

"The next time you want to play with one of my dragons, be a little more careful. I don't like it when people hurt them."

My dragons. Did he mean—

I realized why his eyes seemed so familiar. They were a lot like Nico's. Which wasn't so surprising, considering they had the same father.

"Drakan," I whispered with what breath I had left.

He nodded.

"And you," he said, "you must be the Shamer's son. Dina's older brother. Your name is Davin, isn't it?"

Dragon Blood

That night I learned what Drakan needed his dragon for.

Night had fallen. A big fire had been lit inside the Ring of Iron, and the dragon lay so close to the flames that they washed the gray scales with gold and made its eyes glitter beneath the heavy lids. I too had crept a little closer, even though it also meant moving closer to the dragon. It was that or die of cold. My ankle was so swollen now that it bulged around the iron, throbbing viciously with every heartbeat. My arm, too, was sore, marked by the dragon's claws. But there was something inside me that dwarfed the pains of my body. Inside my head the Whisperers were back, with new whips to flay me.

… your fault… your fault…

Callan. Dead or dying. Rose… what would they do to a girl like her? She had grown so pretty lately, with her fair hair and very nice legs and breasts I couldn't help noticing even though I tried not to. The mere thought that someone might…

… your fault… your fault…

For once in my life, couldn't I have used my eyes and my head before opening my big mouth? Used whatever brains I had, perhaps? For Callan's sake, and Rose's. But it was too late now. I eyed the dragon. Perhaps it would have been better if it had eaten me. Then, at least, the voices would have had to shut up.

I couldn't run away from them this time. Judging from the pain in my ankle, it would be a while before I would be able to run from anything again.

… your fault…

When the first knights emerged from the castle, it was almost a relief that something was happening. At least it might take my mind off the voices and the pain in my foot. They put up torches along the walls so that the courtyard was lit by a flickering yellow glow.

Then Drakan appeared. His uniform looked like the others—perhaps a bit more gold on his breastplate, and I think his cloak might be the only one made from dragon hide—but despite that he stood out immediately. There was something about him, a jittery feeling of power barely held at bay. A sense that he might blow anytime. If there had been a powder keg with a lit fuse in the yard, everyone would have watched that too.

"It is time," he said. And although he didn't say it very loudly, even the knights who had been putting up torches at the far end of the courtyard heard him immediately and came to stand with the others in a half-circle around the dragon and the fire.

There were twenty-four and Drakan. I counted them. I tried to set their faces firm in my mind too, because this was the kind of knowledge that might be useful to the Highlanders in this war, if ever I got out of here alive and was able to give it to them.

One by one the knights stepped forward and bowed to the dragon, like people bow to a prince or the picture of a saint. It seemed to make no particular impression on the beast, but as for me, it made my skin crawl.

"We thank the Dragon for what we are about to receive," they said as one voice. It was eerie to hear so many people say the same thing at exactly the same time and in exactly the same way, as if they were all possessed by the same evil spirit.

"We thank the Dragon for our strength."

There was a loud sound of leather against leather as they all slapped their chests at the same time, with their gloved fists pounding their breastplates at heart height.

"We thank the Dragon for our courage."

A new pounding.

"We thank the Dragon for our wisdom."

Wisdom? Exactly what kind of great thoughts were they expecting to receive from a big dumb animal like that? It might have been cleverer than I thought when it used my chain to drag me within reach. But wisdom?

I looked at the dragon. It had heaved itself to its feet and had begun rocking from side to side, from one foreleg to the other. The neck was swaying, and the head darted this way and that with no purpose that I could see. What was wrong with the beast? If I had thought dragons could have such emotions, I would have said it looked anxious. Nervous. About what?

Drakan, the twenty-fifth man in the circle, stepped up to the dragon. In one hand he held a golden cup, in the other a knife. The dragon retreated from him, step by step, until it could back up no farther. It hissed at him like a cat, but this was a frightened cat.

I could see Drakan's lips moving, but it was impossible to hear what he was saying. What did one say to a frightened dragon: "There, there, easy now, that's a good dragon"? Whatever he was saying, it seemed to work. It lowered its belly to the ground, and then its head, in a curiously resigned manner.

The knife flashed in the torchlight. Drakan pushed the point between two scales on the dragon's neck, and dark blood welled across the knife's blade into the golden cup he held. The dragon didn't move an inch. Was it really so afraid of him that it didn't dare move? I almost felt sorry for it. Almost.

When the cup was nearly full, Drakan withdrew the knife. The scales fell back into place, and the bleeding stopped almost immediately. The dragon shook its head and then sank to the ground like a tired old dog that no longer has the strength to snarl.

The circle of knights had tightened. They were still moving slowly and solemnly, but there was a suppressed eagerness in their steps now and in the way their eyes followed the cup in Drakan's hand. The first of them knelt to his prince, and Drakan held the cup to his lips.

"Drink," he said. "The strength of the Dragon, the courage of the Dragon, the wisdom of the Dragon."

The man seized Drakan's hand and drank the dark blood as if his life depended on it.

It was the most disgusting thing I had ever seen, and yet I couldn't look away.

"What are you drinking?" asked Drakan.

"Strength, courage, and wisdom," said the man hoarsely. And then he laughed, a strangely light and untroubled laugh in the middle of all the gore and solemnity. "Strength, courage, wisdom," he repeated, "and freedom!"

And then he laughed once more.

One by one they knelt. One by one they drank.

When the cup had gone full circle there was still a little of the thick fluid left.

"Get the boy," said Drakan.

The boy? Did he mean me?

"He hasn't been initiated," objected one of the knights. "He has not found his place in the Order of the Dragon."

"No," said Drakan with a narrow smile. "But think about it. The son of the Shamer witch. What revenge could be more beautiful, and more appropriate?"

What did he mean? I wouldn't drink his foul dragon's blood. But even if they did somehow force it on me, where was the revenge?

Three of them came for me. One unlocked the iron—it wasn't easy for him, what with the swelling—while the other two hauled me to my feet. The pain in my foot made my vision blacken at the edges; the two claw marks tore open and began to bleed as well, but it was the ankle that hurt so badly they nearly had to carry me.

"Pitiful," said Drakan. He leaned close and spoke so caressingly that it might have been one of his beloved dragons he was talking to. "But don't worry. Soon everything will be so much better."

He held out the cup. I turned my face away. The fluid was so dark it didn't really look like blood. But the smell—the smell was unmistakable: heavy and sweet and festering at the same time. Like the dragon's own stench, only worse, because of the cloying sweetness.

"Do you turn away from the gift of the Dragon?" he said. "You don't know what is good for you. Hold him."

They made me kneel with a swift kick to the back of my legs, and one of them grabbed me by the hair and forced my head back. I tried to turn my face away or at least to clench my teeth, but one of them edged a knife's blade between my jaws and forced my mouth open. He cut my lip by accident so that, in the end, what ran down my throat was a mixture of my own blood and the blood of the dragon.

They did not let me go until they had made sure that I had swallowed the revolting stuff. And even though I spat and kept on spitting, I knew it was too late. It was there, inside me, in my throat and stomach and body. It made me want to puke.

"There," said Drakan in the same soft tone. "Soon you will be one of us."

I had no idea what he meant. If he thought I was now a Dragon's man—a knight of the Dragon, even—just because they had managed to get me to swallow his disgusting dragon's blood, then he was very wrong.

But something was happening. Something was happening inside my body. My heart was beating faster, my hands and feet were growing warm. Suddenly my ankle didn't hurt nearly as much. No, wait. It didn't hurt at all. I almost laughed out loud. It didn't hurt!

"He's beginning to understand," said one of the knights. "Look at his face."

"Bring him," said another. "Let him see it. Let him try it."

"Naturally," said Drakan. "Did you think I would waste the Dragon's precious gift on him just to put him to sleep with a smile on his face?"

Bring me? Where to?

And then I didn't care. I had just discovered something else. The voices were gone.

The penetrating, whispering voices that had bored their way into my skull, telling me I was a coward, I was a murderer, everything was my fault, and I would never be able to make it right… they were gone. For the first time in months, they were completely silent. More than that: They simply weren't there anymore.

This time, I could not hold back my laughter. It welled up inside me, a soaring rush of freedom, a relief so vast it had to come out somehow. I laughed so loudly that the dragon blinked in surprise. It was a wild and inappropriate laughter, I knew that, but I was not ashamed. Like the voices, my nagging sense of shame was gone. Gone completely and entirely.

Hoofbeats thudded against the frozen ground. The darkness was close and thick, and the frosty mist even thicker, but what did I care? I could see in the dark. I was not afraid. And I was the best rider in the world. No more, no less. One of the others was riding next to me, and right now he was the one who held my horse's reins, but that didn't matter either. We were going the same way: into the night. I felt like baring my teeth and howling like a wolf.

Well, why not?

I did it. A fine, strong howl, which cut through the night like a fang through a vein. Show me the wolf that could have done better! The horse leaped forward as if I had taken a whip to it, and that was fine too. More speed. More freedom. I howled again.

"He's way up," somebody shouted.

"That's how it is," said the one holding my reins. "The first time, we can all fly."

I wasn't quite sure what he meant. But perhaps they were right. Perhaps I really could fly. If I stood up in the saddle and spread my arms—

"Hey! Sit down, boy!"

One foot slipped as I tried to stand up. It wouldn't quite take my weight. I slid down to one side, and the man next to me had to grab me by the arm to haul me back into the saddle.

"Watch it" came a voice from farther down the line. "We don't want him to break his silly neck, do we? At least not until the Dragon is done with him."

I turned and laughed at them. Why would I break my neck? Not me. Not here. Not now.

A call came down from the foremost riders.

"There they are. 'Ware!"

The call went down the line, from one rider to the next. I called too, so as not to be left out. I didn't know who "they" were, nor why we had to beware. But the man next to me had drawn his sword and threw me my horse's reins.

"Here, boy. You'll have to manage on your own for a bit."

I caught the reins easily. Right now all I could do would be to haul the horse around to the left if I wanted to stop it, but what did that matter? I didn't want it to stop. But I didn't have a sword, and that worried me a bit. If everyone else had one, why not me?

More shouting up ahead. A scream that certainly didn't come from a man. Then torches suddenly blazed in the darkness and flew like firebirds, shedding sparks, until they landed on…

A thatched roof, white with frost.

Torches in the thatch.

Something about that wasn't nice. Something about that wasn't right.

"Careful," I told my neighbor. "The whole house might catch fire."

He laughed. "That's the plan," he said. "And it's all right. They are not of the Dragon."

"Oh," I said. Of the Dragon? What did that mean? Were we "of the Dragon"? Yes, there had been a dragon, and it had given me something. And that was why I was feeling so great right now. So maybe I really was of the Dragon? It was a little hard to understand all this, particularly since people were screaming like that all around me, and there was so much fire and darkness. They were using the swords now too, I saw. Why didn't I have a sword?

"Death to the enemies of the Dragon!"

They were all shouting now, all the men. Me too. I didn't want to be left out. But torches in the thatch—there *was* something about that which just wasn't right.

A man appeared under my horse's nose. I jerked at the reins to stop it, but they weren't working properly; all I succeeded in doing was hauling the horse's head to one side so that it stumbled and fell to its knees. Now we'll see if I can fly for real, I thought, and I did fly for a little while before I hit something hard that wasn't the ground. That came later, a second thump. Dazed, I lay on my side with my back against… against a wall, it seemed, a very hot wall. Sparks were dancing in the air like fireflies. It might be better to move away from the fire. I tried to get up, but although I could ride and fly, apparently I couldn't walk.

Oh, well. I would just have to crawl. But someone knocked into me and fell on top of me, and I thought, Why bother? This was as good a place to lie as any. Except that he was lying across me, squashing me. And I was getting wet. Something was running down my neck, along my collarbone, down my chest. I pushed at him, trying to get him off me, and I managed to push him to one side. It was then I realized that this was someone I knew. Not well, just one of Helena Laclan's men that I had exchanged a few words with. Once we had both spent several days looking for Dina and Tavis Laclan.

But he's dead, I thought. A chop like that, right through the forehead, no one could survive that. There was blood in his hair and splinters of bone, and in his eyes there was no life left at all.

I was getting angry. A good man, dead like that. What were they thinking of? And houses burning too.

"Stop it!" I said, as loudly as I was able—I still couldn't breathe very well. "People are getting hurt!"

No one listened. They kept at it until there was not one living, breathing creature left in the village, and no house that wasn't burning.

"Get him up on a horse," said Drakan when they found me. I hadn't made it very far; behind me I could still see the burning houses of the village. I couldn't walk, and my body shook as if with fever.

There were still twenty-four and Drakan. I counted them. And I took note of their faces once more. Twenty-five men had ridden into the sleeping village and killed everyone who hadn't managed to escape. Men, women, and children. There had been dead people everywhere.

They seemed quite unmoved by it. Almost satisfied. What kind of people were they?

People who drank dragon's blood.

Like I had.

Oh, I remembered it, that rush of delight, that sense of being all-powerful. No pain, no shame. Freedom. Perhaps I was just incredibly lucky that they hadn't given me a sword. I had ridden with them, shouted with them, "Death to the enemies of the Dragon." If I had had a sword, would I have killed with them too?

Even now. Even now I felt a stab of longing for another taste of that rush, that freedom. Everything hurt so badly. I felt so completely miserable inside.

Drakan watched me with those eyes that reminded me of Nico's.

"You don't look very well at all," he said.

I didn't answer. What could I have said?

"Tell me. How is he, my dear half brother? Where is little Nicodemus hiding himself these days?"

Did he really think it would be that easy?

"I don't know," I said. It was even true, after a fashion. Who knew where Nico and Dina were right now? Had they reached Dunark? And if they had, what had they decided to do when they discovered Drakan wasn't there anymore?

"Answer when the Dragon Lord asks you a question!"

A cuff at the back of my neck sent me reeling forward. But I didn't say anything else. I just scowled.

"Don't worry, Ursa," said Drakan. "There's no hurry. Sooner or later he'll tell me everything I want to know, just to get another taste."

A Shackle More Cruel

We returned to Baur Laclan in the middle of the night. Sleepsodden grooms were dragged from their beds to tend to the horses, streaked with foam and jittery after the violent ride. The Dragon knights yawned and stretched, patted each other on the back, and straggled across the courtyard on uncertain legs, like men on their way home from a brotherly drinking bout.

"What about that one?" said the knight called Ursa, jerking his head in my direction.

"Chain him up again," said Drakan.

"Here?"

"Where else?"

"It's cold."

"Lend him your cloak if you're so tender."

They had to put the iron on my right foot this time, my left was so swollen that the shackle wouldn't close. Might the ankle be broken? The thought made me go cold inside, because I needed two good legs if I was to have any hope of escaping. And I had to do something. If they forced another dose of dragon's blood down me, might I then tell them everything I knew, and do whatever they wanted me to do?

"Here," said Ursa, dumping his cloak in my lap. "This cold is fierce enough to kill a dead man."

I looked up in surprise. Pity from a Dragon knight? Or was it just that it would be impractical if I froze to death before I had told them where Nico was?

The fire had burned down, and only a few torches now lit the courtyard. I couldn't see his face, and he left without saying another word.

"So he did give you his cloak," said Drakan. "Well, well. Getting soft in his old age."

People as evil as Drakan... it ought to show on the outside, I thought. How else was one supposed to tell them apart from ordinary human beings? He ought to be bigger and uglier. I hadn't expected him to have horns and a tail, not quite, but still it seemed wrong that he stood there looking so ordinary. And so like Nico.

"What is it you want with me?" I asked tiredly.

"Now you're being ungrateful," he said. "Haven't I just fed you precious dragon blood and practically made you one of my knights?"

"I don't want to be your knight. I don't want your damn dragon blood!"

"Really? And here I was, all ready to give you a little gift. But if you don't want it, you can always throw it away."

He tossed something at me, and I caught it without meaning to. It was a small bottle. And I knew at once what it was. Dragon blood.

"Do as you please," he said. "I'm not forcing you."

And then he left.

I stared at the bottle for a long time. I didn't open it. But I didn't throw it away either.

◆　　◆　　◆

Morning came. The dragon lay curled in the ashes where the fire had been, probably because the ground was warmer there. I had wrapped myself in Ursa's cloak and still shook from head to foot with the cold.

"Lad?"

I didn't want to talk to anyone, particularly not to Dragon men.

"Lad, are ye awake?" He prodded me quite gently, all things considered. And then I realized that at least it was a Highland voice. I peeked out from under the cover of the cloak.

It was Ivain Laclan.

For a moment I thought my fever made me see things. Ivain, here? I had to be making this up, probably because I was practically lying inside the Ring of Iron where we had once faced each other. The two things went together in my head; I had never since that day been able to look at Ivain without remembering the taste of blood and gravel and the bitterness of defeat. I closed my eyes, but when I opened them again, he was still there. Wearing a Dragon uniform.

Revulsion rose in me like bile. Traitor! But then an even deeper disgust hit me. I might not be dressed in Drakan's uniform yet, but I was lying here wrapped in Ursa's cloak. I had ridden with the Dragon knights and shouted along with them, "Death to the enemies of the Dragon!" while they were butchering the villagers and burning their houses. I was worse than Ivain. Ten times worse.

"What do you want?" I asked.

"I cannot stand here chattering for hours," he said, "so ye best listen. Something will happen tonight, right after sunset. If ye can get yerself free of that chain somehow, ye can come with us."

With them?

"Out of here? You mean I can get away?"

"That was the plan. Unless ye fancy staying on as His Lordship's special guest?"

And he was gone.

I slowly realized that Ivain was no traitor. The uniform had to be a disguise. Somewhere out there were Laclan men that Drakan hadn't caught, and they were planning an attack for tonight.

How many Laclan men?

Apart from Obain and the other fishermen from Arlain, I hadn't seen a lot of Highlanders here. It didn't necessarily mean that much; Drakan would hardly let the conquered Laclans wander around by the cartload. But on the other hand, grooms, kitchen drudges, castle servants—all the workers who were needed to make sure that Drakan and his knights might be housed and fed and clean and warm—little people like that often simply changed hands with the castle, serving their new lord much as they had served the old. But not here.

I looked more closely at the castle walls. I did remember wondering briefly that there had been so few char marks and scars and other signs of battle damage. Might it be that Laclan had not defended the castle to the last man? Might it be that they had done something much, much cleverer? Like sneaking out the back so that Drakan still had a fighting force to worry about somewhere?

Later that morning a mounted patrol came in.

"Any news?" called one of the guards by the gate.

"We haven't seen hide nor hair of them," grumbled the leader of the patrol. "It's unnatural is what it is. Isn't she supposed to be over seventy? There has to be a limit to how fast the old hag can run."

I sent up a silent prayer that it might be Helena Laclan they were talking about. If she was still on the loose somewhere in the Highlands, Drakan had not broken Laclan yet, not by a long chalk.

Something will happen, Ivain had said. If I could get free of my chain…

A big if. What did he think? That I could somehow rip it off with my bare hands? I couldn't uproot an iron post the way the dragon had. I was only human, and a somewhat battered human at that. I was shaking all over, and I was pretty sure that some of that was from fever. The ankle was still pounding away, and the clawed arm had begun to throb ominously, as if it might be infected. Every time I closed my eyes, new ghosts had joined the throng. It wasn't just Callan's pale face now, or Valdracu's half-cut throat. Now it was flames and darkness and dead people and a Laclan man whose name I couldn't remember, and my own voice shouting, "Death to the enemies of the Dragon!"

And I was thirsty once more.

"Hey," I called at a Dragon soldier. "Can I have some water?"

He just looked at me and went past without saying anything.

Was it on purpose? Had Drakan given orders so that I might end up drinking his vile dragon blood from sheer thirst?

No. I would rather die.

Why hadn't I thrown away the bottle, then? Or broken it? The sharp ends would be a weapon if I needed it. But no. I had tucked the bottle into my waistband and could feel the cool weight of it against my stomach every time I breathed. If I drank

from it, the pain would go away, in my ankle, in my arm and…
inside. For a while.

I wouldn't. I wouldn't do it.

Around noon Drakan and two of his knights came out. Drakan
looked down at me.

"Where is he, then?"

"Who?" I said sourly.

Drakan only smiled. He knew I was stalling for time.

"My beloved half brother, Nicodemus Ravens. He is up here
somewhere, isn't he? But which back of this godforsaken beyond
is he hiding in?"

"I don't know."

"He hasn't touched the bottle," said one of the knights.

"A stubborn one," said the other. "Shall we encourage him
a little?"

"No," said Drakan. "If he drinks it himself, he is mine. Body
and soul. Imagine what that will do to the Shamer witch when
we find her and Nicodemus and that daughter of hers because
her son has become mine and gives me whatever I ask of him.
It is worth the wait. And I don't think it will be a very long wait,
at that."

If I had had the strength, I would have hit him with my
chain. But I wasn't even sure I would be able to stand right now.

"My mother says you spread shamelessness around you like
a disease," I said. "Like a plague rat." The last bit was my own
addition, but he couldn't know that.

He looked at me with clear, deep blue eyes, and somewhere
inside him I could see a spark of fury, a spark he didn't want
to show.

"We'll burn her when we find her," he said slowly. "Like the witch she is. I'm glad she got away last time. Eating her would have poisoned my poor dragons."

When they had left, I watched the dragon for a while. It had made no attempt to get at me today. Perhaps it had had enough of that game yesterday, or else the cold and the loss of blood had weakened it. I had no idea how much losing a cupful meant to an animal that size.

I edged a little closer without getting up. It scowled at me but did not even raise its head off the ground. It didn't look anywhere near as dangerous today, I thought. But maybe it was not really the dragon that had changed. Perhaps it was just that today I had something much larger and more terrible to be afraid of.

To become like them.

If he drinks it himself, he is mine. Was it true?

I had to get out of here. And if that meant tearing up iron posts by the root—

"Dragon," I called.

It looked at me sourly.

"Stupid dragon." I picked a rock off the ground.

"Stupid old monster."

And then I threw my stone.

The first time, it failed. And the second. And the third. By then, the dragon was so irritated that it was ready to eat me just to get a little peace. But the fourth time it tried to attack me; it thrust its head and neck under the Ring chain exactly where I wanted. I kept pelting it with every pebble and small rock I could find, and the beast heaved and shoved to get at me until the post started to lean. And then was overturned.

I snatched at my own chain and hauled for all I was worth. It was still stuck! If the dragon wanted to reel me in like it had last time—

It didn't. It hissed at me a couple of times to make sure I had understood the message. Then it slithered back to its bed of ashes and curled up in the hollow it had made for itself.

A little while later, I inched closer to the Ring again, to the post I was tethered to, the post that had been overturned. If I could work my chain free of the post… but it had not been pulled all the way out of its hole.

I looked around quickly. If anyone had noticed my dragon-baiting, at least they hadn't seemed to work out why I was doing it. But if I started digging openly at the base of the post, even the slowest of guards would become suspicious.

I righted the post so that it was less obviously crooked and leaned against it casually. And under cover of Ursa's cloak, I began my digging. I had only my hands and the chain for tools, and it was no quick and easy job. A good thing there were still hours left before sunset.

Drakan came down again late in the afternoon. He stood there, looking at me, for quite a while.

"If you aren't going to drink it," he finally said, "you might as well give it back to me."

All on its own, my hand went up to clutch the bottle through the thin material of my shirt. Not to give it to him, but to stop him taking it. He smiled.

"That's what I thought," he said. "Just out of interest, how long do *you* think it will be before you drink it?"

He turned to leave, but at that moment there was a clatter of hooves and a lot of shouting by the gate. Two riders came in, or at least, two men on horses. One of them could hardly be said to be riding. He clung to the horse's neck, barely able to stay upright, and the other one had to lead his horse by the rein.

"The Dragon," gasped the wounded man. "I need to see the Dragon."

He was not talking about the monster in the courtyard, or at least not the four-legged one.

"I'm here," said Drakan. "What do you want with me?"

The man attempted to right himself in the saddle but swayed alarmingly instead, nearly coming off completely. One hand was red and black with blood and dirt, but his black uniform made it hard to tell how much he had been bleeding elsewhere.

"We were attacked," he said. "An ambush. Highlanders. They took… they killed nearly everybody and took all the prisoners and the supplies."

"Where?"

"On the road to Farness."

"Which prisoners?"

"From Farness—men and hostage children—and the lot we picked up in Troll Cove."

"Callan Kensie? The Harbormaster?"

"Yes. Those two, among others."

Drakan stood silent for some moments. His face was about as expressionless as the dragon's. But I was whooping with glee inside. A millstone of guilt had just been casually eased off my shoulders. Callan was alive! He and the others had not fallen into Drakan's hands after all. And there were people out there—Highlanders, probably Laclan men—who were resisting, fighting Drakan and his army although their numbers had to be pitiful compared to his.

Drakan spun on his heel, and there was something in his face that made me sit very still. Suddenly I understood completely why the dragon had retreated from him and had stood unresisting while he had stolen its blood.

"You know them," he said.

"Who?"

"These people. The ambushers. You know who they are."

I didn't, not really, except that they were probably Laclan men, and he could make that guess as easily as I could. But I didn't say anything.

"Get up."

So that it would be easier for him to hit me? No thanks. And there was the post. If I got up, they might notice how badly it was leaning. No, I was better off where I was.

He moved so quickly that my tired eyes refused to follow. Suddenly I felt an edge of cold, hard steel against my neck. Drakan's sword.

"Get up," he said. "Or I strike, right here, right now."

He meant it. I could feel the force of his will, in his stance, in the way he held his sword. It was as cold and hard as the blade itself.

I got up. It wasn't easy, but when your life depends on it, you discover that you can do many things—including standing on an ankle that is almost broken.

"Is he doing this? Is he leading them?"

"Who? Nico?"

"Who else?"

"Nico doesn't usually lead people." Not because they didn't want him to, but more because Nico was Nico and did things his own way.

Drakan gauged me with his eyes, probably trying to decide whether I was telling the truth or not. Apparently he believed me, because he lowered the sword a fraction.

"You're right," he said. "Nico could barely lead a flock of thirsty sheep to the water. And still… and still they meant to set that clown on the throne instead of me."

I had to bite my lip to stop myself from defending Nico. True, Nico didn't like to boss people around, but that didn't mean he would be a bad castellan, did it? At least he wouldn't have ravaged towns and villages and killed people. Not Nico.

The sword touched my neck again. "So if he is not running around playing at being a robber chief, where is he? Where is he hiding?"

We had danced this dance before, hadn't we? I knew the steps.

"I don't know."

"This is not a game, Davin. I am sick and tired of Highlanders melting into the dark each time we try to attack them. I am tired of hearing my soldiers complain of the cold and the fog and the ambushes. There is one reason, and one reason only, why I care one whit about this godforsaken place, and that is him. Give him to me, and the Highlands can molder away in peace for the next hundred years."

Now it was my turn to try and gauge his truthfulness. But no. I didn't believe him. I didn't think he would meekly disappear and leave us in peace just because we gave him Nico on a silver platter. And in any case, we didn't have Nico to give, on a silver platter or otherwise. But might it be a good idea to *pretend* that I believed him?

"Do you mean that?"

"What do I want with a lot of rock, a bit of heather, and a few sheep? No civilized people can stand to live up here."

I pretended to consider.

"If I tell you, you will kill me anyway."

"Why should I?" he said. "How does it harm me that you are alive?"

Quite a lot, I hoped. If it was up to me. But that might not be the wisest thing to say right now.

"Give me a little water," I begged, "and I'll tell you."

I let my shoulders sag and tried to look pitiful. Not very hard at the moment.

Drakan lowered his sword and turned to the other men in the courtyard. One of the guards had eased the wounded man off his horse and was holding a cup to his lips so he could drink. Without a word of warning, Drakan seized the cup and passed it to me.

"Here," he said.

There was blood on the rim of the cup. I wiped off the worst of it and drank down the whole thing. When one is thirsty enough, such niceties cease to matter.

"Well?"

"A bite to eat," I said. "And a sweater. This cold is killing me."

Again he was so fast that I didn't see it coming. The blow hit me on the side of the head, knocking me sideways. My ankle buckled, and I collapsed at the foot of my leaning post.

"Do you know it, or not?" He set the point of his sword against my breastbone and put just enough weight on it to break the skin.

I don't know where it came from. But suddenly I knew what to say.

"Skayark," I said. "He's at Skayark."

Drakan hesitated. "If you're lying…"

I shook my head. "It is the most impregnable fortress in the Highlands," I muttered. "Where would you hide if you were him?"

He laughed. He actually laughed. "But of course," he said. "Behind the thickest walls he can find up here. The little coward."

And he turned and walked away, not looking at me or the post or even the wounded man, who suddenly moaned softly and collapsed on the ground.

"Let's get him inside," said one of the gate guards, "while there is still a bit of blood left in him."

They carried off the injured messenger. I slowly sat up. Right now there were no other living creatures out here other than me and the dragon. I put my good foot against the post and shook it like a terrier shakes a rat, and finally it came loose. I jerked the chain out from under it and considered my options. Could I get away now, while there were no guards around?

No, I needed help. I couldn't walk, my ankle would barely support my weight. I had to wait for Ivain and his men to do whatever it was they meant to do. I restored the post to its hole as best I could so that at least the guards would need to come fairly close to discover that I was no longer securely tethered. And during the wait, I might consider what would happen when Drakan attacked Skayark. I remembered those walls, those fortifications. Never yet had they been breached, not in all of the two hundred years Skayark had guarded the Skayler Pass. Let him try, I thought. That nut might crack even a Dragon's teeth.

When the sun began to set behind the walls of Baur Laclan, I brought out the little bottle of dragon blood. I thought about it. Just a tiny swallow. Only so much as it would take to let me walk on that ankle without fainting with pain. If I didn't drink more than a mouthful—

If he drinks it himself, he is mine.

If he was right, then the contents of that small bottle was a shackle far more cruel than the one I had just painstakingly freed myself from. But it couldn't be that bad, surely it couldn't. And if I didn't do it, I was afraid that escape might be utterly impossible.

I drank. A tiny swig. And only the dragon saw me do it.

Back to Birches

Heavy and wet, the snow covered everything—the road, the branches, and us. I was glad of the hooded cloak the Gelts had given me, but it was still a cold, damp, and miserable journey. We kept to the marshes for as long as we could, but on the third day we had to pass through lands where more people lived—plowed fields and wet winter pastures and villages tucked in among the hills.

We had no horses. It was hard not to wish for them when we were in such desperate haste, and I kept thinking of Silky, who was probably still eating her head off in the Harbormaster's stable. But after all horses weren't very practical when one had to be ready to hide at a moment's notice in ditches or shrubbery because a Dragon patrol was passing by.

"I thought you said they were all up in the Highlands," I whispered to Nico.

"Apparently not quite all," he said. "Come on. I think we can get up now."

Carmian had already picked herself up from the ditch.

"Tonight we sleep at a proper inn," she said, coughing hollowly. "And hang the cost. If I have to wade through one more ditch, I'll end up with webbed feet."

Apart from that outburst, she had been curiously quiet since we left the Gelter village. No, since before that. In fact, since

217

she had her way in that business with the marriage contract. Perhaps she was just savoring her triumph. One never quite knew with Carmian.

"We're not very far from Birches," I said, having thought of little else for quite a while. "Nico, we could stay a night at the inn there."

The mere thought of it made my chest hurt with longing. I had to remind myself that there was no Cherry Tree Cottage and no real home to long for. But there was the inn and the smithy and the village and all the rest, familiar and safe. Right then I thought I might be glad to see Cilla, even.

"They know who I am," he said.

"But they wouldn't tell anyone."

He considered it. "Maybe not."

Carmian took off her hat and shook the snow off the brim.

"If this keeps up, we'll need a roof in any case," she said, coughing again.

"Are you coming down with something?" asked Nico.

"No."

"You're coughing."

"So? Sorry if it bothers you."

What was going on? Why did she snap at him every chance she got? If this was the joy of victory, I would hate to be around her at a time of defeat.

Nico didn't say anything, or not about that. A little later he turned to me. "How far is it to Birches from here?"

I looked around. What with the snow, one field looked much like the other, but I thought I recognized the poplars along the road.

"Another hour," I said. "Maybe two, if the weather gets worse."

"All right. Let's do it."

I stared at the pile of blackened beams and broken rubble that had once been our house. In the two years that had passed since Drakan burned it to the ground, no one had tried to clear the site or build anything new. The times being what they were, few people wanted to spare time, effort, and money on something that might be broken by war as soon as it was built.

Nico put his hand on my shoulder. I knew he had seen the tears in my eyes.

"Is this where you lived?" asked Carmian.

I nodded. "Since I was born and… until two years ago."

She didn't say anything else. But from that moment on, she stopped calling me Her Ladyship.

"Let's move on," I said. "Nothing here is worth looking at."

Nico looked as if he might have wanted to spare me the sight, but he couldn't. The house had been right next to the Dunark road.

On the last stretch of road the snow blew right into our faces, and there was so much of it that we could barely see where we were going. It was a good thing I knew my way around, or we might have lost our way entirely. It might be only a little more than half a mile from Cherry Tree Cottage to the village, but in this weather it was quite enough.

It was strange to be back in Birches. I stopped in the middle of the square, with the inn on one side and the smithy on the other. There were no sounds of hammer blows from inside, but it was late, almost dark already because the sky was so heavy with snow.

"Can we go to the smithy first?" I asked. Ellyn and Rikert had almost been a sort of aunt and uncle to Davin and Melli and me, and when Mama was gone on Shamer's business or on a sick call, we could always seek the comfort of the smithy. Ellyn probably loved Davin and Melli better than me, particularly Melli. But I, too, had always been welcome in her house, and I felt sure that hadn't changed. Once before, when Drakan had sought to revenge himself on the Shamer and her children, the smith and his wife had hidden my brother and sister, and even Beastie, our old dog, and kept them safe.

"Smithy or inn, I don't care," said Carmian, "as long as I don't have to be cold and wet anymore."

I don't think anyone saw us. There was no one much about, which considering the weather was only natural. Out of habit I entered through the smithy where Rikert often stood, making nails or hooks or plowshares, or shoeing somebody's horse. Right now it was silent and dark, but he had been at work that day; it was still warm in there and a few ruddy glows from the forge gave off enough light to see by.

I knocked at the door of the house proper.

"Ellyn? Rikert? May we come in?"

It took unusually long before the door opened. Rikert stood in the doorway, not as tall as some men—Callan, for instance—but wider than most, especially across the shoulders. He peered at us as if we had just woken him. It seemed to take him a moment to realize who I was.

"Dina! Holy Saint Magda, it's little Dina."

And then he did something he had never done before. He put both his powerful arms around me and gave me a hug that almost crushed the breath from me.

"Come in. Come inside."

We followed him into the house, into the kitchen with the black iron stove that Rikert had made himself. But there was no Ellyn there, stirring her pans. Actually it looked as if it had been quite a while since anybody had cooked in that kitchen. And in all the time I had known Ellyn, I had never seen her kitchen so dirty.

"Where is Ellyn?" I asked.

Rikert's shoulders drooped.

"Dead," he said without looking at me. "Since… since four days before midsummer."

It was like a blow to the stomach. Ellyn couldn't be, not Ellyn. She had been here always, I couldn't imagine her not—

"How?" I said. "Was it Drakan?" Because whenever something bad happened or somebody took something away from me, he was the first one I thought of.

Rikert shook his head. "She just got sick. Such things happen, Dina. She just got sick and died."

Leaving Birches had been hard, but in a way the village and its people had stayed with me inside my head like a picture: Sasia from the inn, the miller and his large family, Ellyn and Rikert. They didn't move much in the picture inside my head. It was as if they were just waiting for me to come back. And that was silly, of course. That I wasn't here didn't mean that things stopped happening. But Ellyn—

"How are you doing yourself?" I asked. He looked somehow *untended*. Like a horse no one could be bothered to groom. His shirt was dirty, and so was his hair, and behind the sharp sooty smell of the smithy there was a different odor, unwashed and not very nice. Nowhere near as bad as Carmian's old hag, but still… it made me want to heat water and give him a nice hot bath.

"Oh, I do all right. There's always work to do." He looked helplessly around the kitchen. "I don't know if there is anything to eat."

"We can go to the inn later," I said. "But perhaps we could make some thyme tea or something."

"Yes," he said. "There's still some of that around somewhere."

I stirred the embers in the stove into fresh flames and put a kettle on. And it was as if Rikert only now noticed that there were other people with me. He gave Nico a hesitant nod, as if uncertain whether he ought to bow instead. And when Carmian took off her hat and shook her hair, his jaw actually dropped for a moment. Then he rallied.

"Sit down," he said, hastily pushing some of the clutter off the kitchen bench. Carmian graciously sat on the bench, and Nico perched on the stool next to the fireplace.

"I'm sorry about Ellyn," Nico said. "That must have been hard for you."

Rikert looked down at his hands.

"It was nearly fifteen years," he said. "One gets used to having someone there. It's so hard to find things without her." Suddenly he looked directly at Nico. "Her hair was so soft," he said so quietly that I could barely make out the words. "Like the velvet of a horse's muzzle."

The kettle was coming to a boil. Carmian coughed. I went to take stock of Ellyn's pantry and felt like an uninvited visitor, because it had been the only place forbidden to us when we were children. She had rows of jars in there with berries and pickled greens like little pumpkins and beets, and also a generous store of dried herbs. Some of them might even have been given to her by Mama, I thought. I made the tea strong and good and put in some echinacea to ease Carmian's cough.

"Do you see many Dragon soldiers here?" asked Nico.

"Last spring they came here, wanting people to work for them. Craftsmen of all kinds, carpenters and the like, but above all, smiths. I had to hide in the woods for some weeks, or they would have taken me whether I wanted to come or not. And Ellyn had begun to sicken even then." He took the tea mug I offered him without raising his head. "It was hard for her on her own. But the village helped her."

I nodded. When things got serious, the villagers stuck together.

"How did you manage in the woods?" asked Nico.

"Oh, there were folks who were willing to help."

"From the village?"

"Yes. And others." He threw Nico a sidelong look. "You would know them, I think."

"The Weapons Master? He and his people?"

The smith was nodding. "They're called the Foxes around here because they are hardly ever caught, and because they are hard to see even when you know they are there. The Dragon soldiers hate them."

I knew what Nico was thinking. It was still a long way to the Highlands, and as we got farther and farther away from the marshes, there were fewer Gelts who might help. And we did need help. We had no real money, and in this weather it was necessary to secure food and shelter, and to be properly warm every once in a while.

"They would help us," I said.

"Yes. Maybe."

"Why not?"

Nico made an odd grimace. "Because the Weapons Master has his own ideas about me. And about how he wants to use me. And I don't agree with those ideas."

He was right. If the Weapons Master had his way, Nico would find himself at the head of an army of resistance against Drakan. But Nico didn't want to be at the head of anything, especially not something that got people killed.

"You have no choice," said Carmian suddenly. "If Drakan had still been at Dunark, then maybe. But not now. Now you need an army."

But Nico shook his head stubbornly.

"Enough are dying already," he said. "Why should I ask even more people to die?"

We drank our tea in silence. Not even Carmian said anything. Perhaps it was because Rikert was there, or else we were all just too tired to fight.

Finally I got up. We still had to eat and sleep, and it was clear that Rikert could barely feed himself, let alone a crowd of unexpected visitors.

"Stay here," I told Nico. "The fewer people who see you, the better. And there might be a stranger or two at the inn."

He nodded. "May we sleep here?" he asked Rikert. It might be somewhat untidy and none too clean, but the house was warm, and if there were strangers at the inn, this would be better.

"As long as you want."

I put my wet cloak back on and trudged through the slush, across the square to the inn. And it was a good thing Nico wasn't with me. All in all, five strangers were sitting at two of the inn's tables, and even though none of them seemed to be Dragon men, there were probably an awful lot of common folk who had no aversion to earning a hundred gold marks.

At first, I could barely recognize Sasia. She looked all grown up now. Her hair was longer, she was taller… and she had breasts now. She looked really pretty. Lucky her. Not like me, who only grew more and more awkward and peculiar and looked like some kind of underground spirit that had been dragged from a bog.

"Good evening," she said politely. "Just a moment and I'll—" and then she recognized me. "Dina! Dina, is it really you?"

I nodded. There was suddenly a big lump in my throat. Sasia put her tray down and wiped her hands on her apron, looking shy.

"Are you all right?" she asked.

Not really. But I only nodded. How could I explain everything that was wrong with me? No, I'm not all right, I'm on the run with the rightful heir of Dunark and his affianced wife whom I can't stand, people are constantly trying to capture us or kill us, I'm not sure my mother likes me anymore because it looks like I'm turning into a Blackmaster, and oh, I really, really hate my hair. No, it was better not to start on all that.

Sasia put her arms around me and gave me an abrupt little hug.

"I've thought about you so much," she said.

"So have I," said another voice.

I spun. One of the guests had risen from his table and now stood between me and the door.

It was Azuan.

A Rare Pearl

"Who is that?" whispered Sasia.

"My… my uncle." Would I be able to slip through the kitchens and make a dash for the back door?

"There is no need to run away," said Azuan. "I merely wish to speak to you."

Oh, sure. My elbow was still bruised from where he had held on to me the last time he wished to "speak to me."

"What is there to talk about?" I said, taking a small step closer to the kitchen door.

"Your father. Your mother. And you."

I stopped without meaning to. My father, my mother, and me. Well, yes, there might be a few things in that which were worth talking about. But not… not with someone who had tried to buy me like a horse or a dog. If only he wasn't so like my father. It wasn't fair. I felt a huge black hole inside every time I looked at him.

On the other hand, perhaps talking to him here, in the inn, with lots of people about, it might not be so dangerous. Here in Birches at least there were plenty of people who wouldn't just stand by and watch if he tried to make off with me.

"How did you find me?" I asked, stalling for time while I worked things out in my head.

"There were quite a few people in Dunark who knew the name of the Shamer's village. I thought you might return home if you had the chance, and here you are."

Yes. Stupid old me.

"Please sit down, Dina. I'm not going to hurt you."

Sasia was listening to this, and her eyes were getting bigger and bigger, which was no wonder. She had never heard that I had an uncle, or even a father. And up till now this had hardly been the sort of conversation normal uncles had with their nieces.

"Do you want me to call for Papa?" she quietly asked. The inn had no bouncer as such. Sasia's papa was quite big enough to handle that job himself if the need arose, and the mere thought made me much calmer. No, Azuan wouldn't hurt me. He *couldn't*. Not here.

"Not yet," I said, loudly enough for Azuan to hear. "But if he so much as lays a finger on me—"

Sasia nodded, her eyes bigger still. "Just say the word."

Azuan was listening to this with the suggestion of a smile, a smile that reminded me so much of my father's.

"Are you done marshaling your troops?" he asked.

"We can talk," I said. "But don't try to force me to do anything, and don't think I'm going anywhere with you."

He delivered a small bow, still with the same faint smile.

"As you please," he said. "Would the Medamina like to sit?"

I sat.

"What is it you want with me?"

"First of all: where is he?"

My first thought was of Nico, and I sat there in a panic, wondering how much Azuan knew. But then I remembered that he had asked me the same question in Dunbara, and that the "he" was Sezuan.

"He is dead," I said, feeling the tears prickle just because I had to say the words. "He... he was killed at the Sagisburg."

Azuan sat unmoving and silent for quite a while.

"By whom?" he finally said.

"One of Prince Arthos's Educators. Master Vardo. He died too."

Azuan nodded, as if that was to be expected.

"Then I must return without him," he said. "The Matriarcha will not be pleased."

"Who?"

"Her Serenity the Matriarcha Ineze Sina. My aunt. Your grandmother's sister."

I did know that my grandmother was dead and that her sister had assumed her place. This was just the first time I had heard her name.

"I'm not pleased either," I said. "But that is what happened."

"When?"

"Just after midsummer." Almost at the same time as Ellyn, I realized. How strange to think that a person who had meant so much to us had died without us knowing it. Melli still didn't know, nor Davin. In their minds she was still alive.

"And before he died, he gave you his flute?"

I nodded.

"And taught you how to use it?"

"A little."

"You must have been a most apt student. You almost had me slumbering in that small room back in Dunbara."

I looked at him. Even him? What did he mean?

"Are you a Blackmaster?" I asked.

"After a fashion," he said. "But not the ordinary kind."

I had met only one Blackmaster in my life before this, so I didn't know what he meant by "the ordinary kind." Was Sezuan ordinary?

"Why are you so afraid of me?" he asked.

"You wanted to buy me."

"Yes. Ransom you from the clutches of Cador. Or the Crow, as he seems to be called. Were you happy to be with him?"

Hardly. I shook my head.

"So I did you a favor. Or would have done, if you had let me."

"But if you had bought me, would you then have set me free?"

"You obviously wouldn't believe me if I said yes."

I thought about that for a while.

"No, probably not."

"But why? Why do you expect such bad things of me?"

It was the greed. The hungry way he looked at me. And also my mother's fear of his family. But then, she had been scared of Sezuan too, more than she had to be.

"How much did he want? The Crow."

"Seventy silver marks."

I nodded. That was exactly what the discarded cargo was worth, so that made a kind of sense.

"And you would have paid him so much?"

"I think you are well worth it. That and more."

Was I supposed to feel flattered?

"And do you really expect me to believe that you would fork out that kind of money on my behalf and just let me walk away?"

He shook his head, but not in refusal. It looked more like a kind of wonder.

"I don't understand you, Dina. Don't you realize what we are offering you?"

No, not really. We had never got that far.

"The Palace of the Matriarcha is among the greatest in Colmonte. The Sinas possess enormous riches, huge tracts of land. You would be celebrated and admired for your ability. You… you are a rare pearl, Dina, a human being possessed of two such unusual gifts at once. Seventy silver marks! You are worth infinitely more than that, but people here do not see your worth. I heard how the sailors talked of you. Like you were some kind of witch or demon. Your life here is poverty and danger, scorn, fear, and persecution. Loneliness too, I should imagine. Why should you fear the life we want to offer you?"

I didn't know what to say. He made it sound like I was some kind of princess who for mysterious reasons chose to roll in the gutter rather than sit on a throne dressed in velvets and silks. And what he said about the fear and the persecution, that was true. Even my mother… even my mother feared what my father had passed on to me. That which was *in* me, whether I wanted it or not.

"If you buy something," I slowly said, "then it is because you think you can own it."

He looked at me politely and expectantly, like he was still waiting for the point. When he realized that for me this *was* the point, he gave me another of his disbelieving headshakes.

"But we are all owned by somebody," he said. "We all belong to someone or something. The Crow thought you were his to sell, but you tricked him, for which I applaud you. A low person such as he should not own a… a pearl like you. But I think the one you really belong to is your mother. Am I right?"

"I—" I broke off. I was about to say that I didn't belong to anybody. But I found I couldn't. It wouldn't be true. "She doesn't *own* me," I said. "It makes a difference."

"Strong people may sometimes decide for themselves who they want to belong to," he said. "You might be strong enough for that, I think. That was why the Crow couldn't hold you. And why your mother will not be able to hold you either. When I look at you now, I can see that you are no longer fully hers. Some day you will be entirely free of her. But be careful. Those who belong to nothing and no one, they are not human beings anymore."

That scared me to the bone. It was as if huge cracks in the earth were suddenly opening beneath my feet. What if he was right? I wanted so to be my mother's daughter, but if she could love only the part of me that was hers and not the part that was my father's gift to me… I thought of the words of the Spinner: *The thread has twained, but you cannot be two. Choose—before both threads are severed.* Did I have to be either my mother's or my father's? Couldn't I be both? And be myself?

"Who do you belong to?" I asked.

He answered without hesitation. "The House of Sina. My family."

"And you can live with that?"

"I am proud of it. Dina, we would treasure you. You have no idea how highly we would value you. We would teach you to perfect your gifts—both your mother's and your father's. And we would honor you for your perfection."

"And keep me in a cage? Like a rare bird?" Valdracu had certainly treasured me and taken pride in me. His rare bird, his witch and his weapon, obedient to his will.

Azuan actually looked horrified. "A cage! What must you

think of us? Of course not. You would be entirely free to come and go as you pleased."

"And if I wanted to leave you completely?"

He bowed his head. "It would pain us. But it is not a choice I think you would make, Dina. Not once you knew us." He stirred. I think he meant to take my hand and then thought better of it, remembering how I had threatened him with Sasia's father if he touched me. "Dina, how can you reject us so without even knowing us? It is bad enough that I must return home to say we have lost Sezuan. He, too, was a rare gem, and much treasured. But if instead I could show you to them and say, 'This is his daughter, and she is everything he was, and more,' Dina, they would sing and dance and celebrate. They would rejoice. And they would honor you."

I had to blink away fresh tears. He meant it. I could feel the truth in him. And the mere thought that someone would rejoice and… and celebrate me… *she is everything he is, and more*. Here, people tended to cringe and run away from me. Or cross to the other side of the street, at least.

"I can't," I whispered, torn by a strange sense of loss. "I can't come with you."

He looked at me with a piercing intent. "You still belong to your mother," he said.

"No. Or yes, but not in that way. But there are people here I can't just turn my back on." Don't tell him about Nico, I told myself firmly. He doesn't need to know.

"It grieves me," he said. "But you must do as you please."

I frowned. "You mean, that's it, and now you go home?" I felt curiously insulted that he should give in so easily, what with all his talk of rare pearls and treasuring.

"No," he said with the half-smile that reminded me so much of Papa. "But if you will not come with me, I must come with you. Until the day comes when you are ready to make a different choice."

My mouth fell open. "You mean—Do you mean that you will…" follow me around like a dog was what I nearly said, but that would have been pretty rude. "Are you going to follow me?"

"Yes. If we might walk beside each other, I would prefer it so. But if I must walk behind, then so be it. Someone will have to look after you in these barbaric lands where a gift is regarded as a curse and they burn people for having a gift not given to everyone."

I was utterly stunned. "But I don't want you with me."

"No. That is your choice. But you cannot prevent me from being your shadow."

That was the very last thing he should have said. Master and Shadow. My father's brother Nazim. Azuan's brother too, come to think of it, a mad creature, barely human, and yet a man whose life had been ruined and broken because he had convinced himself that my father had stolen his soul and his name so that only Shadow was left. I did not want a Shadow like that. *I did not.*

I rose abruptly.

"Stay away from me," I said, and heard the tremor in my own voice. "Far away. I don't want you."

He regarded me calmly.

"You make your choices, and I make mine," he said. "It is not within your powers to prevent me."

"Dina, should I call Papa?" asked Sasia, who must have been eavesdropping. "Do you want us to show him out?"

"Show him out" in the parlance of the inn meant toss him out on his ear. But I shook my head.

"No," I said. "Let him stay. I'm leaving anyway."

And I staggered out of the inn on legs that felt like they didn't belong to me, out into the darkness and the snow, with no thought for the dinner I had promised to get us.

A Shadow of my very own?

Not if I had anything to do with it.

Nico looked up as I came in and had no trouble spotting my misery.

"What's wrong?"

I hesitated. I didn't want to tell him about Azuan, because that might mean talking about the serpent gift, and there were still a few people left in the world who didn't know I had it. Rikert, for instance, and probably Carmian too. But if Azuan really was intent on his Shadow game, it couldn't be kept a secret for long.

"Azuan is in Birches," I said. "Sitting in the inn, having a beer."

"Azuan?" Nico raised a questioning eyebrow. And only then did I realize that I had never told him the full story about what had happened to me the night the Crow tried to sell me.

"He is Sezuan's brother," I said. "Half brother, anyway." Nico knew how terrified my mother was of Sezuan's family. "Did he... did he hurt you, Dina?"

I shook my head. "No. It wasn't like that. But he said he would follow me. He said he wanted to look after me. And I don't want him to."

Carmian snorted. "That seems to be the effect you have on men, little darling. They all want to look after you."

Nico gave her a sharp glance. "Can't you just call her Dina?" he said. "Instead of all those nicknames."

"Little darling is not a nickname."

"It's not her name either."

"Oh, I do beg your pardon. So perhaps I should call you His Highness Prince Nicodemus Ravens? Because that's your name, isn't it?"

"Carmian, stop it."

"Why? Lessons in etiquette are obviously sorely needed here. We don't want your future wife to embarrass you in public, now do we?"

"Carmian, I said stop—"

"Anything else you'd like me not to do? Burp at the table? Lick my fingers? Just say the word. I'm a very quick student."

She had finally succeeded in making Nico angry.

"First of all," he said in the sharpest and most cutting tone I had ever heard him use, "first of all, you might take note of the fact that not everything in this world revolves around you. And secondly, a little common courtesy would not go amiss."

Carmian was on her feet now. Her eyes were very bright, and you could almost *see* the fury in her, like a shimmer of heat from an oven.

"My Lord Prince must excuse me," she said. "In the future, I shall try to know my place."

"Where are you going?" asked Nico.

"Out. To get My Lord's dinner. Isn't that what the little wife *should* do?"

And with that, she stormed out of the house.

Rikert had followed the row with growing interest.

"Is that true?" he said. "Are you really going to marry her?"

"If I ever succeed in killing Drakan," said Nico, looking as if letting Drakan live seemed quite tempting right now.

"She is… something else," murmured Rikert. "Not quite your ordinary woman."

"No," said Nico. "Ordinary, she is not."

Carmian took her own sweet time in getting back. But when she did return, she brought the finest dinner the inn had to offer: roast goose with apples and a honey glaze, and prune pie for dessert.

"You made them roast a goose?" I said reproachfully. "We could have eaten lamb stew like the rest of them."

"Save your outrage," she said drily. "They were paid handsomely for everything."

"How? You have no more money than the rest of us. Or do you?"

"No. But your friend Azuan has. And apparently nothing is too good for his little princess."

The goose suddenly looked a lot less tempting, despite its spicy fragrance. I really shouldn't eat it, I thought. But when the rest of them dug in, so did I.

That night I dreamed of Shadow. Of his greedy hands, and the way his skin came off in flaky patches. But his face was different. In the dream, his face was Azuan's.

We ate the remains of the goose for breakfast. And during the night, Nico had made his decision.

"Rikert, do you know how we might find the Foxes?"

"Yes. Do you want to do it today?"

"Yes, please. If you can."

Rikert nodded.

"Stay in the house," he said. "I'll see what I can do."

More Than Darkness

Rikert returned late that afternoon, and he brought someone with him.

"This is Tano," he said. "He can help."

The boy was dark-haired, a few years older than me but big and strong for his age, with wide shoulders and large hands. You could tell he would be quite a giant of a man when he reached his full growth.

And I knew him.

I think he was as taken aback as I was.

"You!" he said, and suddenly didn't know what to do with his eyes. I had my difficulties too. I didn't much want to look at him either. Once… once Valdracu had forced me to use my Shamer's eyes on Tano just because he wouldn't stand meekly by while his friends at the Weapons Mill were injured, one after the other, by the hazards of their work.

Valdracu had hit Tano with his wicked chain, right across the palm, where it had to hurt like hell. But that hadn't brought Tano to his knees. No, it took me to do that.

"Do you two know each other?" said Rikert.

I nodded mutely. Tano didn't say anything either. Nico looked from Tano to me, trying to figure out what was going on. But as neither of us volunteered an explanation, he decided to press on as if nothing had happened.

"Do you know who I am?" he asked Tano.

"Yes, Lord."

Nico shook his head impatiently. "Don't call me that. There is no reason to, and I don't like it."

This seemed to surprise Tano, but he didn't reply.

"Who I am is only important because I would like to see the Weapons Master. And I think he would like to see me."

Tano nodded. He gave me a sidelong glance. "Is she coming too?" he said.

"Yes."

"Then I don't know."

Nico raised an eyebrow. "Why? What do you mean?"

"It's just… I'm not sure we can trust her."

"Trust *Dina*? Of course we can—"

"What he means," I interrupted hoarsely, "what he means is that he doesn't dare trust someone who used to be Valdracu's tame witch."

Tano raised his head in surprise for a moment, and I caught a glimpse of his dark eyes. Possibly he hadn't expected me to reveal myself like that, without being forced.

"But, Tano, Dina was Valdracu's prisoner. His hostage. If she did anything that—If she obeyed him, it was only because he would have killed a small boy if she didn't. Didn't you know that?"

Tano shrugged his shoulders evasively. "Some people said that."

"But you didn't believe them?" Nico had spotted the doubtful note in Tano's voice just as I had.

Another shrug. "I don't know. But I'm just not sure we can trust her. How do I know she can keep the kind of secrets that can cost people their lives if they get out?"

"Dina is a good girl," said Rikert suddenly. "Tano, Dina is not one to play you false."

I could have hugged him—Rikert and his steady nature, his big smith's hands, and his steadfastness. And Tano actually seemed to listen.

"Are you certain, Master?"

"Dina is all right, son. I've known her since she was born."

Tano nodded slowly and reluctantly.

"All right, then. If we hurry, we can be there before dark."

"Someone is following us."

Tano was the one who said it, but I had been thinking it for a good long while. It wasn't that I had really heard or seen anything; it was more a sensation. I had hoped I was imagining things, but if Tano had caught it too...

"I suppose it's Azuan," said Nico, grimacing. "He did threaten to do it."

"Azuan?" said Tano. "Who is that?"

"Dina's uncle," said Nico.

"Your uncle?" Tano gave me a brief, cautious glance. "Why is he following you around?"

I shook my head. "He wants to... oh, it's hard to explain."

"He wants to wait on her hand and foot and protect her against all the dangers of this world," said Carmian acidly. "But Dina won't let him."

Tano didn't look as if this was very enlightening. "Why not?"

"That's not all he wants," I said, hoping to avoid any talk of the serpent gift.

I think Tano understood it differently. "Does he want to hurt you?" he said, clenching his fists. "Don't you let him, Dina! You just tell him to keep his hands to himself."

Surprised, I looked at him. At first just because he looked ready to defend me tooth and nail. And then because I finally realized what he meant.

"But he's old!" I burst out. "He must be thirty or something."

"That doesn't always stop them," he said bitterly. "Not the worst ones."

… one of the weaver girls, Miona was her name, who used to smile at him when she saw him. Until she grew all pale and silent and scared and wouldn't look at anybody. And when he found out what the Loom Master had done to her…

"But it wasn't your fault!"

"I should have looked out for her," he said. "She… she had no one to look out for her at all. And he knew that."

"Tano, you can't look out for every unprotected being in this world."

And then we both realized what had happened.

"You saw it," he said accusingly. "You saw it in my head."

Denying it would do no good. I had already admitted it.

"I didn't mean to," I said, remembering how incensed Carmian had been when I had caught a hint of her inner thoughts. "I can't control it. It comes and goes whether I want it to or not."

He kept looking at me, with that same furious, courageous pride that had made him face down Valdracu.

"Do it, then. Go ahead and look. See it all. I don't care!"

He had very dark eyes. Dark like a midnight sky. How could he stand there looking into my eyes when he knew better than anyone what that might cost him? Not even Nico could do that, though he sometimes tried.

I think he was expecting things to happen. But my capricious gift had gone back into hiding.

He frowned. "Something has happened," he said. "You're different."

"I don't have Shamer's eyes anymore," I said. "Not really."

He didn't believe me, I could see that right away. And who could blame him, when I had just looked straight into his mind like that?

"Your uncle," he finally said. "We can't have him trailing along when we get to... to the place we're going to." He didn't want to name it out loud, obviously, and perhaps that was wise. Who knew how close Azuan was?

"No," said Nico. "We can't. But what do we do?"

It was a good question. We were on foot, and the snow was at least ankle high almost everywhere. We couldn't run from Azuan, and he would have no trouble following our tracks.

"Call him," said Carmian suddenly.

"*Call* him? Why?"

"He is your dog, isn't he? If you call him, he will have to come."

"He is not my dog." I glared at her. What a thing to say.

"Protector, shadow, bodyguard, call it what you like. You are his little princess, right? So call him, darling, so that we can have a little talk."

No way. Why would I call out to an uncle I didn't want anywhere near me?

"It might be a good idea," said Nico. "Perhaps we can come to some sort of arrangement with him."

"With Azuan? I don't think so."

Nico smiled. "Oh, most people will talk to you if you can give them something they want."

And what would that be, except for me? I knew Nico well enough to know that he would never just hand me over to Azuan.

"Go on, Dina. Call him."

I felt like an utter idiot. What would I call him? Uncle Azuan?

"Azuan?"

No answer.

I tried again, with the same lack of results.

What if we were wrong and he wasn't there? How long did they expect me to stand here yodeling like a fool?

"He is out there somewhere," said Tano. "Or someone is. I'm sure I heard a horse."

"Do it again, Dina," said Nico. "Just so that we are sure he has heard you."

I took a deep breath and called at the top of my lungs, "Azuan!"

But only the trees surrounded us, black and silent, and I could neither hear nor see any human presence other than our own.

"It's Dina he is following," said Carmian. "If she doesn't go, neither does he."

"And what good is that going to do us?" I snapped. "Do you expect me to stand here forever, while the rest of you go off to take care of Drakan?"

Nico frowned. "That might be the only way. No, Dina, we aren't going to leave you here alone, or even for very long. But Tano and I might go on together for the last little bit of the way."

I thought it was a terrible idea, and I opened my mouth to say so. But at that moment we all heard a horse whinny, a lonely, plaintive sound in the stillness of the woods. And after that, there was no doubt. Tano stopped.

"We can't risk it," he said. "I cannot lead so many strangers to the Foxes' Lair without permission from the Weapons Master."

The Foxes' Lair? Well, if people called them the Foxes, I suppose it was an apt enough name. I sighed.

"All right," I said. "I'll stay here. Just see that you come back and get me before I turn into an icicle."

"I'll stay too," said Rikert. "Can't leave you here all alone, can we?"

I smiled at him gratefully.

"It'll be only Tano and me," said Nico. "Carmian will stay behind as well."

"Oh, will I?" said Carmian, not at all meekly. But Nico drew her aside and said something to her very quietly, and when he and Tano walked on, she stood with Rikert and me, hands on her hips, watching Nico disappear among the trees.

"Well, well," she muttered to herself. "Sweet words and candy smiles. But that's not enough to feed a grown woman."

Then she spun on us.

"What are you waiting for?" she said. "If we are to stay here till our strays come home, at least we have to have a fire."

We moved away from the road a little way and chopped down some pine boughs to make a shelter. After a couple of vain attempts, Rikert managed to light us a fire. We had neither food nor cooking gear, but I had brought a few of Ellyn's dried herbs, and we had two pewter mugs. We filled them with snow and set them on the fire, and soon the tea was brewing.

"How long do you think they'll be?" I asked Rikert.

"A few hours," he said. "Depends how long they talk."

Carmian was restless. She still had a cough, but I think the night's rest in the warm smithy and the tea I had made had probably helped quite a bit.

"Can you play that thing?" she asked, pointing at my father's flute, which I wore in my belt. "Or is it just for decoration?"

I shrugged. "I don't play what you might call real music," I said. "That takes a lot of practice. But what the flute wants me to play, I can do."

"Give us a tune, then," she said. "It doesn't have to be anything I've heard before."

It wouldn't be, I thought. But I set the flute to my lips and started playing.

Tonight, the notes that came were lonely. A song full of snow and darkness and silence.

"It sounds so sad," said Carmian in the end. "Can't you give us something a little more cheerful?"

I shook my head. "Not tonight. The flute is not in a cheerful mood."

"Nonsense," she snapped. "You are the player, right? Flutes don't have moods. Not of their own, anyway."

But whether the mood was in me or the flute, the lonely twilight tune was the only thing I could play.

Suddenly there were four of us at the fire. "Why do you play like that?" said Azuan. "Why do you play so that no human creature can stand being alone tonight?"

Carmian leaped into the air like a cat with its tail on fire. Suddenly there was a knife in her hand, a long thin one, almost the length of a small sword. But before she had time to do anything with it, she gave a strange gasp and flailed her arms wildly for a few moments before keeling over into the snow, the knife still clutched in her right hand. She crabbed her way forward with awkward movements, as if she had suddenly gone deaf, dumb, and blind.

"Stop it!" I yelled at Azuan, because I was certain this was something he had done to her. "Take it off her!"

"She is dangerous," he said. "And she is your enemy. Can't you see that?"

Carmian didn't like me much, that was true, but my enemy? No, I didn't think so. And no one deserved to be as she was now, creeping blindly through the snow. I seized one of the pewter mugs from the fire, though the handle was so hot it burned my fingers. And then I flung the hot tea into Azuan's face.

I didn't know whether I had hit him or not. Because at that moment, something hit me.

It was more than darkness. It was blindness and deafness and more. I could feel nothing, sense nothing whatsoever. And yet I wasn't unconscious. I was aware that something had happened. I was aware that time was passing. But darkness covered all my senses like a blanket, and I felt as if I might as well be dead.

Clipped Wings

I don't know how long it lasted. It felt like forever. When I could see again, there was snow and moonlight, and a horse's neck in front of me. I was sitting on a horse, and someone was holding me. And I was as seasick as I had ever been aboard the *Sea Wolf*.

I didn't have time to say anything or do anything. I just threw up.

That darkness. That more-than-darkness. It was one of the most revolting things that had ever happened to me.

The horse stopped. Azuan got off and lifted me down from the saddle. That nearly made me throw up all over again.

"It will be better in a little while," he said. "Rest for a moment."

"Disgusting. That was *disgusting*."

"Yes. Nobody likes it. Here, lie on my cloak."

I was so dizzy and weak at the knees that lying down was not a choice.

"What is it?" I asked. "The darkness."

"My gift. The only thing I can do, apart from a certain resistance to the illusions of others."

"You take people's senses away from them?"

He nodded. "Not as refined and delicate as what your father could do. But quite effective all the same."

"Disgusting."

He shrugged. "It is the only weapon I have. Is it any prettier to slice people up with a knife, as your long-legged friend intended?"

"She wouldn't have used it." Or would she? I was rarely on certain ground where Carmian was concerned.

"She looked as if she meant to," he said.

"Where is she? And where is Rikert?"

"Still by your little campfire, or so I assume. Unless they are hardier than you are and have started following our trail already. But we have a nice lead."

I tried to sit up, but I was still too dizzy. Azuan put his hand on my shoulder and held me back. It wasn't hard for him.

"You've abducted me!"

"Certainly not."

"Then what do you call this?"

"I saved you."

"Saved me? From what, if I may ask?"

"From people who took no proper care of you. The Highlands are at war now, Dina. Why would you go there? It is no place for you."

"My family is in the Highlands!"

"Only part of it, Dina. You have family elsewhere. You have a House. In peaceful, civilized lands, not this savage country."

He made it sound as if we were all wearing bearskin and carrying big clubs. But perhaps savage was the word for what Drakan had done to Skay-Sagis, turning it into one huge dragon pit where big beasts ate the smaller ones.

"I want to go back," I said, trying to sound firm and determined, or as firm and determined as one can be when one's stomach is still floating about a little too close to one's throat. "I want to go back to the others."

He shook his head. "We ride on as soon as you've caught your breath. It's for your own good, Dina."

Could I run from him? Not on legs that felt like overcooked asparagus. But the flute, perhaps?

The flute.

"Where is my father's flute?" It was no longer in my belt.

"You'll get it back" was all he said. Like Nico, he had apparently decided it was wiser to disarm me. "Come on. Let's get you back on the horse. We have to ride till we find a place where we can spend the night."

In the end, we found a log cabin with just a single room, a fireplace at one end and a sleeping loft at the other. People had been living there until not too long ago, but now there were none. Where had they gone? Had they fled to more peaceful lands, like Azuan wanted us to? Or had it become too lonely and too cold to live here, in the woods so close to the Highlands and so far away from other people? Perhaps the cabin was only used during the summer. I knew some herders built shelters near the summer grazing; this could be one of those.

It meant a roof over our heads, at least, and shelter too for Azuan's poor mount, which had already put up with more than could be reasonably expected from a horse. A long journey and a double burden for the last leg of it—no wonder it heaved a tired sigh when it was finally allowed to stop.

I, too, was about ready to drop from fatigue and misery. What was I doing here, with a man who looked like my father but wasn't, a man who had blinded me and carried me off and still claimed that he was merely looking after me?

"Go inside," he said. "And stay inside. I have to take care of the horse, but you can rest the while."

We didn't talk much as he lit a fire in the fireplace, fetched cheese and bread from the saddlebags, and melted snow for tea in a small pot. Once I tried to explain to him again that I wanted to go back to the others, and that if he really honored me as much as he said he did, he would take me home, or at least let me go. And once more he explained, in the patient voice of somebody talking to a sick child, that my home was not with these people, that they didn't treasure me, and that once I was free of them, everything would look different.

"You could blaze like a sun," he said. "Like a star. Instead you blacken the glass so that the lantern can barely shine. But I will help you."

He sounded so certain, as if it wasn't an opinion or a hope, but merely the way the world was. There was something very frightening about that certainty.

He left the loft to me. He himself curled up on the floor with one of the two blankets he had in his pack. The other he gave me. The cabin was not perhaps toasty warm, but it was still a great deal better than the outside. It would have been easy to fall asleep, tired as I was. But I fought to stay awake.

When I felt sure he had fallen asleep, I climbed down from the loft as quietly as I could. I stepped carefully over his sleeping form and out the cabin door. My body was buzzing and swaying with tiredness, but I had to get away from him, away from all his talk of stars and lanterns, away from that frightening certainty. What if he was right? What if he really could "help" me so that I no longer felt any connection to the people I now cared for and was no longer limited by… by anything, except perhaps the wishes of the House of Sina?

The horse stood, head drooping, in the small shed Azuan had given it for a stall. It wasn't exactly happy to see me, particularly not when I began to saddle it. Falk, our own gelding, would have pounded his forefoot and tossed his head, but luckily Azuan's mare was too well trained for such misdemeanors. It contented itself with a snort and a slight resistance as I led it outside.

"Stop."

My heart leaped in my chest like a startled frog. Azuan stood there, black against the snow, and though his hands were empty, he still looked *armed*. Dangerous, anyway.

"You know I only have one weapon," he said. "I will use it if you force my hand."

I wished so that I could be like Tano and say *Do it, then* and fight on regardless. But I couldn't. I was afraid. It was so awful, that darkness. I had been so helpless it felt as if I was barely alive, and yet I *was* alive. Buried alive, almost.

He could see that I was not going to defy him.

"Go in," he said and took the reins from my unresisting hands. "Go back into the cabin."

I did as he said.

He stood in the doorway, considering me.

"This is not worthy of you," he finally said. "These people are not worthy of you. Don't you understand? They lead you into danger and death, and I cannot be your jailer night and day. I had hoped to bring you gently and in good time to the place where you belong. But we do not have that time. We must sever their hold on you at once. There is nothing else to do."

I didn't understand what he meant. But he went to his saddlebags and brought out a small bag. He filled one of the tea mugs with the last of the water from the pot and sprinkled something from the bag in the water.

"Here," he said. "Drink."

I didn't want to.

"What is it?" I asked.

"Dream powder," he said.

And then I wanted to even less. Dream powder. I remembered Shadow and his greed for one more dream, and then one more, even though every dream pushed him farther into madness. It had all started with the dream powder, my father had told me. A hazardous shortcut, he had called it. *One you should avoid.* I couldn't agree more.

"I don't want it," I said, as firmly and as strongly as I could.

He actually looked regretful. "Then I must force you," he said. "It is demeaning to us both, and I promise you it will be the very last time I do anything of the kind. Once you are free of these people, you will see the proper way of it for yourself."

Force me? I wouldn't make it easy for him. I would kick and bite and fight him as hard as I could. Knock the cup from his hand, run away—

But the darkness hit me like a hammer. And I couldn't bite or kick or fight, because I couldn't see, couldn't hear, couldn't feel a thing.

I hated it. *Hated* it. So disgusting.

Time passed. I had no idea how much or how little. And as for what happened outside the darkness, I had no clue. If he forced the dream powder down my throat—and I suppose he did—I couldn't feel even that. Nothing penetrated the blanket he had muffled my senses with. Not until he himself suddenly stood there. Azuan. In the middle of the darkness he himself had created, bowing to me like you would bow to a queen or a prince.

"Let me lead you to freedom."

Not on my life.

But apparently my will did not matter. With a sudden jerk, we were elsewhere. An eerie gray shining mist surrounded us, a mist full of calling voices.

I had been here before. The Ghost Country, I had called it, and it was no place for the living. Back when Valdracu caught me, one of his men had given me witch weed to subdue me, and it nearly killed me. Somehow I had wandered out of my body and into the gray mists where one usually met only the dead. I had been so close to death myself, back then. Was I dying even now?

"This place is dangerous," I told Azuan. "If you lose your way, you can die."

"I'll look after you," he said, which didn't make me any less anxious. "And there are threads to follow. If you have been here before, how is it that you don't know this?"

Threads?

Yes. Now I saw them. They were what made the mists shine. Delicate, brilliant gossamer threads wove through the grayness like the weft on a loom. Life threads, I suddenly realized, destiny's threads like those the Spinner had told me about. Was this what she was seeing while she weaved?

"Many believe that the bonds of their destiny are unalterable," said Azuan. "But they aren't. We sever and bind with the choices we make. You can choose, Dina. You can choose to be free."

Suddenly I heard the Spinner's voice in my mind. *The thread has twained, but you cannot be two. Choose—before both threads are severed.*

Mother's daughter, father's daughter. Shamer or Blackmaster. That had to be what she meant. But if I had to choose what to be, there was no real doubt. And I knew now what to do.

"Mama," I whispered. And spoke the word again in my mind: *Mama.* I sent out my longing, because in these mists where one couldn't walk from place to place, it was longing that made movement possible. Your own longing, or that of others.

Starry skies. Rocks. And far below me, a small troop of people and horses, and a cart. I knew this road. It was the road to Skayark. And once before I had traveled it at night, a night full of fear and the piercing screams of hungry young owls.

"Sleep now, sweetie. When you wake up, we'll be there."

It was my mother's voice, so clear that it sounded as if I were right next to her. And in one breath, I was. Inside the cart, seeing her holding Melli on her lap, and a bow in her free hand.

A bow? I had never before seen a weapon in my mother's hands. Her eyes and her voice had always been weapon enough.

Except against Drakan. Drakan met her gaze without faltering, shameless, though there was enough for him to be ashamed about. So perhaps he was the enemy my mother needed a bow against?

Maudi was driving, and there were many familiar faces in the small company—Black-Arse and his mother, Callan's old Gran, Killian and his family. Why were they headed for Skayark? And why in the middle of the night?

"Mama," I said, wanting her to see me, though I knew there was nothing really there for her to see. But surely she would hear me, at least?

It didn't seem that way. She stroked Melli's forehead with one hand, the other still clenched around the bow. And then I remembered that it was the Shamer's voice I needed to use if I wanted her to hear me.

I tried. I really tried. I wanted it so badly. But nothing happened. I was no proper Shamer, not anymore. And my mother couldn't hear me.

I would have cried if I had been able to. But my body was elsewhere, back in a cabin in the woods below the Highlands, and if tears ran down my face there, I was not able to feel them. Here in the Ghost Country, only the real ghosts cried. Like Auld Anya, searching for her drowned child…

No. Best not to think about that now. You had to be careful with your thoughts in this place where purpose and longing were more important than arms and legs. Already I could feel the mists crowding more closely around me, already I could hear the calling voices more clearly. I tried to hang on to Mama, Melli, the cart and the people and the horses on the Skayark road, but one of the mist-borne voices sounded nearer than the others, and I was the one he was longing for.

> *Nightbird is flying through the darkness*
> *Nightbird is bringing me a dream*
> *A dream as fine as you are*
> *A dream as fine as you.*

Only one other human being in the whole wide world knew that song, the man who had made it. My own longing rose and took flight like the bird in the song.

"Papa."

I said it before I had time to remember that he was dead. It was so strange. Even though you knew it, you didn't know it all the time, particularly not in dreams.

A campfire by a mountain road, but not the one that led to Skayark. This was the road to the Sagisburg. And by the fire, my father was sitting, singing softly. And I did so long to rest my head in his lap and be the one he was singing to.

He looked up. And he could see me.

"Dina."

"Papa."

"Crying again?"

Was I? I couldn't feel it.

"You lied to me," I said. "You said I didn't have the serpent gift, but you were lying."

"Is that why you are crying?"

I didn't know.

"Why do I have to choose?" I said. "Why is it either or? Why not both?"

"That is a choice too," he said. "But then you will have to become your own woman."

"Mama can't hear me," I said. "But you can."

"Your mama is in the waking world. And that is where you belong as well."

"I'd rather be with you."

And it was true when I said it. I was so tired. I was tired to death of being jerked this way and that, of being scared and in danger, of being alone.

"Dina, I am here only because you long for me."

"But…" But his voice sounded so real. His face, his eyes, the only eyes in the world as green as mine.

"There. You see?" said another voice, very close. "You do belong with us."

Azuan. Suddenly he was where my father had been a moment ago.

"No," I whispered. "I don't want to be the person you want me to be."

"Why limit yourself?" he said. "Why clip your own wings? When I see you here, it is so brilliantly clear. You have shackled yourself. You have broken and crippled your Shamer's powers, and you fear the serpent gift. Take a look at yourself!"

Suddenly there was a mirror where Azuan had stood. And in that mirror I saw…

A girl who wasn't human. A sad and broken statue almost strangled by the vines that covered it. Was that me?

"It is so easy," whispered Azuan's voice, "so easy to break free."

And suddenly, it was.

Not either or.

Both.

The green vinelike tentacles dropped away, like shackles opening. The statue blinked its eyes and came alive. A girl, not quite human in the way others were human, but still no monster. Just me.

"See?" said Azuan. "I knew you could do it. Now, let us get you home where you belong."

The Sting of a Wasp

The cabin was so small. Much smaller than it had been the first time I saw it. And Azuan, he, too, looked smaller somehow.

"Sleep," he said, picking up the blanket. "It has been a hard journey for you, I know that. But at least you may rest a little before we go home."

But I wasn't tired. My whole body was buzzing with… with *power*. And how could I sleep when there was so much to do? I turned to Azuan.

"I'm leaving now," I told him. "And I'm taking the horse. You can follow if you like, but I advise you not to."

He froze as he stood, blanket in hand, as if he meant to throw it over me.

"But you can't—" he began. And then he looked into my eyes. Shamer's gift and serpent gift. Truth and dream. The Ghost Country was inside me now and would always be, threads spun from longing and lives and true dreams. I was a mirror he could look into. He saw himself there, as he had been, as he was, and as he would become. I think he saw all the way to his own death.

He didn't say anything. An eerie moan broke free of him just before he collapsed.

"I don't belong to you and your House," I said. "I don't belong to anybody."

He didn't try to stop me.

"Please don't look at me" was all he whispered. "Please. Not again."

I didn't look at him. I found my father's flute in his pack and left him there. The flute and the horse. That was all I took as I went.

Mist inside and out. A dense cold fog hung among the trees, because the snow was melting. The branches were dripping, and every once in a while a soggy patch of snow slid off and hit the ground or my tired horse. Inside, too, I could still see them, the shining gray mists of the Ghost Country. But that was not all I saw. There were brilliant threads showing me my way through the grayness. My own threads were fewer than they had been. Fewer choices left, fewer destinies. But one of them shone more brilliant than the rest, running like a trail through the mist. I followed that trail, through the waking world as well as the other one. There was no road, no path at my feet other than that trail, and yet the mare followed it as if she could feel my intent without guidance from rein or leg.

My strength wouldn't hold out forever. But even when I began to shake, even when it became more and more difficult to stay on the horse, even then I could see it: the shining thread.

They told me later that I had ridden straight past dozens of guard posts, but nobody saw me. That I was just suddenly there, in the middle of the camp, on a horse so exhausted it could barely stand. They said I looked like a ghost and that at first no one dared approach me.

"Dina!"

I closed my eyes so that I wouldn't look at him by accident, because I knew he didn't like it, and I didn't want to hurt him.

But I felt his hand on my arm, guiding me, and let him help me down off the poor horse.

"Dina, what happened?"

But…

Even with my eyes closed I sensed that this was not as I expected. I had been so certain it was Nico's thread I had followed, with him waiting at the end of it. It wasn't. This surprised me so badly that I had to open my eyes.

Not Nico.

Tano.

Tano? But he didn't even like me! How could he be so close to me already, his thread twined with mine?

I couldn't make head or tail of it, and I was all out of strength. I closed my eyes again and pitched forward into the snow, like a falling tree.

Voices. Voices in the dark.

"… is dangerous. It's just not natural…"

"… telling you, she *shone*…"

I hadn't the strength to open my eyes. My eyelids felt sticky and heavy. I heard the fear in their voices. I didn't need to see it in their eyes as well.

"… Shamers are one thing, but *this*…"

"… look at her. Looks like a little girl. Just a regular little girl. But…"

"… oh no. Real people don't look like that…"

I could feel tear tracks hot on my cheeks. I didn't want them to be afraid of me. I just wanted—

"Go away! Leave her alone."

Who was that? It sounded like Tano.

"We were just looking—"

"Go look somewhere else, then. She's no carnival beast for you to gawp at."

It was Tano, right enough. Tano all up in arms and ready to protect someone. And this time, the one he meant to protect was me.

"Maybe not a beast. But she's hardly a real human being either, Tano!"

A small pause. Then Tano said, "Yes, she is." As if there was nothing more to be said in the matter.

"Dina? Dina, try to wake up."

This time, the voice was Nico's.

Slowly, I opened my eyes. Daylight sifted down through a cover of pine branches above my head, but it was a cold and unfriendly winter light. And I no longer felt strong and brimming with powers.

I needed to pee. I needed to pee so badly it was a wonder the need hadn't woken me up hours ago.

"How are you?"

"Fine," I said, unable to think of anything except my strained bladder. "Nico, I have to… wait a little."

I untangled myself from the blanket some kind soul had lent me and got to my feet in one stiff, groaning movement. Where could I go to…

There were people everywhere, or so it seemed to my agonized eyes. Archers practicing, arrow-makers, people practicing movements with long sticks meant to be swords. The camp was much bigger than I had imagined. And where did one go to pee in peace?

"Dina—" Nico put his hand on my arm.

260

"Back in a minute," I snapped, taking off at a run. Through the camp, into the woods, behind some shrubbery. Saints, what a relief.

Nico was waiting where I had left him, by the shelter that had apparently been my night lodgings.

"All better now?" he said with a crooked smile.

"Much better," I said. "Such a big camp!"

"Yes," he said, the smile vanishing as quickly as it had appeared. "The Weapons Master has gathered more people than I thought he could."

"Isn't that good?"

"I suppose so."

But he didn't sound very happy.

"He has been gone on some business, but he has just returned," said Nico. "And he wants to talk to us both."

"Can I have something to eat first? And a drink?"

He gave me his water bottle.

"Here. There's no time for breakfast, though. He is a busy man, and we had better not keep him waiting."

The Weapons Master was watching the archers with a critical eye.

"Tell number three from the right that he is clutching his weapon too tightly," he told the lean, sinewy figure by his side.

"I did," said the man. "About thirty times, just today. But no one has so deaf an ear as he who does not want to hear."

Rover! It was Rover, standing there looking all normal and untramplike. But there was a bit of rhyming left in him still, it seemed.

"Well met, Dina," he said. "We thought you had decided to play the bear and not wake until springtime."

Play the bear?

"How long did I sleep?" I asked Nico.

"A little over two days," he said. "So if you are hungry, it's no wonder."

No. And no wonder, either, that I had needed to pee.

Two days!

One of the archers was Carmian, I suddenly noticed. Her hair had been tamed and hidden under a tight scarf, so I hadn't recognized her right off. She sent an arrow whizzing toward the painted target, and it hit the bull's-eye, straight on.

After a last sharp look at the archers—especially number three from the right—the Weapons Master turned to us.

"Nicodemus," he said, making it a careful greeting. "Saint Magda be praised. I feared the worst when we heard that Drakan had moved into the Highlands."

Nico looked ill at ease. "I was on my way to somewhere else."

"He was heading for Dunark in order to kill Drakan," said Carmian sharply, lowering her bow. "Alone."

The Weapons Master looked at Nico. "Is that true?"

Nico shrugged. "More or less."

The Weapons Master looked around. "Have you gone stark raving mad, boy?" he said, his voice so carefully low that the archers couldn't hear him.

"It was the best solution I could think of," said Nico tiredly. "I'm not saying it was a brilliant plan."

The Weapons Master looked as if he could barely grasp the scope of Nico's foolhardiness. Or did he think it merely stupidity?

"If we thought an assassination were possible," he said slowly, "do you really think we would have hesitated?"

"I had an advantage," said Nico. "I would have come face-to-face with him in the end. Drakan would never have had me killed without being personally present. And I was going to have a hidden weapon. It would look as if I were bound and unarmed, even though I was neither."

The Weapons Master shook his head slowly.

"Holy Saint Magda," he said, very quietly. "Holy Saint Magda and all her Celestial Sisters. Boy, do you think Drakan's bodyguards are complete morons? Do you really think they wouldn't check? In your wildest dreams, had you imagined that would actually work?"

"I knew it was a risk—"

"A risk! It was madness!"

"But what else was I to do?" Nico's voice rose sharply, edged with despair. "What else was there? It was going on and on, people getting killed every day, and we knew… we knew it was just a matter of time before he attacked the Highlands. What was I to do? Put myself at the head of the line of people his army would slaughter anyway? I might as well do it myself, then."

"Nicodemus Ravens. Have you no concept of your own value?"

"Value? To whom, Weapons Master? For what? I cannot conduct a war. I cannot conceive a strategy that calculates that our left flank will be ground to pieces by his first wave of attack, whereupon our right flank will have the chance to attack from the rear. I cannot sacrifice people like that. I'm not even a very good swordsman!"

"You weren't that bad. Your heart just wasn't in it."

"No! Because I hated it! I still hate it. But if anybody is going to get killed in this war, it had damn well better be Drakan. Or me, so I won't have to see the rest of it!"

The Weapons Master seized Nico's arm.

"Watch your tongue, boy! Don't say such things when your men can hear you!"

"They are not my men," said Nico, but he did lower his voice. "They are yours."

"That's where you are wrong. They aren't here because of me. They are here because they want Drakan gone—and the House of Ravens back on the throne. And if you detest that plan so much, why are you here at all?"

Nico was silent for a while.

"Because I no longer have a choice," he finally said. "If Drakan takes the Highlands, what is left? We will never be rid of the Dragon then."

The Weapons Master nodded. "That is why we have come out of hiding," he said, waving a hand at the camp. "This big a camp, it will not be long before it is discovered. But the days when we could meet in somebody's barn are long gone."

Nico looked at the archers. Number three from the right sent his arrow so far wide of his target he nearly hit a different one.

"They're not ready," he said. "How many have had weapons training before? Half?"

"Barely that. And no, they are not ready. But, Nicodemus, we will always be too few, we will always be too badly armed. If we have to wait until we are 'ready', we might as well give up right away. And it is time. Don't you feel it? You said it yourself. If he takes the Highlands, we'll not be rid of him in my lifetime. Not that my lifetime is likely to be a long one in that case."

Nico kicked at the snow with one foot. "What if this is a war that will not be decided by weapons?" he said. "Or not only by weapons?"

"What do you mean?"

"Have you looked into Dina's eyes lately?"

The Weapons Master glanced at me without really meeting my eyes.

"I know Dina has her mother's powers. But how many people can she look in the eye at a time? No, Nicodemus. I prefer to have as many real weapons as I can lay my hands on."

"Dina has her gift back," said Nico. "You can sense that from half a mile away. But it's more than that. Isn't it, Dina?"

"I… I don't know," I said. "Azuan gave me something called dream powder and it did things to me. But, Nico, I hardly know myself what really happened."

"When you came riding into camp two nights ago, whatever it was, Dina, it was so strong that no one dared go near you. No one except Tano."

"Not you?" I burst out. "Were you afraid too?"

"Tano did it first," he said evasively.

I stared at him, or rather, at his chin, because I knew he would look away if I tried to catch his eyes.

"I'm no monster," I whispered.

"Of course you're not," he said. "But there is no running away from the fact that you are different."

Misery hit me like a club. Nico, who wanted to be neither hero nor monster. Nico who only wanted to be himself, how could he stand there and make it sound like I was some kind of alien creature?

Without another word, I turned and left.

"Now you've upset her," said Carmian, not exactly sounding as if that made her want to cry. "You really will have to learn that little girls have big emotions, Nico."

◆　◆　◆

I didn't know what to do with myself. Everyone else was so busy, but I couldn't really see the point of me trying to learn how to use a bow right now. And if I did get in line with the others, they would probably only run away. Like you would if a monster suddenly sidled up next to you.

Then I heard a familiar sound, that of a hammer pounding away at an anvil.

Rikert. He didn't meet my eyes either; he never had. But I had always been welcome in his house all the same. And I had not forgotten that the first thing he had done when he found me knocking on his door was to hug me.

But it wasn't Rikert doing the hammering. It was Tano. I stopped a little way off and stood watching him. He was so intent on what he was doing that he didn't notice me at first. His dark hair was sticking to his forehead, and he had taken off his shirt. Even during winter and out of doors, the work of a smith could make you sweat, it seemed.

Rikert saw me and came over.

"That boy will be a good smith one day," he said, quietly, as if he was afraid to disturb him.

"That's good," I said. "Are you training him?"

He nodded. "He has the knack, but it's more than that. He can see what isn't there yet. He will be one of those smiths who do things that have never been done before. And there aren't all that many of those."

I looked at Tano's bent back. It was scarred with marks from beatings and burns from sparks from the forge. He looked like someone who had never had an easy time of it but had just kept going anyway. The devil takes care of his own, people said, but I didn't think Tano belonged to the devil. What I didn't understand, though, was how his thread in the Ghost Country had come to be so closely twined with mine. I had hurt him so much already. But on the other hand, Drakan's thread ran close to mine too, and that was hardly because we were the best of friends. There were such things as close enemies.

Then Tano straightened, and I could see what he was working on. It was a shield, a shield with a black raven on it. He smiled at it, pleased with himself and his work, and the smile made his whole face light up.

"Is it done?" asked Rikert.

"Just one boss left to do," answered Tano. "Which is just as well, 'cause I hear we're leaving tomorrow."

"Really?" said Rikert. "Says who?"

Tano shrugged. "Everyone knows. Now that the Young Lord has arrived."

It was more than the Young Lord himself knew, I thought, but "everyone" might turn out to be right after all.

"Take a breather," said Rikert. "Get yourself something to eat. And take Dina with you; she has had neither food nor drink since she woke up."

Not apart from a few swallows from Nico's water bottle. But I didn't think Tano wanted to share his lunch with me.

"I can find my own—"

"Go with Tano, Dina. He'll show you where the food wagon is."

Tano dug up a few handfuls of snow and scrubbed his arms and chest with it.

"Dirty work," he said, looking almost shy. I nodded and thought that I had been right. He wasn't madly keen to be playing guide to the Shamer monster. And he had better reasons to avoid me than most people. Rikert meant well, I supposed. But good intentions were not enough.

"It's over there," said Tano, lacing up his shirt. "It'll probably be kale soup. It was kale soup yesterday and the day before that." He smiled crookedly. "Probably tomorrow as well, if we are still here. But at least the food is hot."

My stomach rumbled. "Anything," I said. "Anything as long as it is edible."

The snow was trampled by many feet, mostly human, but horse and goat tracks were visible as well. I slipped in the slush, and Tano had to seize my arm to keep me upright.

"Slippery here," he said. "Watch out."

I nodded, and felt myself blushing. Now he would think me clumsy as well. But perhaps I should be grateful that he had dared touch me at all and hadn't just let me drop.

He got us two bowls of kale soup from a little old woman stirring a kettle nearly bigger than she was. Some rough tables and benches were set up next to the food wagon, but most were occupied already, and I didn't really want to see people edge away from me, or leave the table because I had joined it.

"Is there somewhere else we can sit?" I asked.

"Over there?" he said, gesturing with one bowl. "On the log?"

"That looks fine."

We ate our soup in silence, and it tasted just fine, even though kale was certainly the chief ingredient. At least Tano hadn't moved away from me at the first opportunity. But then, I already knew that he did not scare easily.

"How did you end up with the Foxes?" I finally asked.

He shrugged. "Not a lot of other places for me to go," he said. "Not once I had escaped from Dracana. The Order of the Dragon takes a poor view of runaways."

I could imagine.

"Was it hard?" I asked. "Escaping?"

"Not easy. Particularly not since, well, there were two of us. And Imrik couldn't walk very well."

Imrik. The boy whose foot had been crushed in the weapons smithy of Dracana. That was what Tano had been most ashamed of—he had promised to look after Imrik, and Imrik had been hurt despite his care. But as with the girl—what was her name? Milena? No, Milona—as with her, I didn't think Tano ought to blame himself.

"How did you do it?"

"I carried him. For two days. Until we succeeded in stealing a donkey."

I looked at him sideways. I knew he was strong, and the man who had once sold them to Drakan had called Imrik a puny runt. But still… two days. He had to have been absolutely desperate.

"Where is he now—Imrik?"

"Life in the woods was hard on him. But he is good with his hands, very careful. Meticulous, like. He is helping the Widow with the medicines. Weighing stuff, and so on."

"But not here?"

Tano shook his head. "Right now they are in a village not far from here. But they won't be able to stay much longer. Not all the neighbors can be trusted."

"Are you two related?"

"No. But neither of us had anyone else."

"Why not?"

"In Hazelford—that's where we grew up—there was an illness. Some said it came from the animals, others that it was the water. But a lot of people died. Imrik's parents and his little sister. I had just my Ma. And then she died too."

So lonely. And as if that wasn't bad enough, the village had let the little peddler take the two boys. Although to be fair, they hadn't known he would sell them to Valdracu and Drakan.

"My papa is dead," I said.

"But you knew him."

"Yes. For a little while."

And apparently that was more than Tano could claim.

"If I ever have children," he said quietly but in an edged voice, "I'll never leave them. Never."

I thought about his faithfulness to Imrik.

"No," I said. "I don't think you will."

It had started snowing again. I put the bowl down and rubbed my chilled fingers. And then Tano did something that took me completely aback. Quietly, as if it was the most natural thing in the world, he took my hand between two of his.

I was utterly stunned.

"Do you *like* me?"

"I might. Is that so bad?"

"No. No, I… it's just… I thought you hated me."

"Only every once in a while."

I couldn't tell whether he meant that for a joke or not. The snow seemed to be falling more slowly around us than it had been a minute ago.

"Do you like me?" he asked. And he looked at me. Right into my eyes, though he knew the cost.

I think I sat there with my mouth open for quite a while. Then I nodded.

"Yes. I like you."

He put his head back and laughed out loud, his dark eyes sparkling.

"What are you laughing at?"

"I'm not laughing."

"Yes, you are."

He shook his head. But his eyes were still laughing. Or smiling anyway.

"Your hand is cold," he said. "It's a cold day."

And then he brought my hand up and blew on it gently, like you do to a child.

"I have to get back to the forge," he said. "I still have one boss left to do on that shield."

"Yes, I know you do."

I wanted to ask him what happened when he looked into my eyes. But I didn't dare. I could barely make myself look at him now. I was utterly confused. Did he like me, or didn't he? Why had he laughed like that? But he must like me a little. I mean, you don't blow on a girl's fingers if you really detest her. Do you?

Tano and "everyone" in the camp were right. The very next day we broke camp and headed into the Highlands, me and Nico, the Weapons Master, Carmian, Rikert and Tano, and a few hundred other people who had had enough of Drakan and his rule.

We were so ridiculously few, reckoned against the Dragon Force—hadn't Nico said something about eight thousand men? It was hard to imagine what we could do. Yet there was a strange mood of… expectation was perhaps putting it strongly, but still.

Some were singing as they walked. And everyone had the feeling that the long wait was at an end.

"They are out of their minds," said Nico. "If my plan was madness, what is this?"

"The sting of a wasp," said the Weapons Master. "But even a wasp may be lethal if you aim its sting at the right place."

A Foul Stench

The sun was down. Not just setting, not anymore. It was down. And still nothing had happened.

Cursing silently, I drew Ursa's cloak more closely around my shoulders. I should have made a break for it. Back then, when the guards were all busy with the wounded rider, I might have got away. Damn Ivain and his "something will happen."

Dragon blood was buzzing through my body. I no longer felt the cold or the pain from my ankle. But when I had cautiously tried it, it still wouldn't bear my weight. How on earth was I supposed to run away when running was impossible? Crawl really fast?

Wait. What was that? Something… something over there, by the stable. A crouched form darting through the doorway, on soundless feet. And then the stable gate opened. And clattering chaos broke out into the courtyard. A horse, no, two… no. More and more horses, ten, fifteen, even. They came trampling into the courtyard, white-eyed with panic. One of the guards at the gate called out, and I decided to steal a horse.

If I could.

The horses were careening around the yard, and the dragon didn't help matters when it suddenly heaved itself to its feet, hissing at them. Now, if only one would come… there. I caught the mane of a small yellow buckskin mare, leaped up with all the power of my one good leg, and flopped onto her back, belly down. That was as far as I got, as we went clattering wildly along, trailing my chain. And right then, there was a hollow roar. The castle gates blew open, and the terrified horses went charging through it, into the streets of Baur Laclan.

I finally managed to hoist my leg over the buckskin's back. We might be out of the castle but not out of the town. The horses thundered through the streets, and Dragon soldiers leaped aside to avoid being trampled. But there were more and more horses. And some had riders. All Laclan. And one of them was Ivain.

They ran the herd through the narrow streets and out of the town, and they didn't stop until we were far away, in the middle of the wilderness.

"Well, lad, you made it," said Ivain when we could finally rest a bit. "Well and good."

"Was that what you wanted?" I asked, dizzy and confused. "To rustle a herd of horses?"

"Och, no," said Ivain, as if I was being more than just a little slow. "That was just to entertain the Dragon-pack. The most important thing... well, it might be they have not discovered that just yet."

The most important thing?

"What is that, then?"

"Ah, some folks were in a bit of a squeeze. Arlain and a few others. Not right, that. So we had to get them out of it. And there are a few ins and outs to the castle that Drakan doesn't know about."

"You mean... did you get the children too? Because other-wise, it's no good at all!" I thought that Obain, at least, would march right back into captivity if Maeri was still hostage.

"That was the idea."

"All of them? You got all of them?"

"I do not have the second sight, lad, now do I? We will know when we meet up with the others."

We met the others shortly before dawn. The Laclans had succeeded in freeing all the children except three. And in the mountains, Helena Laclan waited in her hiding place, ready to receive them. Some of the fishermen chose to go with the children. Others—one of them Obain—joined Ivain's troop.

"The devil will not have an easy time of it up here," said Obain. "Just say the word. Anything to roast his tail."

"Drakan will move for Skayark," I told Ivain. "He thinks that is where Nico is."

"Aye, well," said Ivain. "And just how did that thought occur to His Lordship?"

"I told him."

Ivain looked at me for a while. "Skayark is a big mouthful even for a dragon," he said.

"That's what I thought."

A grim smile split Ivain's weather-beaten Laclan face. "Sometimes, lad. Sometimes ye make me think ye might have half a brain after all."

"Thank you," I said. "But it would be even better if Skayark had fair warning."

"Aye, ye're right." Ivain turned to the rest of the Laclan troop. "Crooklegs. Gevin. Ride hell for leather. Tell Astor Skaya that Drakan is coming. It might be it will take him a fair while, what with dragging along the dragon beastie. But he will come."

Two Laclan men turned their horses and set off as if Drakan himself was at their heels. Which he was, in a way. The rest of us followed at a more leisurely pace, though still too fast to suit my poor, battered body.

"What about us?" I said. "Where are we going?"

"Skayark, of course," said Ivain. "Did ye think I would make ye miss all the fun?"

It was hard riding even for men who were well and rested. For me, only one thing made it possible—Drakan's small bottle. I could not have stayed on my horse without it.

"What is that smell?" asked one of the Laclans riding near me. "Is that you, Obain? Did ye roll yerself in goat's dung or something?"

Obain repaid the insult with an even better one, and the others roared with laughter. But I knew the smell wasn't Obain's. It was mine. My whole body reeked with it—the stench of dragon blood.

It wasn't like the first time. I remembered it well, that rush of freedom and power. It was not like that now. Now I could just barely hang on if I took a small swig every other hour or so. My own revulsion at myself faded somewhat, as did the pain. There was a certain stillness in my head. That was all. I didn't know whether the difference was due to the fact that it was no longer the first time, or whether it was just that I drank as little as possible.

We rode through the night. At dawn, we took a short rest, but no longer than it took the animals to eat and drink a little. Then it was back into the saddle.

"Are ye coping, lad?" asked Ivain, who had noticed how hard it was for me to get back on the buckskin.

"Yes," I said, through my teeth. And I was. After another sip.

"What is that?" asked Obain curiously. "Ye're sucking at that thing like a lamb with a feeding bottle. How about a nip for a friend?"

"You wouldn't like it," I told him. "It's medicine. From my mother." I quickly tucked the bottle out of sight. He might think me an ungrateful lout and my refusal poor repayment for the borrowed socks, but that was nothing to the scorn I would earn if he knew what was really in the bottle. He didn't mention it again, and no one else was curious enough to ask.

Later in the morning, it started to snow. Huge fluffy flakes, crisp with frost. I put back my head and looked into the gray sky, watching the whirl and flurry. It was a dizzying sight, and I had to grab hold of the buckskin's mane to steady myself. The deepest of the claw marks tore open for the umpteenth time. There was a bitter taste in my mouth that was not due only to the dragon blood; it was the taste of fever. Wound fever. The arm was infected now, I knew, but there was nothing much I could do about it.

We passed the road that led to Baur Kensie, but didn't make the detour.

"Shouldn't we warn them?" I asked Ivain. "If Drakan is coming this way soon…" Mama and Melli. Maudi and all the others…

"They already know," he said. "Maudi Kensie has brought the clan into the mountains, weak and strong together. She knows Baur Kensie can't hold against a Dragon Force."

The clan—did that mean Mama too? Yes, it did. I was sure of it. She was as much a Kensie now as anyone could be whose great-grandparents had not worn Kensie cloaks and herded sheep with Maudi's forebears.

We were headed into the mountains ourselves now. The trail climbed and kept climbing, and the snow fell more and more strongly. There was snow around Skayark, lots of snow. On the highest peaks it did not disappear even in high summer. And though the Skayler Pass was no snow-clad peak, still it was quite high enough—a narrow passage between two giants: Eagle Peak to the north, and the Gray Widow to the south.

The mountains rose steeply on both sides of the trail. And ahead of us, Skayark's jagged walls came into view, and the banners flying from the battlements, blue and black with a golden eagle, visible even through the blizzard. The real eagles, of which there were quite a few up here, seemed to have stayed at home, waiting for the weather to improve.

I had been here before, more than once. I clearly recalled the sense of being a nut in a nutcracker. If Skayark closed her jaws on you, you did not get away unscathed. Perhaps not unbroken either. I reminded myself that we were on the same side in this war, and hoped that Astor Skaya saw it that way too.

"Who goes there?" called the guard at the gate.

"Men of Laclan," Ivain called back. "Clan peace, Skaya! Let us in, in the name of clan peace. We're freezing our jewels off out here."

"All right, all right," came the curt reply from above. "On our way. Yer errand boys have already warned us."

The gate opened, and we rode through it. The question was how long it would be before Drakan, too, came knocking at the door.

Too many people. That was what first struck me as we passed into the barbican. More people than I had ever seen here before.

Not just armed men, though there were quite a few of those. Also women and children and old people, and… baggage, I supposed was the word. Boxes, chests, sacks and baskets, even furniture. Every available space was crammed with it.

Ivain looked at it with disapproval.

"What a mess," he growled. "What if they use fire arrows? Astor Skaya should keep them on a shorter leash."

A boy of no more than two or three darted across the barbican, shrieking with laughter. On his heels came a slightly older girl.

"Gully! Gully, come here!"

She nearly collided with my horse, and the buckskin threw up its head in alarm. Again I had to clutch at the mane so as not to come off, and I knew that even with the dragon blood bottle, there was not a lot left in me anymore.

"Much too long a leash," sighed Ivain. "You there! Where do we put up the horses?"

Right then I caught a glimpse of a pair of familiarly fair braids. "Rose?"

It was her. She stopped and whirled, so that the basket of laundry she was carrying nearly tipped.

"Davin!"

A few paces, and she was right next to the buckskin.

"You look sick as a dog," she said. "What will happen once we get you off that wretched animal?"

"Not a lot," I admitted. "I'm not sure I can walk. But Callan. Is he… is he all right?"

"All right might be stretching it," she said. "But better. I think we will get there. Come on, Davin. Let me help you before you fall down yourself."

She put down the basket and took my arm. I let myself slide off the buckskin and took care to land on my good foot. Rose ducked under my arm and set her shoulder in my armpit to support me.

"Phew," she said. "You need a bath."

"I can't remember the last time I had one." How I wished that was all I needed. But a bath would only clear away part of the stench.

Then I put my bad foot down, and for a moment everything else ceased to matter.

"Davin. What is it?"

I couldn't answer. It took all my strength not to scream.

"That foot of his is in a bad way," said Ivain. "And there is something amiss with his arm as well. The lad is in poor shape altogether."

"Then why haven't you done anything about it?" said Rose angrily. "He can barely stand!"

"He is lucky not to be dragon food," said Ivain. "And we have not had the time to stop and admire the view. Obain, give the lass a hand. He is not featherlight anymore."

Obain swung down off his horse and supported me from the other side, and between them they managed to haul me off to what Rose called the sick bay.

The sick bay. Callan. Did that mean—

"Your mama is there too," said Rose. "Come on, Davin. It's only a few more steps."

I felt like taking a few more steps in the opposite direction. Or a few hundred steps, even. Mama. Here. Now. I was relieved to know she was safe, or as safe as anyone might be with the Dragon Force less than two days away. But the thought of facing her—

"Come on, lad," complained Obain. "Ye might do a little of the walking yerself."

After the hustle and bustle of the barbican, the sick bay was rather quiet and empty. Beds waited, but as yet there were not many sick or wounded to fill them. At the end of one row was Callan's bed. And by his side sat Mama, holding his hand.

I think she heard us coming. And I think she let me see her holding Callan's hand on purpose. But when she saw how they had to hold me up, she let go of him and got to her feet.

"Davin!"

"It's not that bad," I said, though I knew she would soon find out about the fever and the infected wound. "I just hurt my foot."

"And his arm," said Rose. "And he's sweating like a pig. Sorry, Davin, but you are." At least she didn't mention the smell.

"Put him there."

They got me to the bed opposite Callan's and let me sit on it. Mama stood at the foot of it, taking stock.

"You have a fever," she said.

"I suppose so."

"Rose, we need hot water. Cloths and bandages. And see if you can find some clothes. That shirt is fit only for the middens. What hurts the most?"

I was almost grateful to be injured, right then. It meant we didn't have to talk about Dina and Nico and Callan right away. I knew it was just a temporary stay of execution, but any respite was welcome right then.

"There is something wrong with my ankle," I said. "And I have a... a cut on my arm that might be infected." I didn't say what had cut me.

She nodded. "Let's have a look."

She picked the remains of Obain's sock off my foot. Rose couldn't hold back a gasp, which was perhaps not surprising. The foot was so swollen it hardly even looked like a foot, and the skin was shiny and bluish black all over.

"What on earth did you do to it?" asked Mama.

"They chained me," I said. "And then a dragon started to play catch with me."

"Honestly, Davin," said Rose in a this-is-not-funny tone of voice.

"If you don't believe me, ask Drakan," I said sourly. "He was rooting for the dragon."

"Well, at least it explains the stench," said Mama.

"Is this how dragons smell?" asked Rose.

"More or less," said Mama. She had begun to press on the ankle, examining it, and I had to clench my teeth, or I would have yelled.

"But it's out of joint!" she said. "How long has it been like this?"

I had to think. Time had gone a little vague on me.

"Four days. Just about."

"It won't be easy, then." She raised her voice. "Allin!"

Mama and Rose were about the only people I knew who called Black-Arse by his real name. And saints, was I happy to see his freckled grin as he came trotting into the sick bay.

"Davin," he said. "Did ye come in with the Laclans?" And then, not waiting for an answer: "Phew! You do stink!"

"Thanks," I said. "You're not exactly squeaky clean yourself, you know." He had a black sooty streak across one cheek, and his hands looked as if he had greased them with goose fat and rubbed them with ashes, the way royalty did in the fairy tales when they wanted to pass for beggars.

He grinned. "Master Maunus and me are working on something," he said. "Just ye wait. It'll knock yer socks off."

Somehow that sounded ominous, coming from Black-Arse. He had not got his nickname for nothing.

Mama gave his hands a disapproving glance. "Try not to touch anything in here," she said. "Allin, I need a strong man."

Black-Arse straightened proudly. "At yer service!" He saluted her boldly, giving himself another black streak in the process, this time on his forehead.

I saw Mama suppress a smile.

"Someone a *little* stronger, Allin," she said. "Who do we know?"

Black-Arse shrank back to his normal size, like a punctured pig's bladder. He threw Rose a quick look, and I knew it was to see whether she was laughing at him. Black-Arse had a weakness for Rose, and it wasn't just because she was a mean cook. Although that was by no means unimportant, if you were Black-Arse.

"Killian is not so bad," he said. "Callan is stronger, but—" He glanced at Callan's bed. Callan had his eyes closed, and I think he was asleep.

"Get Killian, then," said Mama. "And Allin…"

"Aye?"

"Wash your hands before you come back in here, won't you? Cleanliness is important in a sick bay."

"Aye, sure," he said, and was off again. I envied him his two good legs and his ability to run.

A little later Killian Kensie came in. Black-Arse may have warned him. At any rate, his hands and face were a good deal cleaner than usual.

"Black-Arse said ye needed a hand?"

Mama nodded. "Davin's ankle is dislocated. I need someone who can pull it back into joint, and I'm not strong enough myself."

Ouch. And ouch again. That sounded dreadful.

"Are you sure?" I said, even though I knew it was stupid. "What if it's only a sprain?"

"Davin. It is clean out of joint. And if you ever want to walk on it again, we need Killian to put it back."

Oh, for a swig of the dragon blood bottle. A large one. But I couldn't bring out the bottle now without revealing that I had it. And I couldn't stand the thought of Mama and Rose discovering what was in it. Better to be racked and broken by Killian's big hands.

And that was about what it felt like. I am not proud of it. I screamed like a girl. I screamed so loudly that I woke Callan up. But in the end I felt how the joint went back to where it should be. You could even hear it. And right away, so quickly it felt as if someone had waved a magic wand over it, the pain lessened enormously. It was still very tender, yes. But the wrongness and the I-can-hardly-stand-it pain went away.

"It almost doesn't hurt now," I said, amazed at the difference.

"No," said Mama. "Do you still think it was just a sprain?"

Compared to that, the cleaning and bandaging of the claw marks were easy as pie. I even managed to push the bottle under my pillow before they helped me out of what was left of my shirt. But the fever was still there, of course, and they had to help me wash. Very strange. Like being a child again. It was one thing with Mama, but Rose… I didn't like her to see me so weak and pitiful. Mama made me drink two different kinds of tea, one with willow in it, the other some concoction of various herbs which all seemed to be competing for the ghastliest taste. Once all this was done, she went back to Callan's bed.

"Will the lad be all right?" asked Callan.

"Yes," she said. "If he does as I tell him." The last bit was clearly meant for me to hear.

"Good," said Callan. "Because when he and I can both stand on our own two feet again, that boy is getting such a clip to the ear that he'll think he can fly."

I slept for most of the day. But the dreams wouldn't quite leave me alone. Once I woke myself up, yelling so loudly that the sick bay was still ringing with it when I opened my eyes. Callan was watching me from his bed, but he didn't say anything.

Rose, on the other hand…

Rose was sitting beside my bed, looking pale and anxious.

"You're really sick, aren't you?" she said.

I probably was. I was cold all the time, even though there was a great big brazier right next to my bed.

"It'll pass," I said. "Once the fever drops."

"Yes," she said. And then the words suddenly burst from her, as if she had been holding them back for a long time: "I know I'm always nagging you."

Where did that come from?

"It's… I suppose I'm used to it by now." More or less, anyway. Sometimes when she snapped at you, there was a real sting to it, and I didn't enjoy that.

She nodded, as if I had said something important. I didn't know what. Nico had once told me that there were great big books for when you were learning a foreign language. Books full of foreign words. Dictionaries, I think they were called. I wish someone would make up something like that on girl language, because most of the time I understood barely half of it.

"You know, you still stink a bit," she said. But she took my hand all the same.

A Big White Death

Four days later, Drakan came to Skayark with his army. And his dragon.

There were so many soldiers that they filled the entire pass, from mountainside to mountainside. Even if he tried, he couldn't attack with all of them at once. There wasn't room.

I stood on top of the outer wall and watched them as they came. Getting up the steps had not been easy, but more because of the weakness of the fever than because of the ankle. My foot was much better already.

They stopped while they were still so far away that they looked like one being, a snaking people-beast, black against the snow. But one thing was visible even at this distance: the long, pale gray body of the dragon.

"What does he want with that monster?" Astor Skaya seemed to be asking his question of the air. He did not really expect anyone here to answer him. "What good is it? It has delayed him two days already. Does he think we will take fear at the sight of it and run away?" He spat into the snow at the foot of the wall. "It's just a beastie. A big one, I grant ye, but still just a beast."

I knew one reason, at least, why Drakan had dragged a living dragon all the way from Dunark into the Highlands. But I wasn't going to shoot off my mouth about it. And before the day was over, all Skayark knew another reason.

It began when Drakan sent a messenger out ahead of his lines. The messenger approached the walls. And he wasn't alone. In front of him marched a troop of...

Very small soldiers?

No. Even though everything looked smaller from up high, there was still no doubt.

"But they are children!" said the archer next to me. "Children with weapons. Do they expect us to fight children, now?"

"Ye cannot," said my neighbor on the other side. "Ye cannot shoot at children!"

"That is what he is counting on," I said.

It was true. They had weapons, the little soldiers down there, though they were hardly more than ten or eleven. Bows. Crossbows. Spears reaching much too far above their heads. A grown soldier with a full-length sword could mow them down like a farmer harvests his corn. If he could make himself do it, of course.

Soon, they were close enough for us to see their faces. Most were boys, but there were a few girls as well. And there was something icily familiar about the short-cropped hair and the serious faces. They looked just like the children from the House of Teaching. Exactly like them.

"How does he make them do it?" asked my neighbor. "They have no chance against a grown fighter."

How? I knew how. Drakan might not have a Hall of the Whisperers. But I was pretty certain he had Educators somewhere in his Dragon Force. Terrifyingly clever Educators. And when you take children away from their parents...

"What else can they do?" I said bitterly. "Look at them. What can they do except obey the adults who feed them and clothe them and tell them what to do?"

"Skayark!" shouted the messenger, a Dragon knight I recognized, called Voris.

"What do ye want?" answered Astor Skaya. "Ride back to yer Dragon Lord and tell him he is not welcome on Skaya lands!"

"My Prince, the Dragon Lord of Dunark, Solark, Eidin, and Arkmeira—and of Baur Laclan too. Baur Laclan too, sir! My Prince the Dragon Lord has a message for you. He has brought a dragon."

"So we have noticed!" called back Astor Skaya. "Though what he wants with that big dumb beastie is more than I can fathom."

"The dragon is hungry," continued Knight Voris, disregarding the interruption. "Every day it will eat a child."

"What?"

"Every day until Skayark surrenders. And it will not be one of these good children—the faithful, fine children of the Dragon—but a Highland brat. We have enough of them."

He turned his horse and rode back to the Dragon Force, his small soldiers trotting behind in close formation.

"Do ye want us to shoot him in the back?" asked one of the archers on the wall.

"No," said Astor Skaya. "At this distance, ye might hit one of the children."

"Is it true?" asked my neighbor. "Does the devil have Highland children he can… he can use to feed that monster with?"

"He has some, at least," I said, thinking of the three we had not managed to rescue from Baur Laclan. And there were probably others. Not necessarily all of Highland stock, but children were children, wherever they came from.

"The man is mad!"

I wasn't sure I agreed. Sick, yes. But he knew what he was doing. Every time he had taken a city, every time he had used whatever means he had thought most effective, no matter how cruel and revolting others found it. At Solark, poison in the water. And at Arkmeira, *One, two, three, four, you die.* A fifth of the men in the city. And now he had decided that the way through Skayark's impregnable defenses lay… what should I call it? In our minds or our hearts. How many children could we watch die? And it wasn't just the children that the dragon might eat. What if he really sent his army of child soldiers against us? Then we, too, would become the murderers of children. How long could one stand that and still have the heart to go on fighting?

I knew well enough what Nico would have said. Not one. Not a single child should we allow to die. But how were we to prevent it?

"Can we free them?" I said. "The children."

"We must try," said my neighbor. "But look at it. Look at that army. We haven't a hope."

I cursed, slowly and thoroughly. Then I made for the stairs, limping painfully.

"Where are ye going, lad?"

"To see someone I know."

I found Black-Arse exactly where I expected to find him, in the corner of the castle smithy that Master Maunus had invaded and made into his workshop. The two of them had their heads together, bent over the contents of a clay jar.

"It might be ye need more nitrate," said Black-Arse.

"Not on your life, young man. You're not the one we're trying to kill."

"But it has to work quickly—"

"It will work, never fear. The question is, though, how do we get it up there? Oh, hello, Davin. Up and about again?"

"What are the two of you up to?" I asked.

Black-Arse grinned. "A bit of a *boom*," he said.

"Something big enough to kill a dragon?"

Black-Arse raised both ginger eyebrows. "Dragons?" he said. "Has he brought dragons?"

"One. But one is enough. Well? Will it kill a dragon?"

"I should think so," said Master Maunus. "If we can place it right."

Black-Arse looked dreamy. "Imagine us being able to say we killed off a real dragon," he said. "Now, that would be something, would it not?"

"It would," I said. "And especially this one. So come on. Tell me how to do it."

Master Maunus cleared his throat. "Listen, young Davin. What do you think your mother would say to this?"

"I have no idea," I said curtly. "I'm not going to ask her."

We were waiting for the darkness. The Dragon Force was still out there, within sight of the walls but out of range of our arrows. The dragon was at the front, lit by several big fires that were probably necessary to keep it warm and moving.

Master Maunus had promised not to tell Mama about our little outing. I think the clincher was his own eagerness to see if this would really work. And it would not be entirely easy to find two other volunteers for the task Black-Arse and I were about to undertake.

"Are ye sure yer foot is up to it?" asked Black-Arse. "And the rest of ye? Ye were sick as a dog only days ago."

"Of course I'm sure. Or I wouldn't do it."

He looked at me. "Aye. Ye would. Ye've never known when to quit."

"I'm fine, I tell you."

He shrugged. "If ye say so. But if ye drop in yer tracks out there, do not count on me to drag ye back."

I got up.

"Where are ye going?"

"I forgot my knife."

"Hurry, then. It will be dark enough, soon."

I limped across the barbican to the sick bay. In there, it was dark and quiet, and I could hear Callan's breathing. Slow and easy. Hopefully, that meant he was sleeping. I sneaked up to the bed I still slept in, when I slept at all, of course. I wouldn't be getting much rest tonight.

I put my hand under the pillow. Then I lifted the whole thing. Then I shook out the blanket, and finally the mattress. All in vain.

"Is this what you're looking for?" asked Rose.

Startled, I spun on my heel. There she was, in the corner beside Callan's bed. And in her hand she held my bottle of dragon blood.

"Give it to me," I said.

"It stinks of dragon," she said. "What is it?"

"Nothing. Just give it to me."

"I don't think so. Because whatever it is, I don't think it's good for you."

I threw the blanket and pillow back onto the bed. Why did she have to be such a busybody? But I took care to sound calm and relaxed.

"Come on, Rose. It's nothing to get all worked up about."

"Davin, I want to know what it is."

"Just something I got from one of the Laclans. You know. Helps you keep warm."

But she shook her head. "You're lying. And you know what, Davin? You're a piss-poor liar. It shows from a mile away."

I hardly listened. I was almost within reach now. One more step… I flung myself forward, seizing her wrist. The bottle flew out of her grasp and rolled along the floor, so that I had to drop to my belly to catch it before it rolled under Callan's bed. It hurt like hell because the claw marks weren't quite healed yet, but that didn't really matter now. I had the bottle.

"What is it, lad?" muttered Callan sleepily. "Cannot the two of ye find a better place to fight?"

Rose straightened to her full height. "That won't be necessary," she said. "I'm all done fighting him. As far as I am concerned, he can go to hell in whatever way he pleases." And then she walked out on us.

I stood there in the gloom, hiding my little bottle in one hand. A moment ago, all I wanted was for her to leave me alone. But now that I had my wish, it felt all wrong.

"What did ye do, boy?" asked Callan.

"Nothing."

"Oh aye. And ye expect me to believe that?"

"You heard her. We're done fighting."

Callan made a growling sound in his throat.

"Listen, lad. The two of ye fighting, that is all in a day's work. It's when ye do *not* fight that I start to worry."

I unstoppered the bottle in the shadow of the doorway before going back outside. There wasn't a lot left. I drank all of it and tossed the bottle on to the middens. And it was then it really struck me: If Black-Arse and I succeeded, then the dragon would soon be dead. And then there would be no more dragon blood available this side of Skayler's Edge.

It actually made me hesitate. And then I was ashamed of my hesitation. Because if we didn't kill that dragon very soon, Drakan would start feeding it on children.

Shame. There hadn't been enough left in the bottle to rid me of it. And that was probably a good thing.

"Here," said Black-Arse, passing me a white sheet.

"What do I want that for?"

"For when we reach the snow," said Black-Arse. "So we will be less easy to see."

He had a point. I rolled up the sheet and put it inside my shirt. If I put it on now, it would merely make me look like a pale ghost against the blackness of the castle walls.

Of course, there were men on the walls. Guards and the like. But they all knew Black-Arse and me by now, and no one tried to stop us. It wasn't until we started climbing off the wall and up the mountainside that we were hailed and called on to stop.

"Halloo, there. Where do ye think ye're going?"

"We have a little present for Drakan and his dragon," said Black-Arse. "But do not tell anyone. We want it to be a surprise."

"The dragon? Lads, ye do not want to go anywhere near that beastie. The Dragon Lord is sure to have set a guard."

"Don't worry," I said. "We'll keep our distance."

And so we would. You would have to be part mountain goat anyway to climb into the pass from up here. Climbing back up would be impossible. Traversing the mountainside, the way we were doing it, wasn't exactly easy. There were trails here and there, mostly made by animals, and it was possible to walk upright if one was careful. In other places we would have to cling like limpets and use both hands and feet. Black-Arse had packed our dragon present in a rucksack, which we took turns carrying, leaving our hands free, but even so it was no picnic. Try as I might, though, I couldn't keep from grinning.

"What are ye laughing at?" asked Black-Arse at some point. "It is not that funny."

"You don't think so? Aren't you looking forward to... to seeing the dragon's face when our present goes boom?"

Black-Arse couldn't help grinning too. "Aye. That I am. But you. Ye're usually more serious."

"Not tonight."

"No. I can see that."

And so we pushed on through the snow, with the white sheets tied on like cloaks so that Drakan's guards should not catch sight of us. I had no wish to test the range of their crossbows. The cold nipped at our hands and feet, and the breath rose from my mouth like a pillar of steam. But inside, I was warm and happy. It was such a good feeling to be with Black-Arse, my best friend, on a mountainside in the middle of the night—or at least after dark—and to know that this silence would soon be broken by a colossal *boom*. I felt almost like—

Like the night I had ridden with the Dragon knights, thinking I could fly.

Not a nice thought.

But...

But this was different. We weren't going to set fire to anybody's thatch. I wouldn't be shouting "Death to the enemies of the Dragon" tonight. Death to the Dragon, more like.

"Are we there yet?" I asked.

Black-Arse measured the distance with his eyes. "Just about, I think. Master Maunus said…" He looked around, then pointed. "There. Just below the rock that looks a bit like a hare."

I looked up. It didn't look very much like a hare in my eyes, but I knew which rock he meant.

I looked down into the pass. The dragon lay coiled by the fire, almost directly below us. Around it, there were guards, perhaps even Dragon knights. I couldn't tell from this distance, but I could always hope.

"Here," said Black-Arse. "Hold this, will ye?"

He passed me the rucksack, and I took it—with my bad arm, unthinkingly, because right now it didn't hurt. But that arm was not as strong as the other, and the leather straps of the rucksack were slippery with Black-Arse's sweat. I dropped it.

"No!"

Black-Arse moaned as if I had dropped a living baby. But it had not fallen very far. A little farther down, in the snow on a rocky outcrop.

"I'll get it," I said.

"No," protested Black-Arse. "Ye aren't—"

But I had already leaped. I skidded sideways and down, slid on my butt for a little while, and landed as I intended, on the outcrop, right next to the rucksack.

"Davin!"

Black-Arse peeked at me from above, pale behind the freckles. "Are ye mad?" he hissed. "What if ye had missed it?"

I grinned at him. "But I didn't, did I?"

"Pass me the rucksack."

I tried to do as he said, but it was too far.

"That's all right," I said. "I'll just put it on."

"Oh, aye," said Black-Arse. "And now for the hard part. How are ye going to get back up here?"

"Could you lower your shirt, or something? Don't worry, you don't have to haul me up, I just need a bit of support."

He tried. But his shirt wasn't long enough.

"It'll have to be your trousers, then."

"Davin, if ye think I am going to stand here with my rump showing just because you—"

"Black-Arse. Just do it. We have a dragon to kill, all right?"

He sighed. But in the end it took both his trousers and the white sheet, knotted together, to give me the purchase I needed.

"Never do that again!" Black-Arse told me once I was finally back on the same bit of rock with him.

I held out his leather trousers. And grinned into the darkness.

"What now? What are ye laughing at now?"

"You. I don't know. Maybe we got your name wrong. Maybe we should really call you Bare-Arse."

For a moment, he looked as if he wanted to push me back over the edge again. But then he started laughing too. We sat there on the mountainside and laughed till our stomachs hurt. That's the brilliant thing about Black-Arse. At heart, he is crazier than I am.

Finally we pulled ourselves together and climbed the last bit of the way to the hare rock. Black-Arse carefully lifted two clay jars out of the rucksack. They didn't look very big, I thought.

"Are you sure this will be enough?" I asked.

"Master Maunus says so. And he is good at calculating things like that on paper."

Quite possibly. But we needed it to work in real life too.

Black-Arse brought out some metal spikes, a small hammer, and a coil of rope. Carefully he hammered the spikes into the rock and tied the jars firmly in place. Then he uncoiled the fuse from the jars. It was quite long and smelled as if it had been coated with tar or something.

"Ready?" he said.

"Yes."

I fished out the tinderbox I had carried in my belt. At the second attempt, I succeeded in striking a spark and making it catch. The small flame eagerly ate at the fuse, working its way toward the jars.

"Off ye go," said Black-Arse. "No time to hang about."

We ran and climbed as fast as we could, until we were a fair distance from the hare rock. Then we waited.

"How long?" I asked.

"Any second," said Black-Arse breathlessly. "Shut up now!" As if I was spoiling something by talking. Perhaps he was listening to the slight sizzle of the burning fuse.

Then something dawned on me.

"Black-Arse?"

He sighed. "Yes?"

"If the rope was in the rucksack all the time, why didn't we use that instead of your trousers?"

He looked at me, open-mouthed.

"The rope in the pack." He started laughing. "I forgot about it!"

And right then there was a sharp crack from the jars. It was nowhere near as loud as I had expected, and I was a little disappointed. Was that all?

Then there was a creaking sound. Then a huge and hollow boom. And then the rock trembled beneath us, as a whole mountainside's load of snow tore loose and tumbled down toward the pass.

"Holy Saint Magda," I whispered. "Look. Black-Arse, look!"

It was like a floodtide, a huge wave of white and gray, of snow and dirt and rock, roaring down, falling so quickly that the little people at the bottom of the pass had no time to run. Nor did the dragon. It raised its head and opened its jaws, and I think it probably hissed. But then the snowslide hit it, and the monster down there was devoured by another monster, a huge white death many, many times bigger than any dragon.

"Was that you?" said the guards on the wall as we returned.

"Was that you, lads?"

"Aye. That it was," said Black-Arse proudly. "And let me tell ye, that dragon looked *quite* surprised."

I didn't say anything. My ankle had begun to hurt again, and the arm was smarting too. And there wasn't a thing I could do about it, because I was all out of dragon's blood.

"The whole pass is full of snow," said one of the guards. "But is it too much to hope that ye got all of them?"

I shook my head. "At the most a few hundred. But the dragon is dead, so he can't use that threat anymore. And they must clear a passage through the snowslide before they can do anything else. We have gained time, at least."

"Aye," said the guard. "That we have. Two days. Might be three, even. Nice work, lads."

But in the middle of that brief triumph was the nagging worry that they must surely be feeling too. Two days, maybe three. And what then?

The fever came back. I lay in the sick bay, trembling with it, heaving with nightmares, and sometimes I heard Drakan's voice as if he was standing right next to the bed. *If he drinks it himself, he is mine.* And at other times I couldn't help thinking, Does he have a supply of dragon's blood out there, does he have just one more small bottle? And then I was about ready to march right out of Skayark and sneak down to the Dragon camp to steal it from him. Once I got as far as the sick bay door before Rose and Mama stopped me. And all the time the voices were whispering, louder than ever.

… your name is murderer…

… how many dead now…

And I heard myself telling the guards on the wall: *At the most a few hundred.*

The snow ate them. The white death devoured them like it devoured the dragon. And they might not all have been Dragon knights. Maybe there were men who had been forced to serve in the same way as the Arlain fishermen. People who had families somewhere, children and mothers and wives who missed them. The white death we had roused did not distinguish between good and evil and everything in between. It ate everyone. I couldn't even be sure there were no children among the dead.

Maybe I'm not suited to war after all, I thought in a brief, clear moment between attacks. No more than Nico is. And after a while another thought struck: What if no one really is? But what do you do when war still comes?

The fever wouldn't go down. Mama fed me willow bark tea by the barrel. She and Rose packed snow into pillowcases and tucked them around me, but nothing helped. I burned. I trembled. I sweated so much they had to change the sheets every other hour.

That night—or was it the next? Time had become slippery, impossible to track. But it was night, that much I was sure of, and Mama was standing at the foot of my bed.

"Look at me, Davin."

She wasn't using her Shamer's voice, but I still couldn't deny her.

"Was it dragon blood?"

Then I knew that Rose had been telling tales. I didn't say anything, but she read the answer in my eyes.

I closed them, knowing I deserved the contempt she was sure to feel for me right then.

I think it happened a few hours later. I was dozing when I suddenly heard my mother's voice:

"Dina?"

I opened my eyes. The sick bay looked normal. My bed, Callan's bed, and the chair Mama had placed more or less halfway between them. But no trace of my little sister.

Mama had risen. She was staring into empty air, but I couldn't tell what she was looking at.

"Where are you?" she said. And it wasn't me or Callan she was talking to. Her eyes flicked this way and that, searching, and there was something about the way she *didn't* see me that made chills run down my back.

"What do you want me to do?" she asked.

Callan had his blanket off and was halfway out of his bed.

"Melussina?" he said. "Melussina, what is happening?"

But Mama didn't hear him.

"I don't know if I can," she whispered, looking around her uncertainly. "I can't see you."

Callan hauled himself to his feet and took her arm.

"I'm right here," he said. But I think he knew that she wasn't talking to him. He glanced at me.

"Lad? Can you fetch us Rose?"

"I can try."

But before I had time to find out whether my legs would carry me or not, there was a brief gasp from my mother.

"Dina! Of course I do!"

And then she closed her eyes. And a moment later she dropped where she stood.

And no matter how much we called, she would not answer, nor wake again.

True Dreams

It takes time to get anywhere when you are an army, even though it is a very small army. The snow made the going difficult for people and animals, and the closer we got to the Highlands, the deeper it became.

"How long is it till midwinter?" I asked Nico on the second morning, while we were struggling with our packs. With frozen fingers and buckles and straps made difficult by the cold, packing up was a bit of a battle in itself.

He had to think. "Twenty days, I think. No wait, twenty-one."

I nodded gloomily and looked up at the charcoal sky. "That's what I thought."

"Why do you ask?" said Tano.

"Oh, nothing. Just wondering."

But Nico had caught it, quick as he was with things like that.

"It's your birthday today," he said. "Isn't it?"

I sighed. "Yes."

"You are thirteen years old today." Nico shook his head. "I'm sorry, Dina. It had completely slipped my mind."

"It doesn't matter. There are a few things around here that are slightly more important."

Tano looked surprised. "Thirteen? I thought you were older."

"Why? I mean, I look small." And square and trollish and…
not very womanly.

"You seem older. The way you act. The things you say."

Was that good or bad? Mostly good, probably.

Nico had begun to undo the pack he had just succeeded in
closing. He rummaged around in there and brought out a small
leather purse.

"Here," he said. "I don't know if it fits, but, well, happy birthday, anyway. And may you celebrate it in better circumstances
next year."

It was a ring. A ring with his family seal on it, the raven.

"It was my brother's," he said. "It passed to me when he died,
but I've never really worn it."

Nico's older brother had been killed in a bandit ambush
several years ago. The older brother who had been his father's
heir, the older brother who had been good at all the things
Nico hated, swords and fighting and competitions. Was that
why Nico hadn't worn the ring? But it was silver and really very
nice, even if it was a bit too big, having been made to fit a man's
hand and not a girl's.

"I'll have to wear it round my neck," I said. "Or I'll lose it."
I untied the leather thong that held my Shamer's signet and
threaded it through the ring. Then the signal to move off came
down from the front, and I had to hurry with the last stubborn
buckles before I could get back on Azuan's brown mare.

The snow kept coming. It was hard to see where we were going,
particularly for the riders in front. The rest of us could just hunch
down and follow. The trail rose more steeply with every mile.
This was the proper Highlands now.

"Who is the damn fool who decided to have a winter war?" growled one of the archers. "You can barely string a bow without ruining it."

The winter war was Drakan's idea. But of course the archer knew that.

Suddenly there was shouting and commotion at the head of the file, and then the sound of sword against sword.

"Arms!" shouted someone, while others just yelled their heads off.

What was happening? Was it Drakan? But we were nowhere near Baur Laclan…

Then I heard the voice of the Weapons Master rise above the clamor.

"Hold! Put up your swords! These are not enemies. Hold, I said!"

Not enemies? I set my heels to the brown mare, and she leaped forward, already excited at the noise.

"Please let me past," I called, and then, when that did no good, "Make way. *Step aside!*"

That did it. People leaped aside as if they were fleeing a mad dog. But at least it got me through to the head of the column, so that I could see what was going on.

The Weapons Master was standing between two lots of men, all of them scowling fiercely at one another. One man on our side had a wounded arm, I could see; the blood ran down his arm and dripped into the snow. But at least no one was fighting at the moment. These were not Drakan's men at all. They were Highlanders, in Laclan cloaks.

"Laclan," I said, searching their faces for one I knew, "we're not your enemies. Quite the opposite."

"That is easy to say," said a man who seemed far too ancient to wield a sword. "Ye look like enemies to me. Ye look like an army, so ye do."

"But we are not Drakan's army," I said. "You might even know me? Dina Tonerre, who lives with the Kensies? Helena Laclan knows me."

There was a muttering among the Laclans.

"Aye," one of them admitted. "We know you. The Shamer's lass. But what about the rest of ye?"

"We've come to help," I said. And then, although I knew it sounded foolish with an army of only a few hundred people: "We've come to beat Drakan."

The old man barked with laughter. "With that lot?" he said. "Do ye know how many men he has?"

"Yes," said Nico, who had reached the head of the line too, now. "He left with eight thousand. I don't know how many are left."

"Fewer than when he came," said one of the Laclan men with grim satisfaction.

"So Laclan has not surrendered?" I said.

The old man looked offended.

"I thought ye said ye knew us."

It was the Laclans who told us that Drakan had gone from Baur Laclan and had left only what he thought was enough men to hold the castle.

"And he is wrong about that, I think," said the old man. "Another couple of days, and they'll be ripe for picking. But Helena says we must not take back the castle while Drakan is still in the Highlands."

Nico looked thoughtful. "That is wise," he said. "Let them do the taking and the holding. We are too few for that."

"That is what Helena says," growled the old man. "But it is hard on the little ones and the sick and the old, hiding in the mountains at this time of year. We cannot go on forever."

"Perhaps that is why he made it a winter war," said Nico. "In the summer, this would be much easier for you."

"Where has he gone, then?" I asked, my heart cold with fear.

"Skayark," said the old man. "He is laying siege to Skayark. But that is not a nut he will easily crack."

Nico looked less convinced. "Drakan does not wage his war like other people would," he said. "If there is a way to bring Skayark to fall, he will find it. Poison, treachery, hostages, anything. He will do whatever it takes to win."

The Weapons Master frowned. "That is true," he said. "I suppose we must head for Skayark, then. To see if we can find a crack in his armor and a place to aim our sting."

It took us another two days to reach the Skayler Pass. And the sight that met us there was enough to discourage even the fiercest wasp.

From mountainside to mountainside, like a river that had flooded its banks. Men. Thousands of men. And most of them with swords from the smithies of Dracana.

"We are not an army," said Nico softly. "We are just a bunch of people. This… this is what a real army looks like." And then he suddenly stiffened. "What is that?"

"That" was a row of children, children in black Dragon uniforms. And they were training, some with swords, others with crossbows and spears.

"It looks like children," I said. "With weapons."

"Will he... will he use them?" Even though Nico was the one who had said that Drakan would do whatever it took, there was now disbelief in his voice. "He will use *children* to fight his war?"

"Probably he will," I said, because I didn't think Drakan would waste clothes and weapons and training on anyone he didn't mean to use.

We had both been flat on our stomachs in the snow behind an outcrop of rock. Now he stood up, seeming not to care who saw him.

"That does it," he said in a strangely absentminded tone of voice. "I have had enough of this." And he started walking toward the Dragon Force.

"Nico!" I ran after him. "Nico, stop!"

"He is the one who has to be stopped."

"But, Nico, no. They'll just kill you."

"Not without letting me see him. Not without letting me near."

"And then what will you do? Bite him? Because you don't really expect them to let you keep a weapon, do you?"

He didn't seem to hear me. He tore his arm from my grasp and continued.

"Nico. Nico, damn it! I'll do it. Stop, please! I'll do it for you."

"You can't. What you can do doesn't work on him."

"But it works on everybody else!"

A couple more steps and not even the blindest Dragon man could miss us. It was a wonder we had not already been spotted.

"If you go down there, so do I!"

He stopped.

"No, Dina. You won't."

We stared at each other.

"Won't I?" I hissed. "Look at me, Nico. Don't you believe me?"

He had gone deathly pale, but he couldn't look away.

"Dina—"

"Can you see yourself now?" I asked. "Can you see how stupid and how… how spoiled you're being right now? 'The world is not like I want it to be, so I might as well die.' Is that your phrase of the day? Because you know this won't work. You know you won't get him this way."

He dropped to his knees in the snow and finally lowered his eyes.

"But what am I going to do?" he said. "Because I can't stand this, Dina. I really can't."

"You're not going to do anything," I said. "Not yet. I am."

"Dina! You're not going down there!"

"No. That won't be necessary."

"How many people can she look in the eye at a time?"

That was how the Weapons Master had put it, but he hadn't meant it for a real question. He thought he already knew the answer: not very many. I hoped he was wrong.

"Tano?"

"Yes?" He looked up, quickly hiding something he had been filing away at.

"I… Tano, are you afraid of me?"

"No," he said, not hesitating even for a second.

"Why not?"

"Because you…" He had to stop and search for the words. "You are not one who—Some strong people use their strength against others. Or abuse it. Sometimes openly, other times just when they think they can get away with it without being found out. But you aren't like that, even though you are strong."

"You are almost the only one I know who isn't afraid."

He nodded. "Yes. I've noticed."

"That's why I want to ask you to do something for me."

"And what is that?"

"I have to go elsewhere. But my body will still be here."

He raised his eyebrows. "That sounds strange."

"It is strange. And there are people here—Nico, perhaps, or Rikert—who might be frightened and think there is something wrong with me and do all sorts of things they shouldn't do. So, Tano, will you look after me? While I'm gone?"

He looked at me. Straight into my eyes, like almost no one else dared to do.

"Do you promise to come back?" he asked.

"Yes."

"Then I'll do it. How long will you be gone?"

"I don't know. Time is odd there. You'll have to be patient."

"I'm good at that," he said.

I knew I needed both my father and my mother if this was to succeed. And there was only one place it could happen. I lay down on the blanket and looked at Tano one last time. He sat next to me, steady as a rock, the kind of rock you moor ships to.

Then I closed my eyes and let myself slide into the shining mists of the Ghost Country.

I found the thread I needed and followed it through the mists. This time she would have to listen to me, because now I had my Shamer's voice back. But where was she? Sitting on a chair, it seemed, halfway between two beds. In one bed lay

Callan, in the other, Davin. Davin? Was he ill? He didn't look healthy, certainly. Sweat beaded his forehead, and he was very pale. But both he and Callan were sleeping, and I think Mama was dozing as well.

"*Mama.*"

"Dina?"

She was looking in my direction, but not right at me, as if she could hear me but not see me. And she was frightened. When I had been lost in the Ghost Country because of the witch weed, back when Valdracu had captured me, I had tried to reach her through the mists. She had told me to go back. *What you are doing is dangerous.* Later, much later, it was she who had told me that I must have been close to death to travel the mists like that. Did she think me close to death now? I wasn't. I would not get lost in the Ghost Country this time. I knew exactly where I was.

"*Mama, I need your help.*"

In the bed, Callan was sitting up now, looking uncertainly at Mama, but she paid him no heed.

"Where are you?" she asked.

"*Not very far away. Not anymore. But Drakan's army stands between us. I think I can make most of it crumble. If you will help me.*"

Could she still hear me? Yes, it seemed so.

"What do you want me to do?"

"*First of all, come to me.*"

She knew what I meant. She knew it was the Ghost Country I was talking about. And for the first time ever I saw my mother afraid of something that didn't threaten anyone but herself.

"I don't know if I can," she whispered, looking around her uncertainly.

311

"*Give me your hand.*"

"I can't see you."

I hesitated. How could I reach her when she couldn't see me, and probably couldn't touch me either?

And then I knew. It was simple, really. In the Ghost Country, it was desire and longing that moved people and things.

"*Do you want to see me again?*" I said, feeling a pang of fear that the answer might not be a wholehearted yes anymore.

"Dina! Of course I do!"

"*Then think about that. Think of me. And think about how much you… how much you love me.*"

She closed her eyes for a moment, and I think she did exactly what I asked her to do. Already, I could sense that she was closer to me than she had been a moment ago. And I let my longing reach out too, to bring us closer still, until I could finally touch her.

We were both standing in the Ghost Country now. Voices were calling in the mists around us. Mama squeezed my hand in hers, and it felt as real as if we were actually standing next to each other in the flesh. She still looked frightened, though.

Out of the mists came a third figure. And when Mama saw him, she stepped in front of me, still trying to protect me against him.

"You shall not have her," she said. "Not here, nor any other place."

Papa looked at her. He looked at her for a very long time.

"She is neither yours nor mine anymore," he said. "She can make her own choices. But right now she needs us both."

Mama hesitated. "For what?"

"I want all of them to dream the same dream," I said. "A true dream of the kind you cannot run away from."

"All of them?" said Mama. "Who is that?"

"The Dragon men, of course," I said. "But not just them. The clans too. Otherwise I think it might go wrong."

"She has my help," said Papa. "Does she have yours?"

"You never give anything without expecting something in return," she said. "There is a cost. What is the price of your help, Sezuan?"

An odd sort of movement went through his shoulders.

"Will you think of me every once in a while?" he asked. "And not hate me? And will you not hate the part of me that lives on in our daughter?"

"I don't hate any part of Dina!"

"No? *I couldn't bear it if you became like him.* Those were your words, Melussina."

Her eyes narrowed. "Are you really here, Sezuan? Or is this something I am dreaming, since you know things I never told you?"

And suddenly I knew that it wasn't just because I needed him that he was here.

"He wouldn't be here if you didn't still long for him," I said quietly.

Mama spun as if I had touched her with something very sharp.

"I have Callan now. And I have never—" But then she stopped. Her eyes were full of tears.

Callan? Mama and Callan?

Yes, of course. That was why. That was why he sometimes deferred to her, and to me too, a little, when normally he never listened to anyone except Maudi Kensie.

But right now it wasn't about Callan. And I knew I was right. Papa would not be here if Mama did not still long for him.

"Damn you," she whispered. "Why do you have to be so clever."

And then she looked directly at me.

"Yes, I loved him," she said defiantly. "More than I have ever loved any man. And yes. I still long for him."

Something inside me came loose. A deep, deep knot of fear and longing. I couldn't bear for her always to hate him. And now that she herself had admitted it, then surely I too might love him and be like him, at least a little?

My father laughed, and it was very strange to hear laughter in this place of loss and yearning.

"Did it really hurt you so much to say that? Melussina, it is no crime to love another human being."

"Isn't this where you are supposed to tell me that you love me too?" she asked.

"Would you believe me if I said it?"

"I might."

"I told you once, back at the Golden Swan. And you knew I was telling the truth."

She bowed her head. "Yes. I knew that."

"Do you need to hear me say it again?"

She shook her head. "No. You said it when you were alive. I would rather remember that than hear the words from… from a vision that might not even exist." She turned to me once more. "All right, Dina. If a mother and a ghost can help you, let us begin. What is it you want us to do?"

"I want them to dream," I said. "And I want them to dream of you."

The Shamer's War

I raised the flute. Poised between two worlds, I stood in the pass between the snow-clad walls of rock and here, in the Ghost Country, where the notes lit up the grayness like small stars. They went spinning from one rock face to the other, back and forth, as if weaving an invisible cloth. They wove their way into the mists of the Ghost Country, in a world that did not belong to the waking and the living. And they wove a dream.

No nice dream, but a dream of the sort you would rather forget but cannot. It stays with you forever. Because no one forgets my mother, once they have looked into her eyes. And no one forgets the things she makes you remember.

Look at me.

The words were not spoken aloud, and yet everyone heard them in the dream. Dreams will find you wherever you go. You can't hide, and you can't run. And a Shamer's eyes are a pitiless mirror.

Some moaned loudly in their sleep. Others screamed. Most people cried. Because this had been a cruel war, and many things had happened that they would rather forget.

"He would have done the same to me!"

"I was just doing what I was told to do."

"I thought she had a knife. I really did!"

Look at me.

"I didn't know what I was doing!"

"The others did it too! I wasn't the one who wanted to do it."

"It just happened."

"He was no angel either!"

"But they are not—They are not like us. Not human like us."

Look at me.

And there was nowhere else to look, nowhere to go. Little by little, the chorus of excuses fell silent. And shame spread.

It came most strongly on the Dragon Force, where it had been cast out and rejected for so long. There was so much to be ashamed of there. But the clans felt it too, Skaya and Laclan and Kensie. There, too, some dreamers tried to wriggle free and get away, to avoid remembering. But the Shamer's eyes would not let them go.

Remember. And never do it again.

For if you don't remember your evil deeds as well as your good ones, how can you learn? If you do not remember, how can you be sure it won't happen again?

I lowered the flute. With a stab of sadness I suddenly knew that I would never play it again. Other flutes, perhaps, but not this one. It could do too many things. It *knew* too much. Sometimes I felt the flute was playing me and not the other way around.

"They will fear me even more now," said Mama, softly and sadly. "And you too."

I nodded. "I know. But as long as there are a few who don't. A few who know that… that I'm also just a girl."

My mother gave me a rapid, curious glance. "Have you met someone like that?" she asked. "Someone who knows that you're a girl?"

How can one stand in the midst of shining gray mists, in a Ghost Country beyond the waking world, and still be thirteen years old and blushing furiously? But I was.

I opened my eyes. It was morning. There was daylight everywhere around me.

Tano hovered over me. "Are you back now?" he asked cautiously.

"Yes." My voice was so hoarse it was barely audible.

"Were you the one playing?" he said. "It sounded like you, even though you were just lying there."

I nodded. "That was me."

"I didn't fall asleep," he said, "even though the flute wanted me to."

"It's not easy to avoid."

"No, but if I had fallen asleep, I wouldn't have been able to look after you. But even though I wasn't sleeping, I still saw her."

"Mama?"

"Yes. It must have been her. Her eyes were just like yours."

"Was it bad?"

He shook his head a couple of times, like a horse trying to be rid of a fly. "It wasn't pleasant. There are some things one doesn't like being reminded of."

"I'm sorry. It… it had to be everyone. Otherwise some people might try to… to take revenge."

"On the Dragon men, you mean?"

"Yes. And if this worked the way I hoped it would work, they are not in any condition to defend themselves right now."

◆   ◆   ◆

It was a strange sight. Weapons lay in huge piles, or scattered where people had dropped them. There were men who just sat, crying openly or hiding their faces in their hands. Others wandered aimlessly, looking more like ghosts than living human beings. Some had already begun the long trek back to the Lowlands and whatever homes they had left down there, but most seemed unable to move and to act, as if some great disaster had come upon them and left them stunned and helpless—and perhaps that was not so far off the mark.

The small army the Weapons Master had brought with him had been thoroughly shaken as well, and nobody wanted to look at me.

"Nico?"

He was standing a little way up the slope, looking down at the disarray.

"They have fallen apart," he said disbelievingly. "Completely apart."

"You said yourself that this might be a war that would not be decided by weapons."

"Yes. I said that. But still, I hadn't imagined… Dina, what you and your mother did last night, it's like an earthquake. Nothing is the same."

"Anything less would have been too little."

"Yes. I suppose so."

He wouldn't look at me at all. The way he held his head, the distance he kept between us, was he afraid to touch me now?

I was very, very tired, or I might not have said it.

"Nico. I'm not venomous."

He knew what I meant. But this time there was no offer of a comforting hug, no crying on his shoulder.

"I am sorry, Dina. I'm not myself. None of us are." He touched my cheek, very lightly, like he sometimes did. But I saw a hesitation in his movements that had not been there before, and it almost made me cry.

"Drakan is still down there," I said.

He nodded. "I know. And perhaps now you will let me go down to find him? Without calling me spoiled and suicidal?"

Did he mean for me to smile? I didn't feel like it.

"Only if you take the Weapons Master and his men," I said.

"I was planning to." He sighed. "At least we will no longer see children running around with weapons. At least we will be spared that."

Or so we thought. But a little way into the pass we were met by a sight that made us stop abruptly.

Some sort of snowslide had blocked most of the pass, and a narrow passage had been cleared. Across that narrow bit of free road, a line of child soldiers were ranged. Behind them were ten Dragon knights, standing shoulder to shoulder. And behind them, that must have been where Drakan was.

Why were they still protecting their Lord? Why were they not as stunned and shaken as everyone else? The Dragon knights, that I might understand. There were rumors that Drakan let his elect drink the blood of his dragons. But the children?

I stared at their faces. So serious and determined. So unshakable in their obedience. That in itself was so eerie that I could barely stand to look at them, and yet I could not take my eyes off them.

And then I suddenly knew why they were not crushed by a sense of shame. They were only doing what they had been told was right. Some of them might well be Gelt children, taken from their villages and their parents and brought up to believe that the word of the Dragon Lord was the ultimate law. Perhaps the peddler who had sold Tano and Imrik was not the only one from whom Drakan had bought children.

How could one fight these eerie little warriors? One could not use force and sharp weapons against these serious faces. Not if one was a decent human being. Yet if we didn't—

The weapons were real. And the children would use them.

Nico was standing right next to me, and I was sure his thoughts were very like to mine. To him it was a nightmare reborn. An evil dream he thought he had escaped once, and now it was coming true right in front of him. Nico hated swords at the best of times. He would never be able to use a weapon against a child. His anger was so colossal I could feel it even without looking at him. But what could he do with all his fury?

"Oh, the bastard," murmured Carmian and lowered her bow. "What can you do against something like that?"

Even the Weapons Master had grown pale and looked sickened.

"We cannot let him escape," he said, "even if it costs… we'll have to. If we don't kill the bastard, he will find his way back into the Lowlands and the troops he has left there, and everything will have been in vain." He raised his voice. "Break off your arrowheads and spear points," he ordered. "And use the flats of your swords. Perhaps we can overcome them without having to kill anyone."

But "perhaps" wasn't good enough for Nico.

"Drakan!"

His shout echoed between the rock walls that rose steeply on either side. And the second time he shouted, there was an answer. From behind the lines of children and Dragon knights came a voice I hadn't forgotten, even though it had been two years since I had heard it last.

"Little Nico. What are you doing out there? I thought you were hiding behind the walls."

"Drakan, I want to talk."

"Talk away."

"Face to face."

"Be my guest. If you come alone and unarmed, they'll let you through."

I dug my fingers into Nico's arm.

"Don't you dare!"

And for once, Carmian and I were entirely in agreement, because she caught hold of his other arm.

"Nico! Don't trust him!"

"I don't trust him at all," he said. "But there is one bait he might rise to. One way we might avoid having to shoot at children."

"And what way is that?" she asked suspiciously.

He didn't answer her in so many words. He just raised his voice once more.

"Drakan. I have a suggestion for you. And a challenge."

A challenge?

"Nico."

"Be quiet, Dina. For once in my life I know I am doing the right thing."

He looked directly at me. His eyes were calm and deeply blue, and I knew he wasn't afraid anymore. Finally, I was the one who had to look away. He would not be turned from his purpose, and there was nothing I could do to stop him. I had to stand there and listen, ice in my heart, while Nico challenged his half brother to a duel, man-to-man, in the Ring of Iron, the way it was the custom in the Highlands.

Drakan had learned enough about Highland ways to know what that meant: *What starts here, ends here. No aid, no hindrance, no revenge.* Nico would come face-to-face with Drakan, yes. Without having to fight his way through a line of children with weapons in their hands. But if Drakan killed Nico, he could leave the Ring a free man, and no Highlander would try to stop him.

"Are you really that brave, little Nico?"

"Who is hiding now? In an hour, Drakan. In the Ring of Iron. Just you and me."

Carmian dropped her bow in the snow and put her hands over her ears, like a child who doesn't want to hear the end of a scary tale. I had never seen her do anything so childlike before. But whether or not we heard the words, they had still been said. And it wasn't long before the answer came back to us from behind the closed ranks of the child soldiers.

"It will be my pleasure. But know this, little Nico: It will end only in death."

"That was the plan," said Nico.

Man-to-Man

Stamped snow. A circle of swords pounded into the snow. From sword to sword, a rope. That was the way the Ring of Iron looked for Drakan and Nico. Nothing as refined as the Ring they had at Baur Laclan; this was simple, I thought. As simple as death.

Nico raised his shield. It was a new one, made for him by Dina's friend Tano, with the Raven of his family House on it, and it was the only part of his fighting gear that was his. Astor Skaya had offered him his own chain mail, but Nico had refused. It was more hindrance than gain, he said, when one wasn't used to the weight of it. Instead he wore Skaya's scarred old leather armor. The sword was Callan's, and the helmet one that the Weapons Master had loaned him.

I caught a glimpse of Nico's dark blue eyes across the rim of the Raven shield. He looked determined, yes, but… but still somehow unwilling. Even now. Even now, he hated this.

"Do it, Nico!" I muttered. "Pull yourself together! It's not enough to be brave enough to enter the Ring, you also have to have the guts to fight!"

"What is the matter with the boy?" said Callan. "If he wants to win, he has to fight with a will."

Drakan, too, seemed to sense Nico's reluctance. He put back his head and laughed.

"Poor little Nico," he said, lazily confident. "You're so much more the clerk than the swordsman, aren't you? This is almost a shame."

And then he lunged, so suddenly that a hiss went through the audience, and slashed at Nico's legs.

Nico leaped aside.

"At least the lad is quick on his feet," commented Ivain.

But quickness would not be enough, I knew.

When I heard about the duel, I was sitting on a box in the barbican feeling like myself for the first time in months. The fever was gone. And the dream that had haunted us all in the night, somehow it had taken me more gently than the others. Was it because I was my mother's son and had lived with the Shamer's gift all my life? That was part of it, perhaps, but I thought it was more than that.

"You look better," said Rose. "Is your fever gone?"

"Yes."

She looked at me, a sidelong glance that seemed... well, if it had been anyone other than Rose, I would have called it shy.

"Is there room for more than one on that box?"

Surprised, I moved over. "Go ahead."

"I... I heard that... is it true that Drakan forced you to drink the dragon blood? To make you do what he told you to do?"

"I suppose so. The first time, anyway."

But the other times, no one had forced it down my throat.

"You're not doing it anymore though, are you?"

"The dragon is dead, so no."

But even if it hadn't been, right now, the Whisperers were silent. And suddenly I knew why I felt so much better.

So many people feared my mother and my sister—and now more than ever. But once you had been in the clutches of the Educators, once you had spent a night in the Hall of the Whisperers, then you knew the difference. Because Mama and Dina might be terrifyingly good at making people feel ashamed, but they did not try to make you hate yourself. They did not try to break you, to crush you until there was nothing left of the person you once were. All they wanted was for you to remember and accept what you had done—and make a different choice the next time.

Mama was no Educator, far from it. I think the dream I had had in the night had finally shut those whispering voices down. I now no longer had to listen to their incessant accusations that *nothing* I had ever done was enough, that nothing could be forgiven, that nothing could be made right. I might have made stupid mistakes in my life, but I didn't have to hate myself. Only learn from those mistakes and do better next time.

"Why are you smiling?" asked Rose.

It took me a few moments to find the words.

"Remember when Killian put my foot back into joint?"

She shuddered. "Oh yes. It was *horrible*."

"Not afterward. Afterward, it felt *right*. For the first time in a very long time. And that's the way my head feels now. As if something has been out of joint, but now it's been put right."

She stared at me. "You're crazy."

"Yes."

"And you can stop agreeing with me too!"

"Would you rather fight?"

"Yes." There was a looking-for-trouble glint to her eyes that I had come to recognize. "Actually!"

I moved a little closer to her. Even through all the thick winter clothes, I could feel the warmth of her. Would she get mad if I tried to kiss her? And wasn't it wrong to kiss your foster sister? Even if you really, really wanted to?

And that was the moment Ivain chose to walk—no, run—into the barbican.

"Where is Callan?"

"In the sick bay."

"Can he stand?"

"Just about, yes. Why?"

"Because that Ravens boy has challenged Drakan to a duel. In the Ring of Iron. And for some reason the lad wants to apologize to Callan for something first. Just in case."

Drakan did most of the attacking. Blow by blow he drove Nico round the Ring while Nico parried with his sword or shield, or turned away at the last moment. Quick on his feet, yes... and that will keep you alive for a while. But if he didn't soon start to attack as well...

High above the pass, the sky was gray as slate, but now and then a sliver of sunlight escaped the clouds. It sparkled on the snow and glinted in the blades and on Nico's shield. Suddenly I saw Carmian, on the other side of the Ring. Her face was completely expressionless, but around her was an odd little space as if people knew, even in this throng, that it was better not to get too close to her.

Claaaang. Sword against sword. Nico blocked Drakan's sweep and twisted quickly to one side. And suddenly he did attack, a lightning-quick backhand stroke that caught Drakan flat-footed. He saved himself with a hasty parry, the first sight of uncertainty that he had shown. But then he leaped clear and regained his balance.

"Well, well!" he said, only slightly out of breath. "So the mouse has teeth. It wants to play with the cat."

Nico said nothing. Normally, he liked it best when he could do his fighting with words, but he had not uttered a single sound since he entered the Ring.

He advanced on Drakan. Drakan tried a head strike. Nico caught it on the shield, but Drakan pressed forward until they were body to body, with only the shields between them.

I couldn't see what happened. There was a sort of gasp from Nico, but when they broke away from each other, it was Drakan's shield that dropped to the ground.

"What happened?" I asked. Drakan was backing now, away from Nico. He made no attempt to pick up his fallen shield, but instead kept as much distance from Nico as he could. And was that blood on his hand? Yes. His shield hand was definitely bloody. Was that why he wasn't attacking anymore?

But if he didn't attack, Nico certainly did. Suddenly, he had thrown caution to the winds. He charged forward as if all that mattered was to hit Drakan, as if it was no longer important that he himself might be hit as well.

"There is blood in the snow," said Callan suddenly. "Which of them is it?"

"I think it's Drakan," I said. "His shield hand." Was that why Nico was attacking so furiously?

But suddenly Nico stumbled. For no visible reason. On the other side of the Ring, I saw Carmian raise her knuckles to her mouth, as if fighting to hold back a cry.

"Is he tiring?" asked Ivain. "He looks a bit wobbly."

"No," I said. "Something is wrong." Nico didn't tire this easily, I knew that from our bouts in Maudi's barn.

Drakan had seen it too. He stopped retreating. It was obvious now that this was what he had been waiting for.

"Are you tired, little Nico?" he asked gently. "Would you like to sleep? Come here, then. I'll let you rest."

Nico could barely hold up his shield, and I saw his sword arm twitch as if with spasms. The borrowed helmet slid into his eyes, and when he pushed it back, it came off entirely. But his eyes… the reluctance, the dangerous hesitation, all that was gone. Only determination was left. And if I were Drakan—

"Come on, Nico," I whispered. "Just one good strike."

Drakan picked up his fallen shield. Then he advanced, and something in the way he moved told me that this would be the last attack. He didn't try to slip past Nico's parries, he just pounded them, hammering at him, the shield, the sword, blow after blow, while Nico had to stagger back, stagger and fall.

"No!"

Carmian's voice cut through the noise, but she was not the only one shouting. Because if Drakan killed Nico—

But Nico wasn't done yet. His sword came sweeping around in a flat arc, just above the snow, and suddenly it was Drakan's turn to stagger. He dropped to one knee, his boot oddly split. Nico's desperate slash must have cut the hamstring, I thought. And now Nico threw himself forward, bearing Drakan to the ground with him. For a moment they lay still, Nico half on top of Drakan, pinning him more with his weight than with any controlled effort. And I saw that Nico had his sword at Drakan's throat.

"Do it," I hissed between my teeth. "What are you waiting for?"

And then I heard Drakan's voice, cool and drawling as if he were the one on top.

"Lost your nerve after all, little Nico? I thought so. Just like last time."

"No," said Nico. "I may be stupid. But not that stupid."

The sword came down. And Drakan said nothing more.

Some people were cheering. Not me. I ducked under the rope and made for Nico's side.

"Nico? Nico, what's wrong?"

He wasn't getting up. He looked as if he would never get up again.

"What happened?" Carmian was on her knees next to him. "Nico, what happened?"

Nico didn't say anything. He was busy trying to breathe. It was Callan who found the answer: a bloody knife in the snow, a knife with a dragon hilt.

"He had a dagger," said Callan. "He let go of his shield in order to use it. That was why there was blood on his hand. Not his, but Nico's."

"And that was why Drakan had no reason to take any more risks," I said bitterly. "All he had to do was to stay clear and wait until Nico collapsed with the blood loss."

Dina was suddenly in the Ring of Iron too, her face stiff and pale with shock.

"Davin," she said, "he… where is he hit?"

Ivain had already drawn his own knife to cut away the leather armor. Nico muttered some half-choked protest.

"Just taking a look, lad," said Callan. "It might feel worse than it is."

But when we got the armor off him, we could see that his shirt was soaked with blood all down one side. Callan cursed.

"Through the armpit," he said. "That is the kind of wound that's—" He caught Dina's scared glance and changed what he was going to say. "Not so good."

Carmian turned away. She stood with her back to us and her head bowed, as if it was no longer any concern of hers. But I had heard her voice when Nico fell, and I didn't think she was as unconcerned as she looked.

"Mama can help him," said Dina. "Get him inside. It is too cold out here."

Nico was still conscious. His breathing was sodden and troubled, and his face was not just pale, it was grayish white. His lips were blue now, like a child that has stayed too long in the water.

"Does it hurt?" I asked, and then felt like kicking myself.

"Stupid… question," whispered Nico. Four Skayas lifted him onto a stretcher, and he hissed with pain and closed his eyes. "Actually… I'd like it… to stop now."

They carried him inside, and Mama chased us all out, all except Dina and Rose, who were used to assisting her. I limped around the barbican, kicking at the snow with my good foot. Why the hell hadn't he been more careful? He had *learned* how to fight an opponent armed with sword and dagger. But he thought he had been fighting a man with a sword and a shield.

I paced the barbican for a while. Then I went outside. And then I went all the way back to the Ring of Iron, where Drakan was still lying in the snow, surrounded by a string of onlookers. Callan was there too, looking almost as if he was guarding the body, though I couldn't see why.

"What does your mama say about Nico?" he asked.

"Nothing yet," I said, not knowing whether that was good or bad. I nodded to Obain, who was standing with a couple of his fellow Arlain fishermen.

"What about this devil?" said Obain, with a jerk of his head toward Drakan.

"The eagles can eat him for all I care," I said through my teeth.

But Callan shook his head. "No," he said. "We are decent people. Carry him into the sick bay and put a guard on the door. We do not want to tempt the clans."

"To do what?"

"Many have suffered," said Callan. "But to avenge oneself on a dead man, that is no good revenge, and afterward they would feel shamed by it."

I thought it horribly unfitting for Drakan's body to lie so close to the bed where Nico was fighting for his life. But when Callan said something in that tone of voice, there was no disobeying him. I had learned that lesson a long time ago.

Later that evening, Dina came out.

"Get Carmian," she said, and her voice was so thin and tired and scared that I grew even more afraid than I was already.

"Why?" I asked, more sharply than I had meant to. "What does he want with her?"

"He wants to talk to her. Davin, just do it. And please hurry."

Carmian stood on the castle wall looking out across the snow and the mud and the thousands of people who were still out there, crouching by their little fires, freezing cold but also strangely paralyzed.

"Look at them," she said. "There's no one to tell them what to do, so now they do nothing. It's like they can barely breathe without being told how to do it."

Her voice was as bitter as hemlock, and she looked like a ghost. I had never seen her so pale.

"He wants to talk to you," I said.

"Oh, he does, does he? I'm not so sure I want to talk to some damn fool who can't even dodge a stupid knife."

"He didn't know that Drakan—"

But she was already moving down the steps, so apparently she didn't really mean what she said.

I sneaked into the sick bay on her heels. I could well understand why Mama and Dina needed to be left alone while they were working, but surely by now they had finished binding Nico's wounds? And if they were letting Carmian in, I felt I had a right. After all, he was *my* friend too.

Nico wasn't flat on his back the way I had imagined; instead, they had supported him so that he was almost sitting up. And as soon as I entered, I heard the hoarse, rattling wheeze of his breath. I could feel my own breath catch in sympathy; it was not a nice sound, and I almost regretted going in there. Why did he sound like that? Had the knife gone into his lung?

He might die, then.

I couldn't keep the thought from entering my mind, it pushed its way in even though I didn't want it. He is strong, I told myself instead. And the knife wasn't that long, was it? But I remembered seeing it in the snow, a dark metal shadow, bloody almost to the hilt.

Carmian looked down on him.

"Idiot," she told him. But not very loudly.

"Yes," he panted. "Sorry. But. Drakan. Is. Dead."

He could only gasp out the words one by one, as if each one was a whole sentence. It made it difficult to understand what he was saying.

"Oh yes? And what do you expect me to do? Cheer? Clap my hands? Invite everyone to a party?" There was still that anger in her voice, as if he had done something unforgivable. And I might have wanted to call Nico an idiot myself and curse him for not having defended himself better, but what was the use of all that now?

I don't think Nico even noticed her anger. There was something he wanted to tell her, and it was taking all his strength.

"You. Are. Castellaine. Now."

What? I threw a wild look at Dina, who stood near the bed, rolling up a bandage with jerky movements, as if she was as angry as Carmian. And all the while, her eyes were bright with tears.

"They made a contract," she said in a low voice. "A contract of marriage that was to come into effect at Drakan's death. Which is now."

Nico and Carmian? I stared from one to the other. She didn't look like a tender loving wife. More like she wanted to strangle him, actually.

"Marriage contract?" I murmured, making it a question.

"She wanted to be castellaine. To rule at Dunark, or so she said." Dina tucked in the loose end of the bandage, put the roll into a basket, and reached blindly for the next strip of linen.

"Is that what you want?" Carmian looked down at Nico. "To make me your castellaine?"

"Yes." The word was just a gasp, but quite clear for all that. Nico's hair was so soaked with sweat that it glinted in the lamplight, and I could only guess at the kind of pain he was feeling. Still he wouldn't take his eyes off Carmian; still he fought to deliver his message to her.

"Why?"

"You. Understand. Those. Who. Have. Nothing." He had to break off for a moment to gather his strength. "And. You. Are. Strong. Enough. Clever enough. To rule. Those. Who. Have. Everything."

There was sound from her, a hiss of anger and despair and… and something else. I couldn't quite tell what.

"Oh, sure. If you die now, Nico, do you believe for even a moment that they will let me enter Dunark as its ruler? They will scream and howl and fight me. They will never accept me."

"Let. Them. Howl." He made a small movement with one hand, and Mama apparently knew what he meant by it. She held out a piece of vellum to Carmian.

"He sealed it," she said. "With his Raven signet. It is binding, and he is right. They may howl, but there is nothing they can legally do."

Carmian looked at the vellum as if she thought it might bite her.

"It's a will," she said. "A last will and testament."

He nodded, a tiny, tiny nod. He spent what strength he had left grudgingly, like a miser counting out each penny.

"Make. Dunark. A Gelt. Village," he said.

Which made absolutely no sense to me. But Carmian seemed to understand.

"Nico! I can't! Have you seen them out there? They can't even work out how to get home without somebody giving them permission. And you think they can choose who is to rule them? Nico, they don't know how!"

"Then. Teach. Them."

"That would take years. That would take up my whole lifetime!"

"Yes."

The word hung there between them. Nico looked at her until she knew that he meant it. This was what he wanted. This was what he demanded of her. And Carmian looked completely overwhelmed by it.

"Nico. That's not fair. You can't be—you can't just…"

Mama stirred uneasily. I knew she was watching Nico sharply, counting each sign of fatigue, each danger signal. Carmian caught the slight movement and turned to her.

"Don't you dare let him die!"

"I'm doing everything I can to help him," said Mama. But the fact that she let Nico talk at all when he was obviously so weak… I knew well enough that this was because this couldn't wait until tomorrow. And Carmian knew it too.

She looked back down at Nico.

"Don't you understand?" she said. "What you're asking, it's impossible!"

He was silent for so long that I began to wonder whether he had any strength left at all. But there were still a few words that he wanted to say.

"Not. For. You."

And then he closed his eyes, and Mama chased us all out.

All night Carmian paced the barbican like a wolf in a ditch. I felt like pacing too, but my ankle was too sore. All I could do was sit and wait.

"He had better not do it," she said through clenched teeth. "He had better not die!"

"I thought you wanted to be castellaine," I said bitterly. "Wasn't that what Dina said?"

She stopped for a moment and looked at me. Her eyes were more gray than green just then.

"Not without him, you idiot."

It was dawn when Mama and Dina finally came out. They both looked deadly tired, and there were tiny splatters of blood on Dina's face, and larger blotches of it on Mama's blouse. But the worst thing was… the worst thing was that neither of them would look at me.

"I'm sorry," said Mama. "We did what we could. It just wasn't enough."

Dina said not a single word. But Carmian leaped to her feet, and her face was as pale as Nico's had been.

"It's not true!" she said. "You're lying!"

Mama didn't say anything. She just looked at Carmian.

And Carmian turned and ran. Through the barbican, up the steps, to the wall above. She leaned out across the parapet, and even at that distance I could see her shoulders shuddering. She was crying. She was crying so hard it seemed like she might never stop again.

And still Dina just stood there. Wooden-faced and silent, as if she had been turned to stone.

A Hero's Grave

We buried him two days later. It was a bright and frosty morning, and the mists had finally disappeared. The castle folk stood silent and unmoving, their breaths like plumes in the chill air.

Six men carried his body. I would have liked to be part of that, but my foot was still too sore and unreliable. Astor Skaya and Ivain Laclan went in front, with the bier resting on their shoulders.

They had clad him in armor and helmet, with the sword and the shield Tano had made on his breast. You could still see the dents and scars from the duel, the marks left by Drakan's sword. I saw only a brief glimpse of his face, half shadowed by the helmet, and already it seemed alien and strange, not Nico anymore. And I wanted to yell at them and tell them this was wrong, this wasn't who he was. They had made him look like a soldier, and he would have hated that. But that was how you buried heroes, and that was what Nico had finally become, a dead hero.

He would have hated it so much. He would have hated the trumpets and the drums and all the uniforms. I think the only part of it he might have liked was what Dina said at the end.

"He told me to tell you of his last will and testament," she said, and her voice cut cleanly through the crisp air though she wasn't actually shouting. "The House of Ravens has no male heir now, and Dunark has no ruler. But Nico wanted… Nicodemus Ravens married Carmian Gelters, and it was his will that she should be castellaine and ruler of Dunark, its city and its castle. It was all written down, witnessed, and sealed with his signet. But I ask all of you, here and now, to bear witness to the truth of what I have told you."

Carmian was standing next to Dina, dressed in a black robe. It was the first time I had seen her in skirts. But though every eye in the place was on her, she stirred not a muscle. She stood there, tall and straight as a candle, staring into midair, and already she looked like the sort of castellaine one doesn't get around too easily. And besides, when you looked at Dina, you *knew* that every word was true, exactly as Nico had said it.

"We bear witness," said Astor Skaya in formal tones. And some of the men, Skaya and Kensie and Laclan, too, pounded their shields slowly and respectfully to show their agreement.

"Thank you," said Dina. And now she was crying, I could see, for the first time since she and Mama had come out of the sick bay with that awful message. I think only those standing nearest heard her last words:

"I'll really miss him."

There was so much to be done. So many messes that needed cleaning up. Perhaps it was always like that after a war. There were people who no longer had homes, people who no longer had a job to do or a place to belong to. People who had lost everything, or nearly everything. Fourteen Dragon knights had survived, as far as we knew. Three had made good their escape in the confusion, the rest were under lock and key in Astor Skaya's dungeons.

Obain had his Maeri back and returned to Arlain. The Harbormaster was promised Kensie aid in building a new ship to replace the *Swallow*, and from the look Maudi Kensie gave me when she made that promise, I knew I would have to work hard in that effort. Carmian and the Weapons Master gathered what was left of Drakan's army and made for the Lowlands. There was trouble, of course—it would have been strange if there were not—but most of the men seemed pleased, on the whole, to have a commander again. I heard they gave her a nickname, the Lioness, and bragged to the clansmen about how tough she was. I think Nico was right; she would be a good ruler. Not an easy one, a good one. Probably better than Nico himself would have been.

Still, I couldn't get used to it. It was so unfair. Everyone else got to go home, but not him.

Yet another two days went by before we ourselves could return home to Yew Tree Cottage.

"Rikert is coming," said Dina. "And Tano."

Rikert, yes, I could understand that, sort of. But Tano?

"Just who *is* this Tano?"

"Rikert's apprentice," said Dina. But she blushed as she said it, and even though I still hadn't found a girl-talk dictionary, I had no trouble figuring out what that meant.

"He had better treat you right," I said. "Or you come straight to me, you hear?"

"Don't worry," she said, giving up on pretending it was nothing. "He will. He does. But, Davin…"

"Yes?"

"There is one more thing. And I know you are going to be angry. But promise me—promise me, hear?—that you'll say absolutely nothing about this until we're back at Yew Tree Cottage."

What?

"About what?" I said suspiciously.

"First promise." She looked at me, and even though she was my sister and I had known her my entire life, I couldn't refuse that look.

"All right, I promise. Now, what is it?"

"Come this way."

Astor Skaya had loaned us a sleigh for the trip home, the kind that had a canvas hood to keep out the snow and the wind. A dark brown mare Dina had picked up somewhere waited patiently between the traces, with Mama on the box holding the reins.

"Did he promise?" asked Mama.

"Yes."

"Show him then."

I didn't get all this secrecy. Or at least, I didn't get it until Dina eased back the canvas a tiny little bit.

Inside, wrapped in blankets and furs, lay Nico. And he did not look very well. But he was still very far from dead.

At first I was just so stunned I had to sit down. And then I was furious.

"How *could* you let me think—How could you lie?"

"You promised not to say anything before we got home!" said Dina.

"But why?"

"Because I told your mother that I would rather die than be castellan for the rest of my life," said Nico in a paper-thin voice. "I… was not quite myself at the time."

"Sometimes the difference between life and death is very small," said Mama. "And if you don't want to live, it can be very easy to die. So we decided that Nicodemus Ravens had to die. But that Nico might live on."

"But… but Dina was *crying*."

Dina still looked pretty sad, come to think of it.

"He can't stay, Davin. As soon as he is well enough to travel, he must leave. He must go find a place where no one has heard of Nicodemus Ravens, a place where no one will recognize him. So when I said I'd miss him, that happened to be true."

Then something else dawned on me.

"But we buried you. I saw it!"

"No," said Nico. "We buried Drakan. My half brother, who will now get a fine headstone and be recognized at last as a true Ravens." He coughed very carefully. "There is a kind of long-delayed justice in that, I suppose."

I wasn't sure I agreed. When I thought how Astor Skayark and Carmian were already busy planning a real hero's tomb with a statue and everything…

Nico and Drakan. Drakan and Nico. I knew they were related, of course, and I knew they looked alike, a bit.

And Nico would have hated such a place, statue and all. So perhaps it was quite fitting after all.

Snowballs

Yew Tree Cottage sat there with snow on the roof, looking like its old self. Even the sheep were back; Maudi had herded them home the day before. It would be a while before we would be able to fetch Silky and Falk home from Farness, though. They were still chomping hay in the Harbormaster's stables.

"It's weird," I told Tano. "Everything looks so ordinary."

"You were lucky the Dragon men never got this far."

"Yes."

And we were. So many others had returned to find their homes in ruins, like we had once done in Birches. But that was not what I meant. It was more…. So much had happened that it seemed strange that the Stone Dance was still where it used to be, that the paddock and the sheep shed and the apple trees were still there, neither larger nor smaller, nor in any other way different from when we left. When everything inside was so changed. So completely changed.

Callan had borrowed a horse from Maudi, and even though Mama would rather have had him in the sleigh with Nico, he insisted that he was strong enough to ride. I could see how his eyes kept darting from one side of the trail to the other, like a hound searching for prey. Even though he was still not quite himself, he was watching out for us, for Mama, and the rest of us.

"Drakan is dead," I said, partly to hear how it sounded.

"Aye," said Callan. "But there are still a few of his knights out there, so it is no use getting careless."

Rikert was looking around too, but in a different way.

"Is that the brook?" he asked, pointing.

"Yes." It was not easy to see it because of the snow; it was just the faintest shadow amidst all the whiteness.

"Then we might build the smithy there, just beyond the orchard."

"We might," said Mama, "if you are certain that you want to stay. We would be more than happy, but Birches might not be so pleased to lose their good smith."

Rikert made a sound in his throat. "They'll find another," he said. "Now that the Dragon Force is no longer swallowing up all the good craftsmen. And there isn't much for me to go back to. Not now."

Not now that Ellyn was dead, was what he meant. And when I thought of the neglected house and Rikert himself, and the way he had looked like an ungroomed horse, well, I understood his choice. And I was certainly not unhappy about it. I liked Rikert, and there was Tano too.

It was almost as if Tano could feel me thinking of him.

"Do you want to help me put up the horse?" he said. "There is something I want to talk to you about."

Rose was looking at us with wide-eyed curiosity, but she didn't say anything. And in the next moment, she had other things to think about. Davin threw a snowball at her and hit her right between the shoulders.

"You beast," she said, leaping off the sleigh before it had come to a stop. "Just you wait!" She snatched up a handful of snow herself, and her revenge snowball hit my brother on the nose.

"Me too!" shrieked Melli. "I want to play too!"

It was a while before we got around to unhitching the brown mare, and even Rikert ended up throwing a few snowballs before Mama stopped the rumpus to remind us that the fire had to be lit and dinner prepared, and that Nico shouldn't be outside in the cold air longer than he had to be.

After dinner, Tano tried again.

"Do you want to go and see the horses?" he asked.

I blushed. I wish that whole blushing thing would stop, and soon, please! But at least he didn't see it, because we had only the one lamp lit, and the fire in the hearth.

"All right," I said. And this time we succeeded in sneaking out without being noticed by anyone except Rose, and she just smiled, a sort of smug that's-what-I-thought smile.

Outside, the stars were bright in a clear sky, and it was so cold that the snow crunched beneath our feet. Tano halted in the middle of the yard and stopped pretending that he had a keen and deep interest in seeing the stable.

"I have something for you," he said. "It's a sort of birthday gift."

He gave me a small linen pouch that was very pretty in itself. But when I saw what was inside...

"It's just a bit of copper wire," he said. "And pewter. We didn't have silver and the like."

It was a... no, not a buckle. This was jewelry. A clasp for my hair, light and strong, and shaped like a butterfly. And it had three pins instead of just one.

"It has three pins."

"Your hair is so thick," he said. "So I thought the clasp would hold better that way. Do you like it?"

I had tears in my eyes. This was so beautiful, far too beautiful for me. And yet he had made it for me. And he had looked at my hair, and then he had shaped the clasp so that even my thick coarse horsetail hair would have to behave. That was the best part. That he had seen so much, and thought so much.

I couldn't say anything. I just nodded. But I think he could tell how happy I was.

"Can I put it on?" he asked.

I nodded again. His hands were gentle even though they were so big. I didn't know how often he had touched a girl's hair, but he did a fine job.

"Thank you," I said.

He just smiled. He was happy because I was happy.

Suddenly I thought of Carmian. And I'm not sure why, but that nearly made me cry.

"What is it?" asked Tano. "Suddenly, you look so sad."

"It's just… Carmian. I think she really likes Nico. Or did. Or—" It was confusing because Carmian didn't know that Nico was alive. "She said she wanted to be castellaine and that it didn't matter if he loved her or not. But I think it did matter. And now—" Now she was on her way to Dunark to rule the town and the castle that Nico didn't want. Once, the Spinner had said that Carmian and I would do each other much harm and much good. But to let her think that Nico was dead, that was probably the worst thing I would ever do to her. Nico had said that it had to be that way, for Carmian's sake as well as for Dunark's, but it was hard.

"What will Nico do? When he is well again?"

"He wants to be a tutor. He wants to teach children to read and write and… and to trust in themselves, I think."

"That is a fine profession."

"Yes. I just wish he could… that he could have his fine profession a little closer to Baur Kensie."

"He would never be safe here. Sooner or later he would be recognized. It is bad enough that so many people already know that he is alive. How long can a girl like Melli keep that secret, do you think?"

"Melli won't tell." Or at least, I thought she wouldn't.

Tano looked at me for a long time.

"If you could," he said, slowly and carefully, "when you are older, would you then go with him?"

I shook my head, and the slight movement made me feel the weight of the new clasp and the unusual tidiness of my hair.

"No. Not now," I said.

Because even though you don't want anyone to own you, it doesn't mean that there is nowhere you belong.

The New Smith

The winter made it hard to get started on the new smithy. So far, Rikert and Tano had lived with Maudi and shared Master Maunus's workshop, and this made Melli happy. She leaped into Rikert's arms every time she saw him and clung to him so much that I didn't understand how he could stand it. But apparently he could.

It was Rose who said it. I don't know if she meant anything by it or not. I rarely know what Rose really means when she says things.

"Anyone would think she was his own," she said. "Just look at them!"

Anyone would think she was his own. It made me think. I thought about it for several days, and in the end I went across to the workshop and was lucky enough to catch Rikert on his own.

"Rikert, what made you decide to come up here?"

He put down his hammer and wiped his forehead with a corner of his smith's apron.

"You have to have someone," he said. "Or things don't make sense. Since Ellyn died, I'm no good on my own."

"You've always been fond of Melli, haven't you?" I said, fumbling my way. How did you *ask* something like that?

He smiled without thinking.

"Yes. Ellyn was too. Remember? And we never had children of our own, of course."

"Rikert…"

He must have heard something in my voice.

"Did you talk to your mother?" he asked.

"No."

"Maybe you should."

"I'd rather talk to you."

He sighed. "All right then, lad. If you have something to ask, ask it."

"Are you Melli's father?"

He didn't answer right away. He sipped a bit of water from the barrel and then passed the ladle to me, all without speaking.

"Your mother wanted children," he finally said. "And there weren't all that many people she could ask."

"But Ellyn…"

"The first time, that was before I met Ellyn. But with Melli, she knew. It was after we realized that she couldn't herself." He wiped his forehead once more. "She wasn't like most women, Ellyn. She was generous. Never petty or mean about anything. And she knew that she was the one I wanted, right enough."

The first time. But that meant—

He met my eyes just as the truth dawned on me. And nodded faintly.

"Yes. You too, boy. You too."